Sterling Silver

SILVER DONALD CAMERON is the award-winning author of 13 books, including *Wind, Whales and Whisky: A Cape Breton Voyage*, the novel *Dragon Lady*, and the classic from the 1970-71 fishermen's strike, *The Education of Everett Richardson*. He recently became Dean of the School of Community Studies at the University College of Cape Breton.

Sterling Silver

Rants, Raves & Revelations

Silver Donald Cameron

SELECTED AND EDITED
BY RONALD CAPLAN

Silver Donald Cameron

Breton Books
Wreck Cove, Cape Breton Island
1994

Cover Photograph: Ronald Caplan
Darkroom: Grant Young
Production Assistance: Bonnie Thompson
Typesetting: Glenda Watt
Front Cover Type: Weldon Bona

Some of these essays were first published in *Atlantic Insight, The Atlantic Monthly, Axiom Magazine, CP Air Empress, Harrowsmith, Quest, Maclean's, Reader's Digest Canada, Saturday Night,* and *Weekend Magazine.*

OTHER BOOKS BY SILVER DONALD CAMERON

The Education of Everett Richardson:
The Nova Scotia Fishermen's Strike, 1970-71
Seasons in the Rain
Dragon Lady
The Baitchopper
Outhouses of the West
Conversations with Canadian Novelists
Wind, Whales and Whisky: A Cape Breton Voyage
Once Upon a Schooner: An Offshore Voyage in Bluenose II
Sniffing the Coast: An Acadian Voyage

Canadian Cataloguing in Publication Data

Cameron, Silver Donald, 1937-

Sterling Silver

ISBN 1-895415-38-1

I. Caplan, Ronald, 1942- II. Title.

PS8555.A5188A6 1994 C814'.54 C94-950257-X
PR9199.3.C2776A6 1994

Contents

CONTINUES ON NEXT PAGE

Editor's Introduction

STERLING SILVER comes from 25 years of writing by Silver Donald Cameron, gleaned from about 50 stuffed boxes in a basement at University College of Cape Breton, plus another 25 or so at his home in D'Escousse, Cape Breton Island. Silver Donald writes every day of his life, has published consistently, and has saved just about everything.

I have arranged these essays as they worked for me, but they can be read in any order. I chose each one primarily for the way it stood on its own. I wanted to offer a combination of the personal, the person devoted to community, and Silver Donald's sense of community's critical place within Canada. I wanted some of his best writing: good clear prose, focused subjects, often outrageous approaches, all unified by his generous mix of compassion and good humour.

I asked Silver Donald not to rewrite. I added a few notes, edited out confusions. Silver Donald provided a brief Afterword.

These are brave stories out of the shipwreck of our recent world. They are a survivor's tales and observations, clinging to a chip of wood while writing well about the damage. *Sterling Silver* is a hopeful book. It is not desolate. It is resilient, encouraging, often victorious—even at times when Silver Donald, shipwrecked, is not quite out of the water.

I am grateful for his trust, for allowing us to go mining in his archives, for rarely closing the door.

Fellow miners included Laura Peverill, Librarian at University College of Cape Breton, and Laura Verner, Student Intern from the Community Studies Program at UCCB. Bonnie Thompson and Sharon Hope Irwin shared with me the ache of the first reader. Glenda Watt carefully transcribed our choices to computer.

Over and over during this project, Ezra Pound's lines came back to me: "The blossoms of the apricot blow from east to west, And I have tried to keep them from falling." That's all. This is Silver Donald Cameron between the big books. Angry, hopeful, incisive and amused—a few blossoms I would not want to see fall.

Ronald Caplan
Wreck Cove
Cape Breton Island

Sterling Silver

In the Spiral

"NOVA SCOTIANS ARE PROUD," said Charlie Brimer, gazing out over the sunlit cup of a cove on St. Margaret's Bay, "because they were the world's greatest builders of wooden ships. Which is perfectly true: They were. It's not a terribly useful accomplishment any more, but.... Torontonians, on the other hand, are proud that their city is the cultural hub of North America, which it patently is not. That's the difference, right? Nova Scotians are proud of something which is real, but irrelevant: Torontonians are proud of something which is relevant, but unreal."

Charlie Brimer was born and raised in Toronto, educated in Toronto, jailed in Toronto, married in Toronto, divorced in Toronto. Charlie Brimer re-married in Nova Scotia, became a father for the third and last time in Nova Scotia, ran psychological experiments in Nova Scotia, sailed and taught and partied and shot himself in Nova Scotia. Charlie Brimer has been dead for seven years, and I am still groping for the significance of his abrupt and terrible death. Suicide is terrifying not because it ends the lives of those who have nothing left to live for, but because it so often claims those who apparently have everything to live for.

Do you doubt me? How do *you* account, then, for the fact that suicide is one of the major killers of teenagers? What do you make of the doctor who used to treat me in Vancouver, a lovely man—kind, compassionate, brimming with good humour. He had an excellent practice, an apparently happy marriage, kids, a fine home, and he was well-enough respected to be lecturing on family medicine at the medical school. And yet, like Richard Cory, one fine summer night he went home and put a bullet through his head.

Or consider Kaspar Naegele, a sociology professor at the

University of British Columbia, a man highly respected for his scholarship, a compelling and charismatic teacher, a father of young children, an apparently contented husband. One of his academic interests, curiously, was suicide. Shortly after his appointment as Dean of Arts, Naegele plummeted into a deep depression, and threw himself out of a window in one of the taller buildings of the Vancouver General Hospital. Why? Why?

When we came to Nova Scotia in 1967, Charlie Brimer was a young professor in the psychology department at Dalhousie University, where my wife was to work as a postdoctoral fellow. We had scarcely unpacked before Ann Brimer called to ask us to a party at their summer place on St. Margaret's Bay. After three years in England, we were home, discovering a province we had never seen before. We revelled in the massed ranks of spruce, the openness and space, the colourful wooden houses, the shoreline which touched the road and receded again, advancing and retreating like a mirage of rocky coves and tree-tufted islands.

The Brimers had a little antique house on a peninsula owned by Ann's family; her father, Harold Connor, was a senior officer of National Sea Products, the east coast's dominant fishing firm. Perched on a ridge, the house looked down over an immense lawn to a heated saltwater swimming pool and thence to a tiny harbour, with a boathouse and a private dock thrusting out into it.

Charlie loved the place—loved his whole adopted province, indeed, though his affection never blunted his ironic wit. He was a short, wiry, bright-eyed man with a wide, high forehead capped with straight dark hair which lay close to his head, as though it were perpetually wet. He wore a black goatee streaked with early grey, and he had a minor speech impediment which made him pronounce the letter "r" as though it were a guttural "w." The effect was both distinctive and charming.

He had a scientist's affection for facts, and a passion for understanding his surroundings, and a sense of humour which became a way of seeing the world. We talked about sailing a Flying Junior, about tuna fishing in Halifax Harbour, about the fact that the carpenters who had built the old house had numbered the ceiling beams with Roman numerals. He told me about Trotsky's imprisonment in the Halifax Citadel (a common misconception: Trotsky was *not* incarcerated in the Citadel, but in Amherst), and about his own ambition to visit Sable Island. He talked about the things you couldn't get in Halifax.

"Apparently you can't buy kitchen shears in Nova Scotia," he declared. "Everybody in Halifax has them, but nobody in Halifax knows where to buy them. If you ask people where they got them, they say they bought them when they were living in Toronto, or passing through Montreal. Maybe they inherited them from their parents. But you can't get them at Simpson's or Eaton's or any of the hardware stores; I've tried.

"Or take chromium-plated coathooks. That pool down there is saltwater, right? If you hang a bathing suit full of saltwater on an ordinary hook, it's clearly going to rust and stain the bathing suit. You need chromium-plated coathooks.

"First I tried the obvious places—the department stores and the building suppliers and the hardware stores. Nothing. Nothing! Never heard of such a thing! Never had them, never will have them, only a kook would want them.

"Gradually it got to be an obsession. I was *determined* to get chromium-plated coathooks somewhere in Nova Scotia. It was a mania. Any time I went into any business premises, no matter how ludicrously inappropriate, I'd ask for chromium-plated coathooks. If I was in a candy store I'd ask for them. Or at a barber shop, or a restaurant. Naturally, nobody had them. And people were beginning to look at me kind of strangely.

"Well, after a while this mania began to fade away. Then one time we were at the Tatamagouche Festival, away down on the Northumberland Strait, and I happened to go into a general store for some cigarettes. And the clerk said, Will there be anything else, Sir? and it just popped into my head—Yes, I said, you wouldn't have any chromium-plated coathooks, by any chance?

"Yes, Sir, he said, how many would you like? I nearly fell over. He pulled out a box from under the counter, and I bought the whole box."

Academic departments wax and wane, often because of the impact of one or two dominant personalities. In 1967, the Dalhousie psych department was directed by Henry James, a tall, curly-headed Englishman who had transformed a two-man backwater into one of the hottest centres of research and teaching in the country. He recruited the brightest young people he could find, brought them from British Columbia, Pennsylvania, Ontario, Missouri, Sussex. They in turn ran sophisticated experiments, gave papers at important conferences, and reeled in foundation grants like so many mackerel. Other departments trembled as Henry James smoothly appropriated budgets, space, equipment and influence. His highrolling young cohorts admired him, abetted him, and nicknamed him "Prince Henry the Navigator."

Charlie Brimer, in particular, almost worshipped Henry James —with good reason. James was ruthlessly efficient, personally charming, utterly devoted to excellence, smooth as oiled steel. From my perch in the English department, I caught the infection myself: James had a way of projecting a vision of what the university could be, what it *should* be, and of making a young academic feel part of breathlessly exciting and invigorating enterprise.

I have an unorthodox theory about how to spot a good academic department. Creative minds are omnivorous, passionate, eclectic and adventurous. Hence a really hot department is fun, and it's sexy. The men have a certain self-confident animal magnetism, and the women are bewitching. In 1967-68, Dalhousie psych department parties were far more stimulating than most of the university's official activities.

Barbara Clark might be talking intensely and knowledgeably about the music of protest and its new interpreters—Buffy Ste. Marie, Phil Ochs, Arlo Guthrie, Bob Dylan. A graduate student meanwhile tried to convince her husband Jim that LSD really did open up new forms of perception. Bruce Moore explained why the New Left, to which he belonged, was quite different from the Old left, which had become intellectually arid.

Vern Honig, who was an excellent viola player, declared that although he was married to psychology, his mistress was chamber music. John McNulty described four different fishing techniques used by Nova Scotia fishermen of different ethnic backgrounds. Charlie Brimer remarked that he had a friend who used scuba gear to poach lobsters. That's a fifth technique, John smiled.

"I think," said Charlie, "that Don Cameron and I are the only ex-juvenile delinquents currently teaching at Dalhousie." He was probably right. My specialty used to be stolen car accessories; Charlie began with robbing milkbottles, and he had given his mother the singular experience of bailing her twelve-year-old son out of the Don Jail, where he had been booked as a common drunk.

"What did you say when she got there, Charlie?"

"What could you say?" Charlie shrugged. "*Hi, Mom!*"

At fifteen, Charlie was well established as a source of liquor for suburban teen-age parties. Once, however, he left to visit his downtown sources, and one of the other kids squealed. The parents tipped off the police, and Charlie's little racket was subsequently featured on the front page of all three Toronto dailies. One headline, Charlie reported proudly, said BOY BOOTLEGGER FINED FIFTY DOLLARS.

He married early, and disastrously—and in the divorce proceedings, remarkably enough, he won custody of the two girls. He worked in prisons and kicked around a good deal before going back to school and winning a Ph.D. at McMaster University in Hamilton. He came to Dalhousie, rented an old house in Spryfield, hired a succession of memorable housekeepers—one of them, I recall, was eventually revealed as a working prostitute—and he met Ann, who was then a student.

I remember thinking that Charlie and Ann probably laughed a lot in bed. It seemed to be a marriage of lovers who were also one another's best friends—a warm, companionable, vibrantly sexual affair. Ann is dark—dark hair, dark eyes, tawny skin—and she has a dusky, Mediterranean sensuality about her, a quality piquantly at odds with her steady, reliable Bluenose practicality. She has a special knack of making people feel that what they have to say is absorbing and unusually perceptive. She swims like a seal: I'm still grateful for her adroit rescue of my infant daughter from the pool.

She grew up inside the Nova Scotian elite, among large businessmen, prominent lawyers, imposing doctors and political wheelers. The down-east elite is the oldest, best-established aristocracy in the country: Its power is customary, comfortable, discreet and subdued. The Bluenose blueblood is not greatly enthralled with the life of the mind, though he gives dutifully to cultural icons of the approved kind. Rebellious, laughing, iconoclastic Charlie must have fascinated Ann: a reputable professor with a street kid's sardonic vision.

So they were married, and made a son together, and the current which flowed between them was enough to light a small green flame of jealousy in an observer whose marriage even then was far from being a source of joy. Over the next year, the four of us were often together. At Christmas, Charlie introduced us to the pleasure of frozen Daiquiris. He chopped the ice in a blender.

"I was thinking of getting a blender, Charlie. It seems like a handy thing."

"In theory it is, but in practice we use it once a year—for making frozen Daiquiris at Christmas. Here. Cheers."

Can you conjure up a friend by remembering the details? Charlie was a diabetic. He drank Diet Pepsi for breakfast. Lighting an Export, he'd define his view that tobacco was in part a physical addiction, like alcohol or heroin. He'd look at his aging Volvo, sigh, and remark that he and Ann had more or less come to accept that they would always be four or five thousand dollars in debt. We argued about national politics in the spring of 1968: I had fallen victim to Trudeaumania, sorrow be on me, and I managed to sway Charlie a little, but in the end he was faithful to the NDP.

"The man has no policies!" he'd exclaim. "All right, he has a position on bilingualism, but that's it. Where are his social policies? Where are his economic policies? What does he mean by a 'just society'?"

"Okay, but Charlie...."

"Mind you," Charlie grinned, "I understand he went for a canoe trip with a friend one time, and they took two girls and a case of wine. When I read that, I thought, Man! This guy might be all right after all."

In the fall of 1968, we moved to New Brunswick. Dalhousie fell behind us, like an island in the wake of a ship. Its alarums and upheavals became rumours and reports, fainter as the distance increased. Henry James had become Dean of Arts; after a brief and tumultuous struggle for radical reform, he had vacated the job and gone back to research and classroom teaching. Meanwhile, a reluctant Charlie Brimer had become acting chairman of Henry's old department. The department sought a permanent chairman, and after scouting the possibilities, confirmed Charlie in the job.

He didn't want it. Who would want to be Anthony Eden, succeeding Winston Churchill? Charlie was capable, but his heart and spirit were elsewhere: in the lab, in the classroom, in the rounded experience of life away from his job. Large administrative jobs take over the lives of the people who hold them. Like a cancer, the job consumes its occupant, prevents other aspects of his character from developing, shuts down whatever other developments may have already occurred.

Yet Charlie took it. He was proud of the department, and his colleagues wanted him. A new Life Sciences Building was going up, and someone had to see that it suited the special purposes of the psychologists who would work in it. Someone had to fight for the budgets and defend the graduate programme. Henry James himself pressed Charlie to take the job.

Henry was a pioneer, a builder; Charlie's job was to consolidate, strengthen, reinforce. No comparison. Who would compare Charlie and Henry? The answer is simple: If nobody else, Charlie would make the comparison himself.

We saw Charlie and Ann occasionally as they passed through Fredericton, heading for a skiing holiday in Vermont, and driving a gleaming new 1970 Volvo. We saw them on the way back from some conference in Washington. They stopped overnight, and we talked late into the night. Charlie was subdued, and a little weary. The job was taking its toll.

All the same, he had spent his off hours in Washington in the black ghetto, talking to people in bars and along the streets and trying to get a sense of the whole racial scene in that time of burning cities.

"They'd say, You're a brave man, coming in here all alone. Ain't you scared? And I'd say, Are you going to hurt me? Well, no, I ain't, but.... And I'd say, Then what's the problem?

"But they're pretty bitter, and they say that the whole ghetto is going to burn next summer. *Quiet now*, they'd say, *but come summer, I'm afraid it's gonna be Kill Whitey*."

"What was it they said when you left, Charlie?" Ann asked.

"Oh, yeah," said Charlie. "The guy I'd spent most of my time with—really an interesting person—he shook my hand and said, *Well, man, your skin may be white—but your soul's black*."

In 1971, I moved back to Nova Scotia—not to Halifax this time, but to the Strait of Canso, 200 miles away. My life was in chaos. A terrible ending or a new beginning? The question tormented me. My wife and I had separated, but we had agreed not to admit it until we were absolutely certain that our marriage was over. In fact, we were about to enter a tearing, flensing divorce, and battles over the four children would shape the next three or four years of my life.

I had taken a leave of absence from my university job; I would try, at last, to live out a dream; to live, full-time, as a writer. But this meant a double isolation: I had left not only my family, but also a complete circle of friends and colleagues in New Brunswick. I had friends in Nova Scotia, but they would be bound to ask questions I had promised not to answer. Rather than attempt to avoid the questions, I avoided the friends, thus imposing on myself a triple isolation. That summer I drove four times past the stone gates of The Dingle, the development in which the Brimers lived. I ached to go in, to talk to the only friend I had who had been through a divorce. But I had agreed to silence, and I drove on. I bought a house in a village where I knew nobody, adding to my pressures the obligation to make loan payments out of my derisory income from writing and broadcasting. But the house gave me at least a shallow imitation of roots and connections.

I have no complaint, in the end, about the way it all worked out; sometimes I feel that my real life only began in 1971. But that summer and winter were, I hope, the worst seasons of my whole life.

I had a convoluted, intermittent and destructive long-distance love affair. I made enough money in October to cover the Chargex bill; in November I borrowed from the Chargex to buy food. I couldn't afford a decent bed; I slept on a lumpy old ruin I had found in the attic. I had no furniture; I ate with silverware swiped from Air Canada. The only gift at Christmas was a record from my brother, and I had no record player, nor any prospect of one.

Christmas! My children came down for a few days at the start of their holidays. I strained my financial back to get some dishes, some silverware, a few chairs, and gifts. As I recall it, we managed some kind of a tree. And the kids looked at me and said: Where are your presents?

I shrugged, and said they hadn't arrived yet. But they saw through that, and they hurried around and made gifts. Two boards and a couple of nails became a model airplane. They made drawings which I stapled to my study wall and left there for seven years, till I rented the house. My middle son made me a drawing on a piece of wood, cunningly working in a knot in the board as the sun. With a coathanger and a few boughs, my daughter made a wreath for the front door.

I took them home a couple of days before Christmas. Had I ever loved them so much, missed them so painfully? By now, various friends had observed the unadmitted rupture of our family, and offered me a share of their family Christmases. But I have obscure Scottish stiffnesses in places I sometimes find surprising, and I didn't want to be an interloper at the other people's celebrations. I didn't want to have to bear pity or sympathy. I wanted space to be miserably unhappy without having to be polite. And, at some mysterious depth of my being, I wanted to experience to the full my own isolation and failure.

I got home late on Christmas Eve, a bitterly cold night with a howling northwest wind. The furnace had failed, and the water pipes had split. I got the furnace running, and then water spewed over everything. It would be three days at least before I could get a plumber. In the icy living room lay the pathetic detritus of our makeshift Christmas. When I opened the front door, all the needles fell off my daughter's wreath.

If I had to name the very bottom moment of my whole life, I would name the moment those needles fell.

I lay that night in my cold, lumpy bed and when there were no more tears I thought again about suicide. The thought was not a stranger. It seemed to me then that I carried a little nimbus of coldness, cruelty and ugliness around me, and that no matter where I went, what I did, who I met, that evil nimbus would go with me. It occurred to me that if I died that night, it might be weeks before anyone would even notice—and who, really, would care? Why *should* they?

I thought about the marriage, begun so bravely and with such joy and hope a dozen years before, finishing its life in bitterness and fury. I saw the face of my wife when we married, the blossoming young girl, beautiful and fresh and gallant, who had turned into the drawn, haggard, worn-out woman who lay loathing me at that moment, no doubt, alone in the king-size bed which Charlie Brimer once called "a great playground."

I remembered the cool, distant, correct relationship with my mother, which seemed to be all I could sustain. I thought of a brother with whom I had no contact at all, and of friends neglected till the friendship itself had shrivelled. "Clearly"—it was Charlie Brimer's trademark word—"clearly" I was a hopeless pariah, unfit for any profound or durable relationship with other people. What melodrama! I told myself. What a wallow of self-pity!

Charlie, I thought, I'd like to talk to Charlie. Charlie had been through this and come out on the other side, happy and capable and basking in the love of a marvellous woman: He would have no answers, but he would understand the questions.

But I was not going to drive 200 icy miles in order to appear, like some hideous latter-day version of Marley's ghost, to curdle the Brimers' Christmas celebrations.

My mind returned to suicide, seeking ways to go which would be quick and sure, but which would look accidental. My life insurance provides double indemnity for accidental death, and probably doesn't pay at all for suicide. Besides, absurdly, even here I had some stubborn pride: I would not willingly be seen to be defeated.

I thought about a car accident, but that would leave the possibility of being only horribly maimed or crippled. Were there any cliffs handy, off which one might fall to certain death? An indisputably accidental death is actually rather difficult to plan.

I concluded, finally, that since long walks were known to be among my melancholy habits at the time, I would walk out on the harbour ice towards the ocean. Near the harbour mouth, the ice would be thin; it would break, and drop me into the sea. In that gelid water, nobody could possibly last more than half an hour. Even if I changed my mind and tried to get back out, I would almost certainly fail or, at best—at worst?—exhaust myself and freeze to death at the edge of the water.

Was I now prepared to get dressed, go out, and take that final walk?

It would be pretty to say that God spoke to me in a blinding flash, and dissuaded me, or that I suddenly grasped some profound truth which pulled me back from the abyss. But nothing dramatic happened. Instead, I simply fell asleep—and though I was no happier when I woke up, somehow it is ridiculous to commit suicide in the morning, after brushing one's teeth. And then, having made it through one more day, why not another? And another? And here I am, writing this as we launch into another vicious Christmas season, with its inevitable blizzard of gifts nobody wants, and its inevitable crop of corpses. More people kill themselves at Christmas than at any time of the year.

Dissolve ahead now to a sunny morning in Sydney, Nova Scotia, some months hence. I am sitting in Andrea Campbell's kitchen, having coffee with a young psychologist who tells me he taught last year at Dalhousie. Oh, I say, you must know Charlie Brimer! Well, he says soberly, I knew him.

Knew him?

He shot himself six months ago, didn't you know that?

Shot himself? *Charlie*? The room whirls, I gasp and swallow, *Charlie shot himself*? No, no! How? Why?

He can't tell me much more, he doesn't know much more, and I can hardly remember now what he did say; I had scuttled into some tiny corner of myself reserved for pains I cannot share. He said something about the intolerable pressures of chairing the department, about a girl Charlie had an affair with, troubles with Ann, the horrors of making decisions not to promote and even to fire people he had known as close friends. I made my excuses and got into my Volvo—the same colour, the same style as Charlie's—and drove to the village I was learning to think of, fiercely, as "home." Driving helps, at such times: Nobody can intrude, the automatic reflexes reassure you that not everything has caved in, and your mind is free to wander or lie numb.

But the drive ended, and I found myself standing in the house, drinking coffee, smoking, biting my nails. The house felt like a prison, and I paced out, wandered down to the bit of shoreline which always seems to put me back in touch with the long, quiet realities of earth and plants and ocean, but it had no power that day, and after walking my afternoon away I knew that I had to see Ann Brimer—and not for her sake, but for mine.

I drove through the twilight into the darkness, and late in the evening I drove at last through the stone gates of The Dingle and into the Brimers' driveway. I knocked, and Ann opened the door, her face opening with surprise and welcome.

"Don!" she said, and then she saw my face, I guess, and as I reached out to be held I said into her shoulder, "I just heard this morning about Charlie."

"Oh, God!" she said, "it never occurred to me that you didn't know, I just thought you couldn't...."

There are kinds of courage, kinds of love, that we never think to describe. Consider what I asked of Ann Brimer, and what she gave: Reopening the wounds, she talked with me until 4:00 in the morning, when I went to sleep exhausted on the couch. She told me all the details of the story I had heard in outline in Sydney. The pressure of nursing the new building into existence, the pain of exercising power upon friends, the jangling of hormones and enzymes when the body of an exhausted diabetic is pushed beyond endurance, the girl, the quarrels, the last racking hours with Ann at Henry James' home in Tatamagouche and Charlie trying to reach her, his car breaking down on the highway and Charlie setting out to walk the remaining seventy miles in a snowstorm, the frantic, tightening downward spiral leading to a single gunshot in a university laboratory.

But it took him several days to die; and while his body lay fighting for the life which his spirit had already demolished, one of Charlie's daughters said to Ann, "Well, of course it's not the first time he's tried it." *What?* cried Ann, *what did you say?* "He tried to kill himself once before when he and Mommy were breaking up."

Seven years, Ann whispered in the darkness, seven years I was married to him, seven years of sharing a life, we had a baby together, and *I never knew that?* Was that whole life together a tissue of illusion, two lives side by side, just a mutual fantasy of union?

"Could you ever trust that kind of relationship again?" I asked.

"I don't know. Could you?"

"I don't know either."

Perhaps we all walk along the edge of the abyss. Who among us has never thought, at least fleetingly, about ending the current miseries, about having done with the dishonesty, the meanness, the greed and the cruelty we find not merely in others, but also—alarmingly, revoltingly, unbearably—in the very warp and grain of our own characters? "Some made the long drop from the apartment or the office window," writes Hemingway, "some took it quietly in two-car garages with the motor running; some used the native tradition of the Colt or Smith or Wesson; those well-constructed implements that end insomnia, terminate remorse, cure cancer, avoid bankruptcy, and blast an exit from intolerable positions by the pressure of a finger...."

And what of the lesson of Kaspar Naegele and of Hemingway himself: that to talk about suicide, to write about it, is perhaps to render thinkable the unthinkable, to weaken the restraints which stand between us and that terrible, perfect, unanswerable declaration?

Why do we *not* commit suicide?

I can tell you now, I think, why I don't: because eventually I realized that one has the endurance to stay in the game, and live as though it mattered, only after facing the fact that it does *not* matter; that an individual life is of no consequence whatever to the universe. My life is therefore authentically mine, the only thing I have. It has only the meaning I can infuse into it, and its most ruthless, knowledgeable, insistent judge lives behind my own eyes. I will therefore *not* throw it away, and I will not feel guilty or morbid about my weakness, my failures, my corrupt and venal actions. I will do my best with the deformed and petty soul I have to work with, I will give the stunted love of which I am capable, and if at the end I can look back and say I did the best job possible with such unpromising material, I will have met and satisfied the only judge fully competent in the case, the only judge who even cares to consider it. Who can do more?

And yet all these brave existentialist considerations miss another, simpler truth. We do matter to one another. Occasionally, during an emotional turmoil, I commit bad verses. After my long night's talk with Ann Brimer, I sent her a little poem about my own brush with self-destruction, and my grief over Charlie. Most of it is vile, but I am willing to share the last few lines:

...where I walked
People withered, and some kind of desert grew around me.

Oh, Charlie, Charlie! Man, I understand
how it might have happened. You'd have been forgiven
by everyone but Charlie. But could you ever guess
—no, no, you couldn't, or you'd not have gone—
how we who loved you when you couldn't love yourself
were going to miss you?

A Life Lived Outside the Cash Economy

WHEN I HEARD THE NEWS FROM ABU DHABI, I remembered Leonard Bonin.

Jim Morrison and I were putting down a permanent mooring for my boat that day. We had already found an anchor, a worn-out Chev engine from Poirier's Esso. Jim had a buoy and a big chunk of heavy yellow rope he'd picked up from a fishing boat, and we'd rounded up some other necessary hardware. All we needed now was a stout bit of chain between the engine block and the rope, and Jim said, "Let's go see Leonard Bonin. I bet he's got some chain tucked away in his shed."

Leonard Bonin is one of Jim's fishing buddies. Late in the summer I'd see them, often with Stanley Boudreau or Captain Pertus or Leonard's son Mark, gliding out of the pretty little harbour of D'Escousse late in the afternoon when work was over and the sun was just beginning to gild the evergreens on Bernard Island, heading for the buoy at Morris Rock. I'd be rowing out to pump *Hirondelle*'s bilges, or perhaps to take her for a happy little sail before sundown, and I'd wave. They'd wave back, and Jim's trim Cape Island boat would forge on over the quiet water, out into Lennox Passage where the schools of mackerel swam in circles, waiting to be decimated. I remember once meeting them at the wharf at dusk: They had, I think, a hundred and thirty-six mackerel, and they gave me a dozen. Stuffed with butter and onion and a few spices, baked in the oven, mackerel is a dish to dream on. I asked what they'd do with the others, and they said they'd pickle them in brine and eat them over the winter.

So I knew a little of Leonard Bonin. A quiet, industrious, generous fellow, he'd been a farmer in his younger days, and a good one too, by all accounts. Now he's in his sixties, I suppose, living in one of those immobile mobile homes which dot the Maritimes like manufactured measles, moving in that kind of semi-retired, semi-active condition which seems usual for older people in the Maritime villages. People here don't grow old; their lives just run more slowly. In the last few years, Leonard Bonin's life has been running more slowly than it once did.

Leonard has a shed, but it's more than a shed. It's the size of a small barn, and it's equipped with an old wood stove so that even in winter Leonard can work at household projects in the workshop at the back. Leonard thinks the room upstairs might be fixed up for a guest room, and he showed us how easy it would be to furnish the room, because the shed contains all the bits and pieces, dressers and beds and drapery and tools and machinery, that a family builds up over a lifetime. I saw he had a chest of drawers, and I needed one; I asked if he'd like to sell it, but he thought not. He hoped to use it in the guest room. It occurred to me that it must be splendid to have Leonard for a grandfather, to be young and have the run of such an enchanting storehouse. Later in the fall I was back, the night the vegetable truck rolled over, and a bunch of the fellows were standing around the stove drinking white lightning, clear straight moonshine someone had brought home from Glace Bay, and that was right, too.

Leonard did indeed have some chain, a couple of pieces in fact. He rummaged under the staircase, and drew out three or four lengths—good solid stuff, only a little superficial rust. Jim thought one of the short ones would do, but I cherish *Hirondelle* as I cherish no other possession, and the longer the chain, the more weight the sea would have to lift before it even got a good pull at the engine block sunk in the ooze of the harbour bottom. I wanted the longest chain I could get, a piece perhaps twenty-five feet in length.

Leonard's square, honest face assumed a faintly sorrowful expression. That's a lot of chain, he said, and he couldn't afford to give it away as he would a shorter piece. That's all right, I assured him, I was willing to pay for it. When the Chev engine plunged off the stern of Jim's boat later that afternoon, the total cost of my mooring amounted to those few dollars plus a bottle of rum. In a Cape Breton village, people know how to take care of a boat without spending a lot of money.

Business concluded, Leonard suggested a tour of his garden. I never knew he had a garden, since from the road one can see only the trailer, the shed, and the woods stretching back towards the lake. But on the little slope behind the shed were row upon row of sturdy, healthy plants—potatoes, turnips, carrots, cucumbers. Leonard bent down, picked a few cucumbers and handed a couple to each of us, pulled a turnip for each of us, sliced off the tops and threw them in a compost heap. Yes, he smiled with quiet pleasure, yes, he had his winter vegetables.

Then he led us down to a tiny pond I never noticed before, where three fat white ducks swam under a ramshackle framework of poles covered with fishnet. Usually, Jim told me, Leonard had more ducks than this, but this year a number of them died before they had a chance to mature. Alongside the duck pond I saw some big plywood boxes, hastily slapped together from the looks of them, and Jim made for them at once, to "see how these fellers are coming along."

I followed, Leonard accompanying me with seigniorial dignity, and discovered, to my astonishment, half a dozen pigs tramping about in the mud and squealing at one another. Jim looked down with proprietorial interest, and as they talked I realized that Jim had put in his name for a side of pork in the fall, when Leonard would butcher them. Every year, Leonard buys piglets in the spring, fattens them over the summer, and kills them in the fall, keeping enough for himself and distributing the rest to friends and neighbours.

It began to dawn on me that Leonard had supplies of mackerel and cod and haddock, pork and duck, turnips and spuds and carrots, and that he need not concern himself much with the successes and failures of Beryl Plumptre and the Food Prices Review Board. He embodies a Maritime tradition I had thought virtually dead, the tradition of self-sufficiency almost entirely outside the cash economy. And it occurred to me that my neighbours, whose families have lived here for a couple of centuries, really know what the country affords, what you need and how you can get it, know how to live in Canada in a way that an urban-born person like myself can only begin to guess.

Russell Poirier wanted to build a house, so he bought some woodland, cut some trees, and had Austin Nickerson mill them into two-by-fours and sheathing. Terence Terrio got his buck this fall, a couple of hundred pounds of winter venison. Bert Boudreau knows how to hunt rabbits, and rabbit pie is the traditional Christmas dinner in Isle Madame. Charlie LeBlanc gave me some capelin he netted along the Pondville beach when they spawned there this summer. In the fall nights, men in hip-waders splash along the creek beds with flashlights and iron bars, slashing at migrating eels. If you go ice-fishing you can pull in fat and tasty tom-cod, known in winter as "yellowbellies." At the end of my field the summer offers blueberries and blackberries, raspberries and cranberries. One warm evening, a kid down the road showed me how to rake flat white scallops from the bottom of fifteen feet of glass-clear water. Clams, smelt and quahogs need only to be gathered. In the spring fiddleheads grow along watercourses and roadsides. There's no shortage of firewood: Most of my neighbours own some woodland, and they all have bucksaws. You can even find natural psychedelics. The amanita muscaria mushroom, which recent research suggests was the soma of antiquity, grows among the trees down by the shore. Leonard Bonin may not know about the mushroom, but he knows all the other resources.

A few weeks later I drove to Halifax in the early morning, and I heard the news from CJFX Antigonish, CFCY Charlottetown, CBH Halifax: A place I had never known existed, a sheikdom called Abu Dhabi, had cut off oil exports to the United States, a gnat snapping its fingers at a camel. The Arabs were indeed going to use the oil weapon. Soon angry truckers would barricade American highways, service stations would close, year-round daylight saving would be instituted. Energy Minister Donald MacDonald would flutter and dither. Energy crisis, they would call it.

We live in an apocalyptic age, burning up gasoline that might soon be in short supply. Atomic bombs are still flying over us in SAC bombers, the world monetary system lurches from crisis to panic, pollution and violence and racism and sprawl render North American cities ugly and dangerous. The world population continues to bloat, while British and Icelandic gunboats confront one another in what historians may someday record as the beginning of the European food wars. Ottawa fumbles at the galloping food prices, speculators and developers kick the price of land over the moon, ensuring that their new apartments will be filled with people who can never hope to own a home. The Club of Rome says we will change our ways or face collapse and decimation within the century at most, and our record for foresight is not encouraging. Already the Americans have brownouts, but we are still exhorted to Live Better Electrically.

We may get through all these crises, God knows we have to try our damnedest, but you won't get optimistic odds from me. And if the collapse does come from one source or another, don't worry about the impoverished, backward, deprived Maritimer. Worry about the groovy Imperial Oil executive in the downtown highrise. Men like Leonard Bonin are going to have a fighting chance, and the rest of us will just have to learn as best we can the things Leonard already knows. Perhaps we will even come to see such men for what they are: wise men, who treat the earth with understanding; creative men whom the earth, in turn, may be willing to support.

[1974]

Fear of Fearing

TERROR IN BRIGHT SUNLIGHT: It's all wrong. Fear belongs to the night, to the fog, to the stormy winters, not to the brilliant afternoons of August. Let me tell you what frightened me, and what I think I discovered about it.

I was sailing my schooner alone on that part of the Bras d'Or Lake system known as "the big lake," 45 miles long and 15 miles across from St. Peters Inlet to Barra Strait, the entrance to the smaller bays and channels around Baddeck, Nova Scotia. If you've seen the back of a dime, you know what a schooner is: *Hirondelle* looks about like that, but she only carries the three lower sails—the triangular jib forward, then the foresail and finally the big mainsail at the stern.

The forecast called for westerly winds of 10 to 15 miles per hour, just a nice sailing breeze for my little ship, a wind that would whisk her across the lake on one long reach. When I woke that morning in MacNab's Cove, I had barely enough wind to sail out of the harbour, but in summer the wind usually pipes up toward noon and dies at dusk. Just outside the harbour, though, I found it blowing briskly, perhaps 15 knots already and gusting higher. I am a cautious sailor of only moderate experience; I lowered the foresail in case it should blow harder, and smashed onward under jib and main.

It was a superlative morning, the kind of clear breezy day when every detail stands out in crystalline sharpness. The schooner ploughed on, throwing rainbows of spray from her bow, her sails bellying out against their lacings. I tacked up to the lighthouse and set my course for Kelly Shoals buoy, two miles away.

I was enjoying myself, to be sure. But beneath the pleasure of a sunny day on the water ran an undercurrent of anxiety. This breeze is plenty for me, I was thinking, please don't blow much harder.

At Kelly Shoals I eased the sheets, letting the sails out to put her on the reach for Barra Strait. A reach is a schooner's fastest point of sailing, with the wind roughly at right angles to her course, and *Hirondelle* took off like a racehorse. The deck beneath my feet began to drum as the racing water spun the idle propeller. I put the engine in gear to stop its rotation and reduce the drag. The time was getting on for noon and the wind was rising. So were the waves, which by now were three or four feet in height. We went scorching out into the main lake.

About the middle of the passage, a gust of wind laid the schooner over on her side till water foamed along the deck. A whitecap burst under the windward side of the hull. Suddenly she was laboring, pressed down by the wind and thumped by the rising sea. Time to shorten sail. I scrambled up on the cabin roof and lowered the mainsail. At once her motion eased as the wind caught the jib and blew the boat around till she headed straight downwind, frothing along under her smallest sail. On the heaving deck I tied the mainsail down, then scuttled forward, out on the projecting bowsprit, and hauled down the jib. The schooner stopped, came broadside to the waves, and rolled heavily as I clung to the deck and lashed down the sail. I hoisted the foresail alone, and she headed downwind again. I went back to the cockpit and started the engine.

Hirondelle is unlikely ever to capsize, with a ton of lead along her keel, but she has a large open cockpit, where the helmsman sits; if that should fill up with water, she could founder. Objectively speaking, I'm certain that was never likely—but it is one thing to be objective in a warm, still study, another thing to cope with short rough seas about six feet in height by now, breaking occasionally on the afterdeck. Any sailor can be brave in the yacht club bar.

As I crept to windward under foresail and engine in steep seas which lifted the stern and drove the bow into green water, I was shaking with fear. I took off my sunglasses, streaked and clouded with salt spray, and squinted up to the west, where the wind was coming from. Down toward the schooner marched the curling caps of the seas, shining like wrinkled foil, rank upon relentless rank. I put my sunglasses back on. There are things you'd rather not see too clearly.

Let me make it through this, I muttered, watching our agonizingly slow progress towards the Derby Point lighthouse at the entrance to Barra Strait, and I will sell the boat and never go outside my own little harbour again. It's perfectly possible, I realized, to do something egregiously wrong through inexperience, panic, or misjudgment—to be thrown overboard, say, while the ship plunges on—and to be drowned just as efficiently in sight of Derby Point as in the greybeard seas of the Southern Ocean.

I'm doing this for *fun*, I thought incredulously, and I cursed myself for an addicted fool. I remembered the time and money I had lavished on *Hirondelle*, and I recalled Cyril Connolly's dictum that "the true function of a writer is to produce a masterpiece, and that no other task is of any consequence." Where, I asked myself bitterly, was my masterpiece? Had I not wasted on this wretched obsession with sailing the hours which might have gone into that brilliant, singing, passionate book?

At least, I thought, let me vow not to lie about this. I will admit to anyone, any time, that I would gladly be anywhere else on earth at this moment, that I do not feel any easy confidence in my ship nor in my own abilities. It is so unbelievably easy to make port after such an experience and to shrug and say, "Oh yeah, blowin' pretty fresh out there," as though there were nothing to it. It is easy actually to forget what it was like, what you felt, and to build in your mind a different set of memories. After all, you did make it uneventfully, didn't you? *Hirondelle* did handle it admirably, didn't she? You are one hell of a crusty old salt, aren't you?

No, I'm not. But I watched a big ketch struggle up past Pipers Cove and slide into the strait, and a few minutes later I came into the shelter of the land and pottered through the swing bridge myself. I lowered the foresail in calm water—though the wind was still screeching in the rigging—and motored up to the wharf. The ketch was already moored, and her crew took my lines.

"Dirty out there," said the young Viking in command.

"I was really scared," I said, remembering my vow.

"Were you?" He was genuinely surprised. "I kept looking over at you, and you were doing fine. Every time I looked you were coming right on."

It was my turn to be surprised. I looked at him and my little vessel, dwarfed by his ketch, and I felt a surge of affection. Well, well I thought, you did all right, little ship. And I suppose I did all right myself.

It seemed to me suddenly ridiculous to think of selling her, ridiculous to quit sailing, absurd to do anything about my fear except face it down and go on sailing. What I didn't understand then, and don't understand now, is that I can find no fault with my black analysis of things in the middle of the lake. Sailing *is* expensive and demanding, it *does* deflect energy from the work, it *can* indeed be dangerous. From any rational point of view it's a thoroughly stupid enthusiasm.

Can it be, though, that fear and isolation are what a sailor seeks? Am I, in some obscure way, demanding that I measure up to some idiotic, self-imposed standard of manhood, testing my own self-reliance?

I don't know, but I have a hunch that part at least of the lure of cruising in a sailboat *is* the inevitability of fear. Suppose one sailed always in fair, moderate breezes, ending each day in a secure anchorage, drinking a sundowner while the evening flared and died. No: Who wants cruising under sail to be as regular and reliable as railway travel? Cruising means making the wind and sea serve your purposes; it means being able to cope with all the moods of wind and weather.

But beyond all that I believe that some of us actually *require* fear.

Look at all the strange things people do for fun—especially

men, macho idiots that we are—which involve some element of danger, and thus some legitimate fear. Flying light planes and gliders. Riding kites off mountains. Racing cars and motorboats. Scuba diving. Skydiving. Ski jumping. Hunting, mountaineering, canoeing. Why do so many old soldiers come alive when they talk about the war?

I'm talking here of physical fears, chiefly. Most Canadians probably don't experience physical fear very often. We're frightened about our children's education, about financial problems, about the ache in our chest that could be lung cancer or heart disease, about the disintegration of our jobs or our families. Those are real fears, and they can be crippling. But they aren't the same as physical fears which strike like a blinding realization: *I'm going to get hurt. I could be killed. Right now.* Skating on a lake, you hear the ice crack. You can't find your way out of the woods. Repairing your roof, you lose your footing and slide helplessly towards the eave. On a snowy road the car's wheels seem to slip out from under you and the world turns sideways as you twist into a sickening slide. *Oh God, this is it.*

That kind of fear, once passed, can't even be recalled. Like the experience of pain, it seems unreal in retrospect, the memory of a dream or a scene from a powerful film. Memory won't give you that nauseous lurch in your stomach. The reality of fear is easy to deny.

Not only that. Men are almost forbidden to admit their physical fears.

The most humane spirits among the feminists have always pointed out that sexism imprisons men as well as women. Men are obliged to be strong, unemotional, relatively inarticulate, and rather unimaginative. Men may rage, but they don't cry. In perilous situations, courageous men comfort terrified women.

I am not going to lie about this. I vowed to myself in the middle of the lake. When a friend we'll call Roy asked me about my summer's sailing, I told him I'd crossed the big lake in a 35-knot breeze.

"Lor', I wish I was there, I guess she was goin' like stink."

No, I told him, you wouldn't have wanted to be there. I didn't want to be there. The seas were mean, the boat was heaving like a drunkard's stomach, and I was scared stiff.

He looked at me as though I'd told him I had leprosy.

"Scared?"

"You bet I was scared."

Roy thought for a moment. "You know," he said, "that's not an easy thing to admit."

"I want to figure it out. If I don't I'll probably quit sailing."

"Would you?" asked Roy. He paused a moment. "You know something? I don't think I ever said this before, but I been scared out there by times myself."

"Yeah?"

"You remember that time I told you about, when we steamed right over the shoal in a blow and a wave dropped us right on the bottom? Lord liftin', I thought that was it. What a crack when she hit: broke every piece of glass in the wheelhouse. Well, Mister Man, I was some scared then. Just wanted to go hide in a bunk till the storm was over."

"But you can't."

"No. And another time...."

He was off, and his stories came in a rush, as though they were a burden he had carried for years, and was eager to unload. He had been afraid not once, but often.

Many men, I have found, are like Roy. Again and again I've told about my terrifying afternoon on the lake, and the reaction is almost always the same: a shocked distaste, then a recognition that it takes a bit of effort to be candid about fear, and finally the flood of stories and fellowship. "Every season," one man told me, "I have a couple of days so bad that I swear I'll never set foot on a boat again. You know, you wind up praying: 'Dear God, just let me get ashore this one time, just this once, I swear I've learned my lesson.' And every spring I can't wait to get her back in the water."

There's the nub of it. *Why* do we court danger, why do we almost yearn to feel fear?

Maybe we are simply bored.

The good life held out by the schools, the advertisers, the churches, the media—the good life we still recommend to our children—is absolutely stupefying. Is life really just a matter of NHA housing, consumer goods, fringe benefits and pensions? Are we genuinely expected to be thankful for a lifetime spent repeating pointless chores in cell-like offices or on the treadmill of a production line? What our institutions teach us is that we are small moving parts in a Rube Goldberg apparatus which everyone takes seriously even though nobody can figure out exactly what the damn thing is *for*.

The good life is a crime against humanity. But even an *interesting* life in the affluent society conceals some home truths. I sit in my oil-heated house, working by electric light, with a phone to call the doctor or the fire department, with unemployment insurance and welfare to fall back on if I can't work. I make more money this year than last, and expect more again next year. I am surrounded by books and music; I even get to talk about ideas.

It's easy to forget I am only a hairless animal.

It's easy to forget I can freeze, burn or drown, that I can lose fatal battles with organisms I can't even see. It's hard to recall that life is precarious, that the universe cares no more about my welfare than about that of an individual sculpin or sea urchin.

Oh Lord, runs an old sailor's prayer, *Thy sea is so big and my ship so small*. Even a modest gale on the Bras d'Or lakes puts you in touch with chastening realities. Perhaps fear is nothing more than a sudden recognition that you simply don't matter.

Late in the season I met Charles Vilas, the king of the Washabuck River, which flows into the lakes. Carl is retired, and lives six months of the year in the Washabuck aboard his famous old cutter, *Direction*. He is a thoroughly experienced offshore sailor and editor of the newsletter of the Cruising Club of America.

Carl came alongside *Hirondelle* one gusty evening in his little motorboat *Highland Heart*, and invited me to join him for a drink. We puttered around a point and through a barely discernible opening in the trees, dropping the anchor in a perfectly enclosed little pond no wider than a country road. The wind ripped through the treetops, the rain pattered on the flat water, and we sat under the shelter of the wheelhouse drinking Scotch and eating olives. I told Carl how I was feeling.

"You *should* be afraid of the sea." Carl said. "That's plain common sense. If more people were afraid of it there'd be fewer drowned."

"But that much fear really destroys the joy of sailing."

"You'll get over that," said Carl.

He paused to crunch a potato chip.

"From what you say, I probably would have turned back that day. Sailing is for pleasure, not for punishment."

"I was already halfway across," I said. "Besides, there are times when you can't just turn back."

"That's right. That's when it's really scary."

We looked around at the swaying trees, at the lemon-coloured sky of early evening. *Highland Heart* swung to a stray puff of wind. A cormorant, flying crabwise in the breeze, stroked his way across the little patch of sky between the trees. We might have been the only people in the world. The warm light of tranquillity, rendered luminous by the black backdrop of fear.

"If we know it's dangerous, and we're frightened," I said, "why do we do it?"

"That's easy," said Carl. "We do it so we can have moments like this."

[1976]

How I Faced the Fuel Crisis

Ah, the hiss and snap of burning hardwood! The roaring flare of blazing birchbark, the sweet bouquet of a maple fire! No Arab or Albertan has jurisdiction in the forests of Cape Breton. T-shirts in January! Heat you can afford!

"A HUNDRED AND TWENTY BUCKS FOR OIL!" I moaned. "It's obscene!"

"And it won't last three weeks," said my wife, Lulu. "Say, we've got that old wood stove in the shed, haven't we?" Indeed we did. I had paid $35 for a moldering piece of Victoriana back in 1970. "Can't we just hook it up?"

"Why not?" I cried. "Why not?"

Nothing is that simple.

I nearly burned a building with that stove ten years ago. This time I was determined to Do It Right. I consulted John Vivian's authoritative book *Wood Heat*, and discovered that a suitable chimney should have a flue liner, no rotten mortar, no crumbly brick, no air leaks, no dark streaks where sooty water had seeped through. Book in hand, I inspected my chimney. I found rotten mortar, crumbly brick, air and water leaks, and no flue liner.

Better do it right. I called in a cheerful, chunky mason named Teddy Poirier, and left home for a week.

I returned to find the house ringed with heaps of broken heritage brick, piles of sand, hardened slops of mortar, unused flue liners, buckets, wheelbarrows and bits of roofing. On the peak of the roof sat Teddy, blithely buttering bricks as a mammoth column of masonry grew inexorably skyward. "I think she'll draw pretty good," Teddy called down. She drew just fine. She began by drawing $1200 right out of the bank.

Still, that was a bargain. John Vivian estimated $3000.

Teddy left his brother-in-law, Mike Johnston, to stucco the chimney inside the house, and seal it with tar where it had pierced the roof. Did I have some tar? Mike asked. "Sure," I said, "there's a gallon in the shed," Mike peered at it doubtfully. "I think it looks kind of gooey," he said.

"I don't want to go buying new stuff," I said, with a distinct Scottish burr. Where money is involved, I'm tartan all the way.

An hour later, I was screaming at Mike to stop. Coal tar was dribbling down the stucco, onto the bedroom floor, then *through* it, to puddle on the kitchen floor.

"How would you get that stuff off of stucco?" Mike asked curiously.

I tried solvent on a rag. The stucco ripped the rag, and the rag smeared the tar. I tried a nailbrush with solvent. A diluted brown circle of tar, like a dirty freckle, spread everywhere the nailbrush touched. And there was tar on the floor, well away from the chimney. How did it get over *there*?

I examined my toddling son's feet. Tar. I wiped the feet and the floor and ran outside. A small river of tar flowed down the roof from the chimney and dripped over the eave. I found tar in the grass. In the gravel. On the handle of the shovel. On the cat. Turn your back on the stuff and it migrates. We chased it for weeks. It laughed, and attacked my pant cuffs and the typewriter keys. I drove it from the office. It returned on the knives and forks. On the hibachi, on the fence. We slowed its advance in the yard. It counterattacked on the fenders of the car, the guitar, the milk jug.

The use of coal tar on chimney flashings, I decided as I clambered to the top of the house with a can of plastic cement, is False Economy. "Is that what it is?" called Lulu, painstakingly restuccoing the chimney inside. "I thought it was damn foolishness."

The cottage hearth, where, while the children play,
The plowman bids adieu to weary day....

Charles Pomfret (1703-1747) is only one of the poets who loudly trill the praises of hearth and fireside. None of these rural ruminants tells us about the joys of *building* these delightful hearths.

The estimable John Vivian decrees that the stove should be 18 inches from anything combustible—including the floor. Moreover, since "sparks do fly," the hearth should extend 18 inches all round the stove. I cut a piece of plywood to size, to act as a base. It covered half the kitchen floor. Our stove would evidently make the room warm, but worthless.

"The stove is round," Lulu pointed out. "How about rounding the hearth at the front?"

"Good idea," I admitted, "except I don't know how to lay bricks in round patterns. I don't know how to lay bricks *at all*."

"Oh," said Lulu. "Well, if you *could*...."

Which of us is not engaged in a vain struggle to be a hero to his wife? How can you disappoint a ravishing woman who believes in you? I went to town and bought a mason's chisel, a couple of trowels and a bag of masonry cement. I needed sand, and I live among beaches—but now that Nova Scotia is showing Respect for the Environment (provided it doesn't inconvenience industry), a citizen can't just go take a bucket of sand from the beach.

Late one night, a Volvo rolled onto a Cape Breton beach, with its lights out and its engine muffled. A silver-haired man and a small boy furtively opened its doors, and took out buckets and shovels. An overnight rain erased the tire tracks and footprints. The RCMP were baffled, and the malefactors were never apprehended....

I cut the plywood into the curve of an arch. A friend working in construction made me a gift of mysteriously-acquired 3/8-inch asbestos board. Teddy Poirier gave me advice about mixing mortar and splitting bricks. I cleaned up some venerable bricks from the perished chimney, and set about acquiring a New Skill.

The indefatigable Vivian told me that "a single sharp crack with the hammer" on a mason's chisel "splits best and cleanest."

Maybe so: I can say from experience that such a crack certainly hurts the left hand if you miss. My bricks, unfortunately, had not read Vivian's book. I rapped sharply, and nothing happened. I rapped more sharply, and the chisel bounced. I gave the damn thing an almighty lathering, and the brick exploded into dozens of worthless bits. The yard was littered with shards of brick by the time I created, more or less accidentally, the shapes I needed to fill in the sunburst pattern of the hearth.

We cleaned, plastered and restored the stove. We replaced its dinky mica windows, wire-brushed the word TIDY over the loading door, and painted it with gleaming black stove enamel. We muscled it into the kitchen and set it on the hearth. One of its three ornate legs landed on a patch of allegedly cured mortar, and promptly sank out of sight. We rearranged it to sit directly on bricks, patched the hole and got out the measuring tape. I hied myself to the sheet metal shop and demanded two elbows and an 8.5-inch length of pipe, diameter 5 inches, plus a damper to fit inside the pipe.

"We don't have a damper for 5-inch pipe," said Joseph Marchand. "All our stoves and furnaces use 6-inch pipe. You'll have a hard time to find a damper for a 5-inch pipe."

I plunged into the retail bazaars of Cape Breton. LeBlanc's Dominion Hardware. LeBrun's Home Hardware. Canadian Tire. MacCulloch Build-All. Never heard of such a thing.

Days later, I fetched up in the fishing port of Petit-de-Grat and tried George Samson's Plumbing and Heating.

"A damper for 5-inch pipe?" grinned George. "Sure, I got all kinds. Doesn't everyone?" He fished one down from a rafter.

John Vivian at my side, I drilled holes and metal-screwed the elbows to the stovepipe. I bored a hole in the pipe and winkled the damper inside it. I screwed the whole thing onto the TIDY, and banged the other end into the hole in the chimney, which for some reason is called a thimble.

The thimble was too big.

"An adaptor is what you need," grinned Joe Marchand. "And we do have one of those."

Now, at last, we dropped crumpled paper into the stove, then twigs and splinters, and on top some real wood. I lit a match under the grate. The TIDY took a deep breath and bellowed. I closed the draft a little and the bellow subsided to a roar. Through a crack around the thimble, I could see flames spewing into the new flue. The stove got hotter. I closed the draft further. It got hotter yet. I snapped the draft shut and closed the damper. The stove started to smoke: acrid, choking fumes that made our eyes water. I opened the damper. The stove continued to smoke.

"Where is that smoke leaking from?" I coughed.

"Everywhere," said Lulu. "Look, it's coming up the front, and off the pipe, and—oh, no!"

The paint was cracking and curling on the smoke pipe.

"Let's get out of here."

We went outside and peered in through the window at the murk. Smoke billowed out the open door behind us, borne on a hot draft of air like the exhalation of a furnace. "It works, anyway," I said. Said Lulu: "Maybe we will be able to live in the *other* rooms."

"WOOD IS A BIT OF NATURE," carols the romantic Vivian, "a reminder that this log was once a tree in a forest, home to squirrels, birds, perhaps a raccoon family. The feel of wood is good. The roughness of the bark, the occasional splinter you have to dig out of a thumb...."

Actually, the appeal of wood heat has little to do with economics, pleasure or even common sense. Its real attraction is that it marks you as Socially Responsible, one who derives his energy from a naturally, renewable resource, not from filthy oil tankers, sinister reactors, flooded valleys, ravaged mountainsides. With no garden, no solar heat, no maijuana patch, no composting toilet, no bicycle, I was in danger of losing my accreditation as a geriatric hippie. My right to vote NDP was under review. Burning wood ranks with jogging, growing house plants, eating yogurt and drinking herbal teas. It marks you as healthy, progressive, compassionate, concerned, earnest, boring and narrow-minded.

To get full marks for social responsibility, you must also *cut* your own wood. All you need for this is a sturdy pickup truck (preferably with four-wheel drive and winch), a peavey, wedges and mauls, a chainsaw, a block-and-tackle or a fence-stretcher, plus one acre of mature hardwood for every cord of wood you burn in a winter.

I had none of the above, except for an almost-suitable truck. Cringing with shame, I addressed myself to Alyre Petrie, of Creignish Rear. For $41.25 per cord, Alyre brought me 8 cords of white birch and rock maple. The bill came to $330. But this was green wood, which burns cold, makes a lot of steam, condenses the steam as flammable creosote in your chimney, and, while failing to heat your house, burns it down. Bought this summer, it would be excellent a year hence. But what about *now*?

A friend who works for the local paper mill discovered that the company had aged, dry hardwood stockpiled in its woodlands. The catch? You had to buy it in lots of 12 cords or more. That may not mean much to you, but to me it meant a flat-decked semi-trailer pulling up beside the house and lifting off a full load with its big hydraulic pincers. The pile was about six leagues long and four rods high, and I owned it jointly with two neighbours. We eyed each other, and the pile, carefully. Each of us took a third of the 12 cords—ending up with three cords apiece. Figure that out.

Soon my yard was filled with wood almost ready for the stacking. *Almost* ready because it first had to be cut into stove lengths, "junked up" as we say in Nova Scotia.

I invited a vigorous lad with a casual attitude toward the safety of his limbs to ply his new chainsaw on my wood. He quit after making $15. But a couple of daredevil brothers-in-law stepped in and finished the job for nothing. Then my wife and I built two woodsheds—one handy to the house, the other a little farther away.

All that remained was the splitting. I went out every fine day with my new splitting maul, and mauled away. Soon I'd split enough to need a woodbox in the kitchen—which meant building one, which I did. Then I went back to splitting.

Splitting wood, I can report, is extremely bad for you. It makes your back hurt, it puts fingers and toes at risk, it is very slow work and not very compelling intellectually. A year later I'm still at it.

WHEN THE WOODBOX WAS FULL, we lit the stove again. This was the moment sublime.

"Peter Lougheed," I cried, "you can come begging for birch when oil runs out."

"We're going to be nice and warm when the power goes off!" Lulu grinned.

"Let the Western rascals freeze in their bank vaults!"

"And just think of all the money we're able to save!"

That stopped me short. "We're not saving money," I said. "We're doing this for Higher Reasons. Respect for the Environment doesn't come cheap."

"I thought we were cutting down the oil bill."

"We are, but that's different. Look here: chimney, $1200; woodsheds, $500; wood, $530; stove, $35; sawing the wood, $15; maul, $27.95; stove pipe, damper enamel, mortar, plywood, furnace cement, lumber for the woodbox, metal screws, plastic cement—another $100 anyway. It adds up to $2407.95. Then there's my time: I have already spent about a month on all this, in bits and pieces. That's worth $2000. Our capital cost is around $4500. At 20-percent interest, that $4500 costs us $900 a year. Maybe we'll save $300 on oil—after all, we're still using the furnace at night and when we're not at home. So we end up losing $600 a year on the wood heat."

"Oh," said Lulu. Then she brightened. "It really puts out a nice heat, though, doesn't it?"

"Yes."

"And it looks beautiful."

"Does it give you fifty bucks' worth of pleasure a month?"

"Yes," said Lulu, firmly.

"In that case," I said, kissing her sooty face, "it's a bargain."

[1981]

At the Hour of Our Death

"THE LORD BE WITH YOU," said Father Dan, lifting his hands in a graceful gesture.

"And also with you," responded the village. In the polished wooden coffin lay the silent figure of Artie Samson, 54, electrician and neighbour, abruptly launched into the mystery.

Our little island has had too many funerals just lately. Old Annie MacDonald lost her sinewy battle against death only a couple of weeks ago, at the age of 93. On the morning of Artie's funeral the priests had been to the neighboring village of Petit-de-Grat, to bury a little boy struck down by a car. That same morning our own village was jolted by the death of Chesley MacDonald, dropped by a heart attack at 41, beheading a family with four small children.

I am not Catholic—which makes me almost unique in D'Escousse—but I generally go to the funerals. In some unfathomable way this village has laid its hands on my heart, made me part of itself, and this is how the village purges its grief. In all of eternity there was only one Artie Samson. There will never be another. He lived among us, and we knew him and cared for him, and now he is gone. We have gathered here to contemplate these facts.

"Lord, hear our prayers," Father Dan asks, "and be merciful to your son Artie."

Wherever you went this weekend, people paid their own tributes to Artie, as they did to Annie, as they would to Chesley. *Artie would always give you a help. Artie was honest. Artie was good at his work.*

At the gas station, Hazel Britten remembered his care in putting her washer and dryer in place, how he got them flat against the wall even though it took extra work to do it. "And if he made even the smallest mess," she declared, "he *always* cleaned it up. Now, how many workmen do that?"

"He had had a heart attack already," mused Ernest Poirier of Nu-Way Radio TV. "He had inherited some money, too, you know, he could have sat back and taken it easy. Probably I would have done that, or you would have. Not Artie. No way! He was always a worker, Artie."

Yes, and I have my memories, too. I remember calling Joe MacNeil to check over the wiring in a building. Joe took one look at the wires running straight as pencils, neatly stapled every sixteen inches, and said, "I seen all I need to. That wiring's perfect. Artie Samson done it."

Godfrey Gaudet and I were trying one night to fit a copper housing around the rudder shaft of my boat. We couldn't get it watertight; only silver solder, it seemed, would do the trick. So we went to Artie's house at the head of the wharf, and Artie soldered it up. Silver solder is not cheap but he wouldn't even allow me to replace what he'd used. "Glad to help," he said, and waved his hand and grinned.

Artie was a slender, handsome man. His wife Clarisse, whom I see every day at the post office, is a merry and attractive woman. She kneels now, crying quietly, in a front pew.

Remember Artie, whom you have called from this life. In baptism he died with Christ; may he also share in His resurrection....

I am becoming much too familiar with the Funeral Mass.

EVERYONE IS HERE. I ran into Artie on Friday, at the hardware store; that night he called at my house to return something his niece had borrowed, and by the next sunrise, his heart had stopped. John LeBrun, who owns the hardware store, is sitting here with his wife. Don Boudrot, from the high school. Marshall Bourinot, printer and historian, and his wife, Ina. Simon Samson, who built the shed I have spent my spare time enlarging. Pretty

Paula Doyle, 17, who has been driving the family car ceaselessly since she got her license. Mathilde Landry, principal of the elementary school. Anita Joyce from over the road, Artie's third cousin. Paul Fougere, 10, my next-door neighbour and assistant carpenter. Leonard Pertus, last of our sailing-ship skippers, who has interrupted a hunting trip for the funeral. The skipper will be 87 on Friday.

"Artie paid his bill at Landry Brothers Friday, said he wanted to pay all his bills before he died. He was only joking, sure, but it's a queer thing all the same...." Benny Landry is here.

The pallbearers: Claude Poirier, from the Esso station, Mark Bonin, artist of the front-end loader, solemn in their best clothes....

The church, a modern brick building which replaces the great old wooden church which burned twenty-two years ago, the church is full.

There are many rooms in my Father's house; if there were not, I should have told you. I am going now to prepare a place for you, and after I have gone and prepared you a place, I shall return to take you with me, so that where I am, you may be too....

Art Terrio, retired from the Fisheries Department, reads from the Gospel. His wife Mimi read at old Annie's funeral.

Four priests: old Father Albert Doucet, from West Arichat; Father Jimmy Mombourquette, who after nearly a decade in D'Escousse moved just last year to the neighbouring parish of Louisdale; Father J.J. MacDonald of Arichat, a huge Scot, president of the Nova Scotia Credit Union League, fluently bilingual; and Father Dan.

Dan Doucet is nobody's idea of an Acadian parish priest. Thirty-five years of age, with a beard and a flowing mane of black hair. I know him well, but as a friend and ally rather than a cleric: a quiet activist, an effective youth worker, a summer student at the Esalen Institute of California, a puzzled pilgrim, a good man with whom to drink rum and sing lustily.

But this is another Dan. This is not my friend with the human perplexities and confusions; this is a supremely graceful, artistic celebrant of the Eucharist, the central mystery of the Christian faith. Like a superb dancer, this white-robed figure moves with assurance and compassion through the intricate choreography of the Mass, and suddenly I am struck, as I have been before, by the profound understanding Catholicism shows towards the needs of human beings for familiar ritual and established ceremony.

When one of our people dies, he is "waked" by mourners who carry out a vigil by the casket, usually in the church, while the friends and relatives come, pay their respects, and express their fellowship. Then this Mass, which Dan does not perform by rote but infuses with mingled sorrow and resignation, in which we gather as a community to say our farewell. After this cathartic event, the water of life will begin to flow into the gap where Artie once stood, and the process of healing will have a right to begin. The Mass seals Artie's death, and thus helps us move beyond it.

In a moment of revelation, I grasp the importance, the honour, of the priestly function. We need this process. It brings home to us the reality of what has happened, and holds us steady while we confront these awesome facts.

Father Mombourquette speaks the eulogy. *I am going now to prepare a place for you*. Death is not, for the Christian, an entirely sorrowful event. Our sorrow is for ourselves, not for Artie. Father Mombourquette speaks of the splendours of Heaven, the perfection of the next life. "Help us always to remember," he prays, "that life is short, and the day of our death is known to you alone." Death is an occasion for us to contemplate our own lives, the extent of our readiness when we are—as we will inevitably be—called home ourselves.

For me, this is not difficult. My father died young, when I was only 14, and since then life has always seemed to me precarious and death a constant possibility. I intend to live to be a hundred, but if I die tomorrow, I am ready.

I find I am having a small vision.

It occurs to me that I do not want eternal life, any more than I would want perennial wakefulness without sleep. I can conceive of no life more perfect than this one, and mentally I float out of the village church, to the dramatic play of sun and cloud over the autumn landscape, the sea, the islands, the enfolded harbour. It shakes me to contemplate the towering beauty of the world out there, the fellowship of human community, the magnificence and poignancy of love, the sturdy courage of men and women walking every day a further mile along the road that leads to the grave. But if it did not lead to the grave, would life have that unbearable sweet wonder which draws me so powerfully towards tears?

Dan Doucet holds a little mace-like affair made of silver, with which he sprinkles water over the white cloth that covers the coffin.

"In memory of our baptism we use this holy water, and call on the Lord Jesus to welcome Artie into the glory of eternal life."

He hands the mace and the water to one of the village children who is also wrapped in a white robe; on the other days he performs kamikaze feats with a bicycle and terrorizes the poultry. Dan takes a silver censer, smoke issuing from its scrollwork, and walks around the coffin, swinging it toward Artie's remains as he goes.

"As a sign of respect for our brother Artie, we let this incense rise to God, who has called him to share in His glory."

Water, Dan, and incense! What puny, insignificant gestures on which to rest our hopes of uniting with the forces that rule the cosmos! How trivial! How childlike!

I am traveling up and away from the church at the speed of light, watching myself and my people diminishing like ice in a furnace, till we have shrunk to sparrows, to flies, to nothing at all—busy and invisible and trivial as atoms, particles of energy which form and vanish too quickly to measure. Artie is dead, sweet Clarisse will die, you and I are rotting where we stand. We flicker like candles, and like candles we gutter into darkness. Our culture and languages are fading away. Continents will sink and new continents rise. As the universe traverses its endless flux, the planet and humanity itself will be annihilated. Our great loves, our global crises, our games of art and war stand as nothing against the infinite backdrop of mystery.

And we dare to describe and measure and name the forces

that drive the mystery; we name them by the names of our gods and our God; we promise one another life everlasting and call on the universe to treasure our fleeting existences as we treasure them ourselves. With our crosses and censers and holy water we seek to identify with a mystery so vast we cannot even imagine its fringes. Absurd, capering creatures on a minor satellite of a minor star in a minor galaxy!

But what else are we to do? The playwright Samuel Beckett does not trust language, yet he continues to use it. Why? they asked, and he answered, *Que voulez-vous, m'sieu? Il n'y a pas de l'autre.* What would you have me do, my friend? There *is* nothing else.

O Lord, runs one of the greatest of the prayers, *be with us now and at the hour of our death.* And be with Artie Samson, for he was one of us, and we loved him. *Il n'y a pas de l'autre.*

[1977]

Cape Breton Soul

IMAGINE IF YOU WILL, a plywood hut unpainted on the inside, with a rack along one wall for all the violins, and a piano. At the piano sits May Belle Chisholm Doyle, long-waisted, tall and pretty, beating out the clear racing notes of a reel, and behind May Belle stand 15 fiddlers, *fifteen*, pouring forth that foot-stomping, stepdancing, hot wild Scottish music that makes your whole body pound in time until you are sweating as much as the 15 fiddlers themselves.

It's a private show, this. Outside on the green hillsides of Glendale in Cape Breton's Inverness County, the largest fiddle concert in Cape Breton history—which may mean the largest fiddle concert in history, period—has just ended the first of its four sessions, and the general public in droves has gone up the hill past the barn and the Catholic church to the parish hall for a square dance. What's here are 15 fiddlers who played solos tonight, 10 or 12 minutes each, and that's nowhere near enough, my dear man. In the old days the fiddling went on for three and four days at a time without stopping. When the music's on you, my friend, you want to play forever; and so 15 faces scowl in concentration, 15 arms flash up and down in unison, 15 bodies vibrate, strung out as tight as fiddle strings themselves.

This is the tuning room, fiddlers and invited guests only. By the door stands a table cluttered with empty bottles of whisky, rum and mix. People are crowding in the doorways, pressing in against the fiddlers, thrusting their Sony microphones as far forward as they can reach, hanging through the windows—and if you go outside you'll see that some of them have fiddle cases in their hands. It must be 90 degrees inside and it's been hotter than that outside on the grounds at the end of six rainless weeks in the driest summer for years. The grass is brown and stiff, the fire warnings are ominous, and there's a suggestion of mid-summer madness, of Celtic abandon, about the whole event.

The fiddlers drive on, lost in the soaring, rippling, wailing tunes, tunes whose origins are lost in the mists of the ancient Highlands, other tunes composed perhaps by Dan R. MacDonald of Judique, who sits on the chair at May Belle's left elbow. Dan R. is a huge man, pot-bellied, his glasses held together with Band-Aids, a veteran—of what wars, I wonder, aside from the usual ones? Dave MacLean of the Antigonish radio station, CJFX, who is recording everything and will play it back throughout the next year, says Dan R. is "the greatest thing ever to happen to Cape Breton fiddling." He's composed between 2,000 and 3,000 tunes, he doesn't remember how many, and dozens are lost, written on the backs of calendars, on scraps of paper and old bills; but he is still the fiddlers' fiddler and when he plays the others listen. Who knows what new tunes he may have?

"Dan R. wants to play! Dan R. wants to play!"

So now Dan R. plays alone, a new tune, slow and sweet, and everyone else listens—Carl MacKenzie from Washabuckt, who is now the town engineer of Antigonish; Clifford Morais from Big Pond, a mechanic by trade; Malcolm Dewar from Dunvegan, Ontario. The fiddlers at Glendale come not only from Nova Scotia, but from Prince Edward Island, from Boston and Detroit, from Toronto and Sudbury. Some of them are natives of those places, but a good many are Cape Bretoners home on holiday from locales where a good living is easier to find—Donald J. MacEachern of Glendale, home from Toronto; Bill Lamey, whose Cape Breton Society meets monthly in Boston for fiddling and fun. One of the fiddlers to play Sunday will be John Donald Cameron who makes a living now on national television with his brother, the celebrated John Allan Cameron. Here in Glendale is the music that formed

John Allan; these are the people he grew up with, the people he is related to, and the music is so much a part of them that, as Clifford Morais says, "your arms and fingers seem to have a life of their own when you play it." John Allan Cameron is no accident.

Dan R. concludes, people applaud, and someone mutters, "Dan R. wants a drink."

"A drink!" Others take up the cry. "A drink for Dan R.!" A glass, full of some Highland fire, is handed forward through the crowd.

John Morris Rankin plays next. John Morris is perhaps 15, a thin, almost ethereal boy with brown curls and freckles, and he looks as though he should be scampering through the crowd and pestering his father for hot-dog money. Instead he plays as seriously and intently as Dan R. himself, plays with bite and verve, a fiddler among the others, a man among men. Son of a violinist, brother of guitarists and singers, John Morris plays the bass guitar as well, but now he concentrates on strathspeys and reels, and smiles shyly at May Belle Chisholm when she glances up from the piano.

"Give 'er hell, Rankin!" shouts a bass voice. John Morris does.

He's called John Morris to distinguish him from the other John Rankins, from the grey-haired parish priest of Glendale, for instance, who stalks the grounds like a worried shepherd. Father Rankin—Father John Angus, pronounced J'nANGus—is a pianist and student fiddler, and a well-known authority on Cape Breton Scottish culture. He leads the grand finale Sunday night when all the fiddlers play together. A week hence, he will lead the finale at Broad Cove too.

Glendale's festival is being held now for only the second time and Ron MacInnis, who shyly played a solo tonight and who stands in the tuning room now with an arm around his lady, beating out time with his foot, is largely responsible. MacInnis, a black-bearded young Haligonian of Cape Breton ancestry, made a film for CBC television four years ago. Called *The Vanishing Fiddler*, it was a tribute to what MacInnis perceived as a musical tradition killed off by records and television, by good roads and mass communications. In Cape Breton the Gaelic language was virtually gone, the French language was going, and the music was fading. Mass society levels us all out; as the philosopher George Grant observes, liberal capitalism and its technology are the universal solvent of tradition.

But another mood is abroad these days, a mood of rebellion against mass culture, a mood which treasures human difference and local tradition. In Cape Breton the response to MacInnis' film was a slightly shamefaced roar of outrage. The fiddlers are *not* vanishing! They *can't*!

Father Eugene Morris recalls discussing *The Vanishing Fiddler* with Frank MacInnis, a teacher at the vocational school in Port Hawkesbury. Were the fiddlers vanishing? Maybe, but a good many were still around, and perhaps a massive festival for fiddlers only would encourage them. They drew together a committee of like-minded people including Anne Marie MacDonald, a legal secretary and the daughter of a celebrated fiddler; Hugh MacPherson, a judge; Rod Chisholm and Archie Neil Chisholm, joint masters of ceremonies, a highway engineer and a retired school principal respectively; and Joey Beaton, a paper mill accountant who bobs up and down in the tuning room now, his round face beaming, his black hair shaking, leading the fiddlers. Joey is a stalwart of Scottish concerts, conducting groups of fiddlers, playing a nimble piano accompaniment for one solo violinist after another, part of a musical family from Mabou. Indeed, for a portrait of pleasure, you could do worse than Joey at this moment, leading 15 fiddlers playing for sheer delight, playing together for the sake of the music long after the audience has moved on.

The festival committee knew dozens of fiddlers themselves and those fiddlers suggested others. Father Morris and Frank MacInnis went on CJFX to discuss their idea and the letters poured in, applauding and suggesting fiddlers to invite. The committee wrote to Cape Breton fiddlers in Boston, Toronto, Detroit. It took two years to set it up, tracking down performers, arranging the grounds at Glendale, setting up catering, publicizing the event. But in July, 1973, 130 fiddlers played at Glendale for crowds that, over the three days, totalled 10,000 and more.

At the Sunday night finale, 102 fiddlers stood on the stage and played together—102 vanishing fiddlers with a sound you'd have to hear to believe, a sound like wind rising and falling, a sound full of exile, bogles, fury, joy, poverty and pride. A sound to make you dance, a sound to make you laugh. A sound to make you cry.

If you can't hear it, more's the pity, but perhaps you can see it: a field with a red barn at the top and the Catholic church of St. Mary's in the background, its steeple black against the burnished sunset, and in the foreground a field, a real working field, mind, with at least one pile of horse buns between the bleachers. I know, I stepped in them. Slanting down from the barn are rows of benches and at the bottom stands a wide plywood stage and a simple bandstand. To the left is a canteen and the tuning room. Behind the stage are the sound trucks of half a dozen radio and television crews from Antigonish and Sydney.

It's like a rock festival for the whole family. Kids are wrestling on the sidelines, mothers are pouring juice, grandma sits in a folding aluminum chair shielded from the sun by a vast black umbrella. Down front a shaggy black mutt frisks with a couple of toddlers, pausing to lift his leg on the front of the stage. That's the music critic, someone whispers, from the Cape Breton *Post.*

Ron Gonella comes on stage. One of the most famous of old Scotland's current fiddlers, an adjudicator at the National Mods, Gonella has played around the world, cut records and starred with famous Scottish dance bands. There's no question of his talent, but his style makes it clear that what Glendale offers is not really Scottish fiddling so much as Cape Breton fiddling. Cape Bretoners weave their stamping feet into the rhythm of the music; Gonella only waves his knee. The Cape Bretoners play with passion and abandon; Gonella plays with polish and finesse. It's the difference between ice hockey and grass hockey.

"We call it Scottish music, but it's really become a regional thing," explains Father Greg MacLeod, a professor at the College of Cape Breton in Sydney, who is discovered wandering the grounds in a sports shirt and a Caterpillar Tractors cap. He points out a dark, hefty man in an orange shirt. "That's Wilfred Prosper.

Now he's one of the best, and he's a Micmac Indian from Barra Head. You've heard Joe Cormier and Didace LeBlanc from Chet-icamp? They're Acadians. There are Ukrainian fiddlers and Irish fiddlers, you know, you name it. It's really a Cape Breton thing now, more than a Scottish thing. And I really like that. I'm pleased that the culture has drawn others to it rather than turning in on itself. I've been at fiddle workshops where in the breaks between the music you'd hear conversation in English, French, Gaelic and Micmac, all the languages of Cape Breton."

That's both true and splendid. Yet the music remains at its core the expression of a Highland culture which is both Catholic—which it shares with the French and Micmacs—and Gaelic-speaking, a very different matter from the thin gruel of diluted Presbyterianism I knew as Scottish culture when I was a child. The Scots of Cape Breton are descended from the clans which made up the army of that romantic Catholic insurrectionist, Bonnie Prince Charlie, the clans which were slaughtered at Culloden and sold out by their own chiefs in the Highland Clearances. They have been loyal to their leaders, their faith, their language, and their loyalty has cost them dearly. Indeed, one story has it that the Highlanders originally took up the fiddle when their English conquerors banned the bagpipes. No wonder there's a sadness to the music, plaintive and persistent under the exultant beat.

That loyalty, of course, has its rewards as well. Others may puzzle about their identities, but not the MacInnises, the MacEacherns, the Beatons or the MacDonalds. And by some paradox, the very strength of their traditions seems to evoke talent and innovation. How else can you explain the dozens and dozens of fine fiddlers produced in a few square miles, who make Cape Breton the North American heartland of Scottish culture?

This music is *part* of a life, not its focus; it is an enormously important strand in the web of associations that makes a community. It is the music of a working people. From such roots arise the popular stars of Canadian music, an amazing number from the Maritimes. Don Messer, Hank Snow, Anne Murray, Stompin' Tom Connors, John Allan Cameron. Peter Gzowski has suggested that in Canada such music should really be known as "country and eastern." But the music is not justified by such people; their emergence is in a sense irrelevant; the music has its own logic in the lives of families like the Beatons.

Something needs saying about the spiritual bases of such music, too, as Father Rankin walks up the hill to say Mass between the two Sunday concerts. Father Morris is involved in the charismatic revival in the Catholic church, and he makes the hesitant suggestion that music is a spiritual gift, an outpouring of praise, and that it may not be so very far from the gift of speaking in tongues. Perhaps the combination of church, language and music has a more profound importance than one might expect. "Some people," he says, "call this Cape Breton soul music, and that's really what it is."

My own suspicion is that genetics may even play a part. After all, I am of Highland ancestry, though my family has been six or seven generations from Scotland, lost the Gaelic at least a century ago and worshipped the grim deities of Calvin and Knox. But once, fooling with a harmonica long before I heard a Cape Breton fiddle, I stumbled on a tune I had never heard before and that tune was distinctly Scottish. We know very little about how people perceive sounds. Gary Karr, the great bassist, remarked that though everyone in his family plays a different instrument, all of them seek a similar quality of sound, a dark sensuous lushness which he suspects is attractive to each of them because the whole family hears sound in the same hereditary way.

Where did my little Scottish air come from? Is there a distinctly Scottish way of hearing sound, an inherited Highland sense of melody and rhythm? Am I, despite my feeling of independence and liberty, manipulated by Celtic approaches to experience?

I don't know. But I do know that as all the fiddles joined in the grand finale of the Sunday night concert at Glendale, Little Joe MacNeil and his brother Raymond stood up in the front row and danced a jig together, and if I had acted as I really felt, I would have danced there with them. Ah man, it would tear the clansman's heart out of you to hear those fiddles, those urgent, ecstatic tunes with their exotic and homespun titles: "Hector the

Hero," "MacLean's Farewell to Oban," "Haste to the Wedding," "Mary Jessie MacDonald's Jig," "Clach na Cudain March" and my favourite, "The Boy's Lament for His Dragon."

More than 200 fiddlers had played, 160 were still there in the wee hours to play the grand finale. One pianist accompanied them: Joey Beaton, his shoulders canted, his right leg dancing. "It was one of my greatest moments in Scottish music," he says, "playing with 160 fiddlers!" The music wheeled and flew, chuckled and wept with a sound of being born Scottish and exiled, as one Gaelic poem puts it, to the dismal forests of Nova Scotia; a sound which spoke of being born in Cape Breton and exiled to the Boston States. A sound derived from hard winters and short, intense summers, from labour on poor stony farms and on small boats fishing a cold sea. A sound refined in the kitchens of two Canadian centuries, the wood stoves crackling, the blizzards whistling at the windows. A sound about the hysteria of love and the onset of death. A sound of frenzied, defiant joy. A music of fellowship. A remark, hard, bright and resigned, about the human condition.

That sounds like a lot of emotional freight to be carried by a few dozen fiddlers in a Cape Breton glen, I know. But you could hear it, hear the melancholy at the heart of the most exuberant reels, hear the acceptance in the most mournful of laments, hear the release this music offered to a normally self-contained people.

Soul: What you heard came straight from the soul and that, more than language or culture, is what makes the music so moving, so addictive, so capable of involving very different people. Our life is a brief splendour and all our roads end at death. The magic of the fiddlers is that somewhere in their violins they know about such things and, speaking passionately through their Gaelic strings, they contemplate for all of us the only themes which really matter.

Thig crìoch air an t'saoghal, runs a cherished Gaelic proverb, *ach mairidh ceòl agus gaol.* An end will come to the world, but music and love will endure.

[1975]

The Immortal Volvo

A MAN STANDS BESIDE A NEW VOLVO station wagon, outside the Volvo assembly plant in Halifax. He speaks into the cameras of CBC-TV's *Market Place*. It is 1971. The man in front of the camera explains that he is unhappy with his new Volvo. It was expensive, and he expected quality. But the engine will not stay in tune and the front end will not stay in line. The roof rack dismantles itself and panels drop out of the dashboard. The jacking system dents the doors. The chrome developed smallpox after the first winter salting of the roads. Parts are grotesquely expensive—when they are available. Servicing is so bad that some Volvo owners have formed clubs to service their cars themselves.

The man sums it up. "Shoddy workmanship and lousy service. Volvo cynically exploits a good reputation and a fund of consumer goodwill which it just doesn't deserve. My Volvo is the most disappointingly overrated car I've ever owned."

The next sound you hear is the slap of writs being served. Volvo Canada sues the CBC and the broadcaster. Volvo magisterially demands a full apology during prime time. The CBC's counteroffer would pit the president of Volvo Canada in an on-air debate with the broadcaster. Volvo is emphatically Not Interested. The company's suit, like a weary snake, winds its slow way through the legal system. Long before it reaches the courtroom, it gasps and dies.

Dissolve now to 1981. A seedy-looking, ancient Volvo, primer painted, rust pocked and overloaded, roars across the Canso

Causeway onto Cape Breton Island, trailing clouds of blue smoke behind it. Great waves crash in from the Gulf of St. Lawrence, dashing spray in heavy sheets across the roadway. The Volvo sways in the gale but forges on. It has covered about 170,000 miles. It is just returning from a 2,300-mile round trip to Montreal and Ottawa. It is the same car, driven by the same man. The man is opinionated and forceful, but not unfair. He decides it is time to tell the other side of the story. The car is still a nuisance, with little failures constantly in need of correction. Parts and service are still a problem. But the car is certainly durable. Indeed, it is a good deal more than merely durable.

Olaf the Volvo appears to have become immortal.

SINICE 1971, I HAVE PARTED from one wife and gained another. I have moved to another province, pursued another career, bought three houses and sold one, become a father again, bought and sold one cruising sailboat and built another, written five books and worked in ten elections. Colts have turned into horses, beards have turned grey. Stanfield and Twiggy have faded away. And Olaf?

Olaf has covered the highways of six provinces and seven states. Other vehicles have mauled his front, his back and his left front door. He has investigated more ditches than I care to remember. He has been mired to the axles and frozen in ice to the belly pan. At 80 mph, he has crossed Newfoundland with eight people and all their baggage aboard, including a canoe stuffed with packsacks on the roof. He has been driven over beaches, fields and logging roads. He has carried firewood, lumber, pig lead and a quarter-ton of coal. I have cooked in that Volvo, slept in it and made love in it. I once gave Olaf away. A few months later he was back, with a burned-out engine. I scavenged another engine and drove on.

There was a time, about 1977, when I feared Olaf would soon be worn out. Today, by any reasonable standard, he *is* worn out. He is costing me hundreds of dollars a year in repairs. He is saving me thousands in depreciation and interest charges. With all the repairs, though, his condition is constantly improving. By 2001, when a kiddycar will cost $200,000, Olaf will be the wonder of the known world: the indefatigable 1971 Volvo, the perennial 1971 Volvo, the perfected 1971 Volvo. The 1971 Volvo as it exists in the mind of God.

VOLVO, AS EVERYONE KNOWS, is a Swedish company. Sweden was once the home of the dauntless, world-voyaging Vikings. Among the Vikings' less amiable habits were pillage, theft and extortion. The Volvo parts department is a worthy heir to the Viking spirit.

The secret of Volvo immortality is beating the Vikings. As ancient peoples from Newfoundland and Iceland to France and Istanbul can attest, beating the Vikings is no trivial challenge.

Suppose your Volvo is two years old. The disc brakes on a Volvo are very efficient and very finicky. You have to overhaul the front brakes. You take the car to a dealer. The bill is $600, of which about $400 is the cost of parts. Since the value of the car is perhaps $8,000, the bill is proportionately small.

But suppose the car is six years old, rusty and worth $1,000? Then the bill is outrageous. For $400 more, you could buy the whole car. At this point, people give up and trade in. Viking pricing has cloven the consumer to the chops. Warriors with horns on their helmets stand victorious over the smoking ruins of his bank account.

At this moment, the battle hangs in the balance. It is possible to win. As others scrap their cars, they provide a pool of cheap parts for yours. Forget the dealer. Your warranty has long since passed into history, and dealers have to maintain showrooms, inventories and three-piece suits. The local vocational school has no need of these. Nor do its teachers when they moonlight in their own carports. Nor does the little repair shop in the back alley. Take it to them, and watch your labour bill sag to match your parts bill.

Better yet, learn to do it yourself. A saving of 100 after-tax dollars is not a bad return for an evening's work. All over this country there are networks of ancient-Volvo freaks. They buy wrecked Volvos, strip them, swap parts, rebuild entire cars. They know their way around a Volvo the way Hiawatha knew his way around the hunting trails. With pop-rivets, an electric drill, some sheet metal and a fibre-glass kit from an auto-supply house, they rebuild the naves and arches of Volvo bodies. They do this for fun. They do it for economy. They do it because they believe in ecological conservation. They do it to beat the Vikings.

When your Volvo fails in a strange town, sniff out the local Volvo network and the workingman's garages. Here is how it worked during Olaf's Christmas trip to Ottawa.

The morning we left, Olaf failed to start. I hooked up jumper cables to my father-in-law's car and we departed. Olaf started five times en route and failed again in Fredericton. I went to see Jon Oliver, architect, conservationist and Volvo freak. With Alan Roy, Jon once built a Volvo out of three wrecks and converted it to run on methane gas, which can be generated from domestic sewage. Jon's basement is full of Volvo parts. Two Volvo engines lurk under the card table on his sun porch. A fading Volvo 122 crouches, crumpled, beside the house. A 1974 Volvo 142 carries him on his professional travels around New Brunswick. Jon thought Olaf probably needed a voltage regulator. So did his own car. He apologized for not having one in stock. Next morning I took Olaf to Sunset Motors.

Sunset Motors is a newish Volvo agency, run by a couple of young men named Reg Drummond and Peter MacMillan, who have degrees in subjects like anthropology. Before Sunset rose, Volvo service in Fredericton compared unfavourably with the post office. Jon Oliver has unearthed reports of a Volvo dealer in England who will go anywhere in Britain to rescue a stranded customer. Jon contends that this noble Briton forms an excellent model for Sunset Motors. In the face of such exquisite standards, Reg and Peter are moved to offer a commendable level of service. Olaf was placed in the hands of Moe, their most experienced and dignified physician. Moe replaced Olaf's voltage regulator.

The cost of labour was $13.74. The cost of parts was $84.70. The regulator alone cost $57.93. Last summer I paid $15.95 for a regulator for my Dodge van. A *radiator* cap for Olaf cost $12.49. In the remote distance, I heard the vicious sound of Viking laughter.

We reached Montreal. Among other things, the signal lights had started to work erratically and the heater fan was dead. A Volvo agency called Uptown Auto told me that Vikings demanded $100 for a new motor for the heater fan. I preferred to shiver. The signal lights need a small relay. They promised to have it the next day. The next day they reported they would have to order it from Toronto. They would not have it until the Tuesday after Christmas. By that time I was scheduled to be back in New Brunswick. We left for Ottawa. Twenty miles out of town, the battery belched forth a putrid odor of boiling sulphuric acid. The old regulator had been feeding the battery too little current, but the new one was feeding it far too much. The service manual shows how one may adjust a 1971 Volvo regulator. The replacement regulator, however, was a completely sealed unit, impossible to adjust. I heard Viking war cries. It was Christmas Eve. Auto-electric repairmen were wrapping presents and drinking eggnog. Five people and their luggage were relying on Olaf to carry them to a family reunion that evening. We filled the battery with water, turned on everything electrical to drain off as much current as possible and boiled on to Ottawa.

The day after Christmas I stopped a cabby outside the Four Seasons Hotel and asked what he would do about such a problem in the middle of a holiday weekend. He told me he would take Olaf to Beaupre Automotive Service on Gladstone Street. Bernie Hayes is the resident auto-electric wizard at Beaupre's. Bernie said a heavy-duty Dodge regulator might be enlisted. He installed one. It worked fine. It cost $18.95. On its open, honest face is an adjusting screw, clearly labelled. I rehearsed poetic flights of vituperation to unleash on the heads of the Vikings through Sunset Motors when I got back to Fredericton.

The Dodge regulator chivied all its neighbours back to work too. The signal lights saluted and blinked obediently. The interior lights took up their duties. The horn bellowed lustily. The rear window wiper slashed across the glass. Olaf grinned. Vikings glowered.

We left Ottawa. Olaf had some chronic ailments. An oil ring was broken in number three cylinder and the car used two quarts of oil to a tank of gas. We carried six quarts of heavy oil. Oil in the combustion chamber fouls spark plugs. We carried two extra sets of spark plugs. Over several months, the car had been developing a heavy vibration, particularly when pulling away from a stop. I developed misgivings about the clutch. Now I discovered a heavy clicking sound when I stepped on or off the gas. This vindicated the clutch but cast deep suspicion on the universal joint. Alert to these dangers, we cast off and steered for Cape Breton.

It snowed hard between Ottawa and Montreal. Olaf plowed through it. After Montreal, the road was awash in brine. Olaf surfed over that. Freezing rain put 15 cars off the road between Trois-Rivières and Quebec. Olaf picked his way daintily along. I thought kind thoughts about the roll bars imbedded in Olaf's roof, the twin braking system, the reinforced fire wall, the recessed door handles. We reached St. Leonard, New Brunswick, early in the evening. Olaf had developed a sparkplug cough. While we ate dinner, the local garage changed the plugs. When we left St. Leonard, the motor ran smoothly, but the other vibration threatened to bounce us out of the car. The universal joint was handing in its resignation. I drove to Fredericton without shifting gears, easing up and down on the gas pedal. As we pulled away from our first stoplight in New Brunswick's picturesque capital, the whole car shuddered and hopped.

Next morning I returned to Sunset Motors, with the treacherous Viking regulator in my hand. With vivid imagery, I expressed my dismay. Reg blanched. I told Peter that the universal joint appeared to be seeking a pension. Peter asked to try the car. He made one slow, brief circle of the parking lot.

"Don't drive that car *anywhere*," he said, tossing me the keys, "at least until you're prepared to leave your drive shaft lying on the road."

This is one of Olaf's peculiar merits. In 10 years, he has managed, time after time, to hobble to a convenient garage before any organ fails utterly. He will not quit at the roadside. Evidently he is allergic to tow trucks.

Moe eased Olaf into the operating room. Two surgeons removed the rear section of the drive shaft. The universal joint had reduced itself to rusty fragments of theory. The cancer had spread to the drive shaft itself. Reg reported that the drive shaft was available only as part of an assembly that also included a spline, a plate and two universal joints. The assembly commanded a mere $305. Reg did not have one in stock. It could only be ordered from Toronto. The background sound was the ghostly whistle of Viking broadswords.

We phoned Jon Oliver, who checked his stock of drive shafts. We needed one 31 5/8 inches long. Jon had only 29-inch ones. We tried Glen Barker. He had none suitable. Reg called a man named Arnold. Arnold trudged out through the snow to discover his ruined 140 had no satisfactory drive shaft. The Vikings massed for a final charge.

"Hello, Don!"

I looked up. It was Don Gorman, a jazz bass player who sometimes jams with my son, and a Volvo freak. Don had dropped by for a tune-up consultation with Moe. What had brought me here? I showed him my disintegrating drive shaft. He led me to his spotless 1966 Volvo and drove across the river to his apartment. Burrowing in the basement, he came up with a drive shaft. It was 30 7/8 inches long. It came from a 1968 Volvo 123GT. It was probably long enough for Olaf. We took it back to Moe. Moe nodded. An hour later, Olaf was on the road. His ride was as smooth as a bagman's pitch.

"Listen," said Don Gorman, "if you ever get into trouble in Cornwall, Ontario, there's a guy you should know about. His name is Gerry Joanisse and he runs Gerry's Import Auto Service. He's wonderful. I met him when I was driving from Toronto to Halifax for a CBC gig one time. I couldn't afford to fly. My water pump let go on the 401 just outside Cornwall. I called a wrecker, and we drove around town looking for someone to fix it. It was

Saturday afternoon. There wasn't even a train that would get me to Halifax on time. We drove around for five hours with my car hanging off the back of the wrecker, until we found this guy. He's wrecked any number of Volvos. He went to work on it. He also fixed up a couple of other things he noticed that were going. He didn't like the way it was running, so he gave it a tune-up. While he was doing all this, his mother gave me a hot meal. Then he charged me 50 bucks and sent me on my way. You don't owe me anything for that drive shaft. I'm just passing on the favour. You can take me for a sail in your boat some time."

Don is becoming a semipro Volvo freak. Last year in Saint John he picked up one of the last Volvo 1800s ever built. The 1800 is the delicious sports model driven by the Saint in the TV series. It is now a collector's item. Don expects to have his 1800 on the road next summer, in sparkling condition. He will have spent $2,200 on it. It will be worth about $8,000. It is becoming immortal too.

Olaf cantered on to Cape Breton. When we got home, he was coughing again. I took him to his friends at Britten's Service Centre.

"Listen," I said to Dean Samson, "I know it's New Year's Eve, and almost closing time. But I just want you to pull out number three spark plug, clean it and put it back in. It's only got about 700 miles on it, but I'm sure it's fouled."

Dean twisted his wrists twice, and the job was done. Olaf purred. Vikings cursed. I asked what I owed. Dean said it was a Christmas present.

YES, I ADMIT IT'S COSTLY, time consuming and sometimes infuriating. But look at it this way: Almost any car more substantial than a tin can will cost you a fortune today. If I spend even $2,000 a year in repairs to Olaf—and I don't—I'm money in pocket. Lots of money.

Mind you, Olaf cannot accurately be called a 1971 Volvo any more. He's just Olaf. He boasts a 1974 engine with a 1969 distributor. The points come from a 164 series Volvo. When first and second gears failed, I inquired, out of scholarly interest, about repairing them. The parts alone would have cost $250. The entire transmission from a 1970 wreck cost $35. I extracted it from the wreck myself and got Richard Britten and Dean Samson to install it. Olaf has a 1973 windshield, a radio aerial by General Motors, a jack and wheel wrench by Canadian Tire. The vent windows come from the car that supplied the engine.

And the body? Under the assault of Nova Scotia's salty air and briny roads, even a Volvo needs rust repairs and a paint job every two years. I missed one round of bodywork and it proved nearly fatal. Nova Scotia's safety inspections forbid any holes through the body. With inspection due, Olaf was distinctly perforated. I took him to the plastic surgeon.

Claude Poirier cut strips of galvanized sheet metal and built new rocker panels under the doors. He covered the floor with acres of fresh steel. Strange, curling shapes became wheel wells. Strips of aluminum tape covered the roughest of the rough edges. Hardly anything remained of the windshield frame. Claude puttied up a new one of fibre glass. He bedded the new glass in black mastic and used two bits of green plastic, metal-screwed to the doorposts, to hold the windshield in place while the mastic set up. They are still there. He dusted the repairs with green paint. The bill was $265.

IT MAY APPEAR THAT I BEAR some continuing ill will toward Volvo Canada. Utterly untrue.

As a manufacturer of durable cars, Volvo is unmatched in anything resembling the affordable price range. If I had to buy another new car (from which I trust Olaf will forever preserve me) I would buy another Volvo, or build one.

And so I apologize to Volvo Canada for my splenetic 1971 telecast. What I said was not the whole truth. How was I to know that parts would stop falling off as Olaf grew older, and that his general performance would mature like a vintage Burgundy? (I may yet paint him burgundy. He has earned the royal purple.) I do not even complain seriously about the Vikings in the parts department. The Vikings are wily brigands who unquestionably know how to press their advantages. But what player of any good game relishes an inept and unworthy opponent? A thousand years ago, beating the Vikings was the greatest challenge in the world. It is still a pretty good alternative to chess.

[1983]

Farley Mowat, Prophet

THE WORM OF FEAR IS TURNING in Farley Mowat's guts, melting his knees into jelly, making him ready to scream. Around him stretches a featureless, nightmare landscape of stinking mud, fog, smoke and overcast. The air reeks of cordite, sweat and putrescent flesh. After three years of war, Mowat is ready to break.

The scene is somewhere south of Ortona, Italy. It is Christmas Day, 1943, and Farley Mowat is 22 years old. He has written about that campaign in *The Regiment* (1955). But that book was a history. What did it *feel* like, that terrible time? What did it do to men's minds and spirits? This fall, Mowat tells that wrenching, private story in *And No Birds Sang*. It's an occasion: his first complete book of new work since *A Whale for the Killing* in 1972. It's been, he grimaces, a long dry spell. Cornered by hyenas of the mind.

What's he like, this most celebrated of our storytellers?

Around the corner of my old cottage, one summer evening, came a smiling, curiously tentative reddish beard surmounted by a pair of merry eyes.

"Oho!" I said. "It's Farley Mowat!"

"That's who," he said. "How are things?"

I had known he was around. At first I discounted the rumour he was buying a place across the bay from mine. The rumour persisted. The local realtor who sold Farley the place had been sworn to secrecy. As a result, the story made CBC radio. Farley's arrival was imminent. Months went by. Farley was impending. More months. Farley was still impending. Farley was in the Magdalens, in Manitoba, in Ontario. Farley was impending.

The hell he was. I relaxed. The last thing I want is an influx of writers and artists and Deep Thinkers into my corner of Cape Breton. Why share paradise? I have problems enough already, without having to deal diplomatically with prima donnas and dipsomaniacs.

"That's precisely why I came here," said Farley, plunking a bottle of Lemon Hart on the kitchen table. "There's hardly any place left. On the other side of Cape Breton, it's all Winnebagos heading for the Cabot Trail. When I first went to the Magdalens, you never saw a tourist. Last year, there were over a hundred thousand. *A hundred thousand!* I had tour buses stopping at my gate. *This is the home of Farley Mowat, the famous author.* Can you imagine it?"

I can imagine it.

"We've taken serious measures. We don't live in the house here, you know. Oh, no! We live in a travel trailer elsewhere on the property. We don't answer the phone. But you know what happened the other day? I just happened to be at the house washing some dishes, which we do once a day. And the phone rang. Like a fool, I answered it. You know who it was?"

I hate to think.

"*The Globe and Mail*! The bloody *Globe and Mail!* How the hell they got hold of the phone number I'll never know. By the way, I'll write it down for you."

"Farley, isn't that sort of a contradiction? You come down here to get away from all that, and the first thing you do is seek out the only other full-time writer for miles and give him your unlisted phone number."

"I'm not hiding from *you*, I'm hiding from the bloody tour buses!"

He was full of questions. How long had we lived here? Were the people mostly Acadians? How did they make their livings? How did they react to having a writer in the village? Did I still have my schooner?

An attractive, humorous bit of a man, full of stories and passionate opinions, puffing sporadically on a huge briar, helping himself to the occasional cigarette, radiating good will. Emboldened, Margo confessed she once wrote him a fan letter after reading *People of the Deer* in a college course. She deplored the way the book had been dismantled and ransacked. And Farley wrote a personal reply.

"Good for me!" Farley grinned. "What'd I say?"

"You said, 'Keep fighting the bastards, they'll never win.'"

"Good for me again!"

At the end of the evening, Margo wondered whether he'd like to sleep away the Lemon Hart, but no, said Farley, he was all right.

"Look," he declared, his square body framed in the doorway, "I'm really glad I came here tonight."

"So are we."

"I wasn't sure what kind of reception I'd get, you know."

"What?"

"Well, younger guys who are struggling along, you know, and I've made it, I don't ever have to write another word. That's why Claire didn't come. We've had some nasty experiences...."

No doubt. No doubt.

OVER THE NEXT TWO YEARS, I saw at least three Farley Mowats. No doubt there are more.

Farley In Public is the famous bad boy of Canadian letters: the rum-drinking hell-raiser who rampages into the homes of CBC executives at three in the morning, demanding drink and women; the kilted Roaring Boy who offers his bare bum to the sedate citizens of Orillia, Ontario; the quarrelsome eccentric who makes headlines by being bounced from motels in places like Picton, Ontario, for disorderly opinions about the owner's ancestry. Farley In Public is compounded of lechery, exhibitionism, fish gurry and raw caribou meat. He misbehaves on television, terrorizes bureaucrats, makes the stuffy get sniffy and suggests that the snotty get stuffed. The Only Living Farley Mowat in Captivity and, emphatically, Not Housebroken.

Farley In The Books is the inventor of a form I call the "mowat." A mowat is not exactly fiction, not exactly fact. It follows Mowat's Maxim: "Never let the facts stand in the way of the truth." A mowat is personal experience trimmed and shaped to convey something true and important about the lives of whales and wolves, the destruction of native people, the skill and courage of those who live by the sea. Farley In The Books is a powerful historian, a successful anthologist, a prize-winning humorist, and the author of four excellent novels for young people. Farley In The Books is a spacious, droll, rebellious spirit.

Farley In Private is astute, irreverent and generous. This Farley virtually gives an outboard motorboat to a young neighbour. Farley In Private doesn't drink at all when he's working. "Times like this," observes a rural friend, "Farley *looks* like he's drinkin' but there's no bubbles in the bottle." Farley In Private belongs to the NDP in three provinces, and gives it time and money. He loves dogs, boats and northern countries. He's a reliable friend. And Farley In Private, I sense, is subject to moods of black despair.

Farley In Public has been deliberately created by Farley In Private to serve the professional needs of Farley In The Books. We all know Farley In Public because he was created to be known. "I have an image of you," I told him. "This funny little kilted rapscallion is dancing and carrying on, paralysed drunk in public places. But he's made out of cardboard. You're standing a couple of yards behind him, pushing him in front of you with a long stick, and smiling quietly to yourself as you watch him drawing all the attention, like a lightening rod."

Farley smiled, those blue eyes twinkling.

"That's pretty close."

"And it's a way of having fame and eluding it, too."

Farley nodded. Fame is a strange thing. For Canadian writers, selling in a market flooded with American and British books, fame is an absolute necessity. The happy few who live on their royalties are adept not only at writing marketable books, but also at marketing them. Here's Templeton on radio, Berton on TV, Charlie Farquharson tickling the Rotary Club, Dennis Lee chanting with children. W.O. Mitchell addresses a convention while Margaret Atwood reads at a college. Authors lead a life rather like that of a politician. Farley In Public is a master of the art. Heading out on my first publicity tour, I asked his advice.

"Don't talk about your book," he insisted. "The book is *death*! Be outrageous, tell stories, insult the interviewer. Hold your audience. If you deliver a good show, the interviewer's going to be eager to have you back. Talking about the book makes you sound like a cheap promoter. But if you just come across as an interesting person, people will buy the book because they want to know more about you."

Really?

"Absolutely! *Refuse* to talk about the book!"

It works. Almost every Canadian knows a story about Farley In Public. And in bookstore after bookstore, whole racks are devoted to prominent displays of his work. His publisher's representative in the Maritimes once told me that he owes his job to Mowat. Without Mowat's sales, the Maritimes wouldn't warrant a full-time rep.

But Farley In Public will eventually vanish. A century from now, only Farley In The Books will remain. Farley has written or edited 25 volumes since *People of the Deer* appeared in 1951. Most of them inhabit a kind of no-man's-land of literature where journalism, scholarship, fiction and autobiography interchange and overlap. Farley's craft fuses them into seamless mowats.

FARLEY IN THE BOOKS describes himself as a "saga man"—a storyteller like the anonymous authors of the Norse sagas, who preserve the heroic and poignant experiences of the tribe, creating the mythology which holds the tribe together. He is openly nostalgic for tribal life, with its web of conventions and values so deeply ingrained that they needed no enforcement. Inevitably, he travels beyond the reach of regulation and burcaucracy, always seeking people who sustain this lusty natural anarchy.

Institutions and bureaucracy thus seem to Farley contemptible warts on the shapely bum of humanity; he is, he remarks, "in favour of anything that takes the mickey out of duly constituted authority." Here, indeed, is one of Farley's great themes: the conflict between rigid authorities and the infinitely subtle shades of human practice. No law requires the oldest, most enfeebled Inuk to offer himself as food when starvation threatens; all the Inuit understand the reasons for such terrible sacrifices, and the old one can hardly imagine disobedience to a tradition so brutally realistic. But the white authorities have laws designed not for Inuit life, but for the wildernesses of Toronto and Montreal. When the two collide, the result is inevitably tragic.

Hence, too, the profound sorrow of Mowat's work. Despite his award-winning humour, he is fundamentally a conservative man, in the root sense of the word, and thus, like all conservatives, a sad and angry man. His books are either bitter laments, or celebrations of a heroism which no longer meets with honour. He celebrates nameless heroes, men and women and other animals who confront death and do what they have to do in the teeth of their own mortality: the native people, the deep sea tugboat men, the Vikings, the Atlantic fishermen, the trappers, the infantrymen of Ontario.

"Mankind," Farley said in his first book, is "the only living thing that could deliberately bring down a world in senseless slaughter." He was reacting in sick horror to his war experience. But war is only the most spectacular of civilized man's barbarities. Equally destructive is what Mowat calls "the bitch goddess of technical progress," the goddess of a species which disregards the truth that man lives on the land, by the land, from the land.

Farley In The Books finds his true ancestors in the Old Testament. "For leaders of this people cause them to err, and they that are led of them are destroyed," rages the prophet Isaiah. "The earth is utterly broken down; and it shall fall, and not rise again."

In the end, Farley In The Books is writing about the most grand and terrible theme one can imagine: the end of humanity. He is the prophet of nature's revenge. "I have heard an oracle," rages the prophet Mowat. "If we who have brought such massive discord and such wasting sickness to this planet cannot bring an end to our blind orgy of destruction, then, most surely, shall we perish from the earth."

Farley In Private is Farley In The Books, and a good deal more beside. He is a great-great-nephew of Oliver Mowat, a Father of Confederation. He is the father of Sandy Mowat, a merry, elfin young man who recently stood for Parliament in the Toronto Rosedale riding as candidate for the Apathetic Party. "Sandy's theory," Farley explained solemnly, "is that there are more apathetic voters than there are Liberals, Conservatives and New Democrats put together."

Farley In Private lives with his second wife, Claire, generally in Port Hope, Ontario, or in Cape Breton. For several years, they have shared their lives with two black water dogs, Edward and Lily—named, I suspect, for the Mowats' old friends, Their Excellencies The Schreyers. Last year Lily had a litter of pups, which were so fetching—well, now there are *three* water dogs living with the Mowats.

Claire met Farley in St. Pierre, during the long string of misadventures chronicled in *The Boat Who Wouldn't Float.* Ever since, she has been part of his migratory life, living in Burgeo, Newfoundland, in Ontario and the Magdalen Islands; in Manitoba, where Farley briefly served the Schreyer government as an adviser on northern development; in Iceland and Siberia and....

"We're an aberrant species," he continues. "We're like a cancer in nature. And writers, my friend, are an aberration within the aberration. Writers don't belong anywhere. You can live a hundred years in this village and love it with all your soul, and you'll never belong. You have this insane compulsion to write things down and to tell the truth, and sooner or later you're bound to write down truths that the people around you can't stand. And they'll wheel on you and destroy you."

Farley speaks here from an open wound. One night he talked about it, about how the Mowats lived seven years in Burgeo, and how they loved the place. About the petty tyrannies, and the closeness of people, and the unexpected eloquence and kindnesses. About Claire's notes on how things changed when the telephone came in. And then Farley got involved with the whale that came ashore, and brought the whale to the world's attention. But some of the younger men thought it sporting to shoot it, and when it died, the outside world condemned all the people of Burgeo as savages.

And Burgeo, stung, turned on Farley the publicist.

"Do you have any idea how it feels," asked Farley, very quietly, "to have your closest friends, people you've known and loved for years, turn away and refuse to speak to you when they meet you on the street?

"You don't belong here!" Farley cried, seeing in me the romantic refugee he once was himself, willing me not to repeat his terrible misconception. "You'll *never* belong here! And don't you ever forget that, because someday it's going to happen to you!"

Occasionally I glimpse other Farleys, ones I will never really know. Farley, the devoted but difficult husband, for instance. Claire is a perceptive and lovely woman who might well have had an outstanding career as a writer or artist. Instead she has usually been seen as an adjunct of Farley—a difficult role for someone with her own pride and her own imperatives. She keeps extensive journals, which Farley plunders mercilessly, and for some time she has been working on a book of her own. But—*Mrs.* Farley Mowat? They like and trust each other. But there must be days....

Farley, the son. Angus Mowat was a leathery, whiskery, opinionated Scot, a great librarian, a formidable outdoorsman. He sailed all his life—even, miraculously, in Saskatchewan. He scorned mediocrity, championed good library service and, when well into old age, set up housekeeping with a woman thirty years his junior. Farley blew into my workshop one January night with his adopted brother John, a full-blooded Mohawk transmuted into an Ontario banker. Farley is "amazed at the quality of the workmanship" of the boat I'm working on, but I know its many flaws: gaping joints, poor finishing, sags in the varnish.

"Nobody's ever going to notice those but you," scoffed Farley. "Hell, nobody's even going to be able to see half of them. That bit along the keel is going to be under the floorboards."

"I know, I know, but...."

"Yeah, sure, *you* know it's there," Farley snorted. "Who does he sound like, John? Haven't you heard this crap before?"

"Yeah," John grinned, running a finger over the wood. "He sounds just exactly like Angus."

Al Purdy wrote a poem about the loving care with which Angus rebuilt a 60-year-old boat on the Bay of Quinte. Once, I asked Farley why he didn't write novels. "My father wanted me to be a novelist in the style of Conrad," he said bluntly, "but that wasn't my route. He was always disappointed in me because I wouldn't—couldn't—do that."

Farley may be the dominant prose writer in the country. His books sell briskly in New York and Moscow. To many of his countrymen, Farley Mowat is the *only* Canadian writer known by name.

"*My father was always disappointed in me*."

I felt a flush of anger at Angus. And yet, all the same, if a man had to choose a father he could do worse.

Farley sits at the kitchen table, reading aloud the final pages of the new book. The book germinated when he ran across his own letters from overseas and thought he might write a wry and astringent mowat about youth and maturity. Instead it proved to be a ravaging study of fear. Glasses low on his nose, he reads too quickly, shy about his work and its reception. But the images of the pounded, churned Italian countryside, the slithering tanks and ruined men, the worm of fear: These are so strong, so vivid, that they overmaster even the author's anxiety. As the last words hang in the air, Farley is crying. He's not alone.

"Well, kids," Farley says, with false heartiness, "I guess my long drought is over."

Welcome back, saga man.

Farley suffers from Canada's small-minded resentment of flamboyance and achievement, but some of us know his worth. "From the day I first met Farley back in 1956, he's been my closest friend," says novelist Harold Horwood. "I have the greatest respect and affection for him on every level, as a man and an artist and a public figure whose public stances have been right all along the line."

His public stances. The essential Farley Mowat is the saga man and prophet, Canada's Cassandra. Nature never loses: That's the truth. And that truth is what Farley Mowat's life is all about. He sits at the kitchen table, the sunlight glinting in his coppery beard, staring sombrely out over the green land and the glittering sea. His sidelit face could be chiselled from stone. "Nobody who watches the way human beings behave can possibly doubt it," he concludes. "We're going to destroy ourselves and our environment. And the world will be better for our going."

[1979]

When the Dory Failed to Make it: the Legacy of Stan Rogers

THEY DON'T LOOK AS BIG AS THEY ARE, those three men down there on the stage of the Eric Harvie Theatre in Banff, Alberta, but the sound they make and the spirit that flows through their music is enormous. Jim Morison, bass guitar, from Red Deer. Garnet Rogers, lead guitar and violin, from Hamilton. And Stan Rogers.

Stan Rogers!

It's February 26, 1983, and I have been looking forward to this live concert for six years, ever since I heard Rogers's first album, *Fogarty's Cove*, in 1977. The joy I took from *Fogarty's Cove* was like the joy of a homecoming—for here, at last, was a music rooted in my own place, a music that turned Nova Scotia's melancholy resignation and irreverent gusto into something crystalline and timeless:

> *How still lies the bay in the light western airs*
> *Which blow from the crimson horizon;*

Once more we tack home, with a dry empty hold
Saving gas, in the breezes so fair....

In their lack of innocence, their skepticism, the Maritimes are unique in Canada. They have known promise and power—and then stagnation and loss. Maritimers, for instance, were not traumatized by the recession. They were stoical, having learned centuries ago the limits of hope and possibility.

Oh, the year was 1778,
(How I wish I was in Sherbrooke now!)
A letter of marque came from the king
To the scummiest vessel I've ever seen

God damn them all!
I was told we'd cruise the seas for American gold
We'd fire no guns—shed no tears!
Now I'm a broken man on a Halifax pier
The last of Barrett's Privateers.

That graphic account of youthful optimism, followed by disillusion and rage and the blighting of a life, has become a folk classic. *Fogarty's Cove* bristles with such muscular and vivid songs, full of poignancy, love and occasional manic high spirits. I have listened to it over and over again—sailing, washing dishes, building a boat, driving, dancing. It is a rare and precious album.

But Rogers is not singing those salty ballads on this cold Rocky Mountain evening. He is not a Maritime songwriter, he is a Canadian who knows and loves the whole of his country. He has devoted an entire album to the West, where he is now a familiar figure. He packs the clubs and halls of Winnipeg, Edmonton, Lethbridge. He takes the voice of a grain farmer with the same intensity of identification he gave to the inshore fishermen.

Watch the field behind the plow turn to straight dark rows.
Feel the trickle in your clothes,
blow the dust cake from your nose.
Hear the tractor's steady roar, Oh you can't stop now.
There's a quarter-section more or less to go.

We're right there, on that tractor seat. The song conjures up my grandfather, who farmed wheat in Manitoba. I never really knew him; he lived far away, and he died when I was eight. But now in Stan Rogers I seem to hear his voice, as though he wanted me to understand, four decades later, what his life was all about:

For the good times come and go, but at least there's rain;
So this won't be barren ground
when September rolls around.
So watch the field behind the plow turn to straight dark rows,
Put another season's promise in the ground.

The line hits like a blow. *Put another season's promise in the ground.* That's what my grandfather must have felt, that long, resigned rhythm of good times and bad, that revolution of the uncertain seasons, that coaxing forth of life from the earth to feed people he would never see. One could hold one's head high, being a farmer.

The rich baritone voice pours out Stan Rogers's chronicles of Canadians, songs that seem to come from inside the people. Songs that speak for sailors, ranchers' wives, old men, broncobusters, refinery workers, criminals, pacifists, runaway kids, everybody. Tragic songs, satiric songs, lyrical songs. Not all of them are his own, but most of them are. Songs of the Canadian people.

Down on the stage now, the three men are singing "Northwest Passage," the title song from Rogers's newest album. They are singing a cappella, just the three big men with the three big voices, with an occasional sharp *thwack!* on the body of the guitar for rhythm. The song is riveting in its almost casual blend of the western past and present, calling up the spirits of Franklin, Kelsey and David Thompson as the narrator drives restlessly over the highways to the Pacific, "tracing one warm line through a land so wide and savage [to] make a Northwest Passage to the sea."

The three of them have an organic sound like a single harmonic instrument—and it's *so right*, the words bitten off with split-second precision, the heads snapping back to snatch breaths, the knees flexing, the bodies dancing out the rhythm. They're incredibly light and accurate on their feet. There's not a ragged edge anywhere.

Their a cappella numbers—"Barrett's Privateers," "Northwest Passage," "Rolling Down to Old Maui," "The White Collar Holler"—have caused a minor vogue for unaccompanied singing, just as the restless sweep of Rogers's imagination has put fresh energy behind the impulse to create authentic Canadian songs. I used to wonder whether we would ever have a songwriter like Woody Guthrie, someone who would move among our people like a fish in the water, as Mao said a good revolutionary should move. A musician who would celebrate our stories, give voice to our people, help us to understand who we are.

We have him—live, on this stage in Banff. And he's *better* than Guthrie.

"I was in a turtleback trawler out of Hamilton one time," Rogers tells his audience. "I was in the wheelhouse, looking out the window—"

"The *window*!" his brother cuts in. Garnet is slim, angular, acerbic, with a cascade of hippie-length hair, in sharp contrast to his bald, hefty brother.

"The window!" Garnet repeats, in total disbelief. "Ships don't have windows! The *porthole*, you fake!"

"Well, all right—"

"Ladies and gentlemen, this man has passed himself off for years as a seaman, a salty old sailor—and he says the *windows* of a ship. He's a complete fraud."

"Well, the porthole—" Stan concedes.

"Window," sniffs Garnet. "Did you get up to the pointy end of the boat too?"

But Stan is off on another story. His songs are dramas, compressed into a few short lines. Their melodic inventiveness and taut inevitability make them go off like explosions in the mind. One of them, "Harris and the Mare," was actually converted into a drama by CBC radio in 1982.

Oddly enough, though I have never met him, I have worked with Stan Rogers on another radio drama. In 1979, our mutual friend Bill Howell was producing my radio play *The Sisters*, based on a chilling Nova Scotia legend, and he commissioned Rogers to write and perform original music. Rogers worked at his home in Ontario, I worked aboard my boat in Nova Scotia. He wrote a haunting, lovely song, and our play went into international circulation. But tonight is the first time I have ever laid eyes on my collaborator.

The concert ends. There are certain class places to play in Canada, Rogers tells the audience—the Rebecca Cohn Auditorium in Halifax, the National Arts Centre in Ottawa, the Banff Centre.

"It's been a privilege to play here," he says, and he makes it sound as if he means it. "Thank you for coming out on your Saturday night to hear us. Good night."

We get him back for two encores, but that's it.

THE BANFF CENTRE'S READING ROOM is a bar, with no books. After the concert, Stan Rogers sat among a dozen friends and admirers, expatriate Nova Scotians, folk music buffs. I bought him a "touch of the father": the Glenlivet, neat.

He was not just a big man, he was a giant; six feet four and a half, 250 pounds, prematurely bald with a little ruff of reddish beard under his jaw. We talked about his growing reputation—not just in Canada, but also in the United States, in Australia, Japan, the Philippines, England. His little record company, managed by his mother, not only carried all his own records and his songbook, but had branched out to record other artists, too—notably Grit Laskin, songwriter, performer and instrument maker, who built all Stan's guitars. ("It astounds me the support he gave me," Laskin has said. "He would come back from his out-of-town gigs with deposits and names and addresses of people who had passed on an order just because he talked about my instruments so much and loved to show them off. I've never had anybody that supported me that way.")

We talked a good deal about ships—*Bluenose II*, and my own little vessels, and *Blue Dolphin*, the Nova Scotia schooner being restored by a dogged and dedicated man in Sarnia. We talked about the spacious old house I was about to renovate, swapped notes on mutual friends, discussed our current writing projects and the state of the nation.

I was startled by the firmness and severity of his social attitudes. He was scathing about terrorism: His most recent song "The House of Orange," was a searing indictment of the sterile mutual barbarism of the Irish conflict. He favoured the death penalty not just for terrorists and murderers, but also for habitual criminals, and for politicians and civil servants who plunder the public purse ("They should be tried for treason, and if they're convicted they should be hanged") and for rapists.

Nobody argued. Who does battle, on a social occasion, with an impassioned giant? Especially if you admire him? There would be other occasions, lots of them.

So we had another round, told a few jokes, and said our farewells, promising to meet in Halifax in May, or later on, down in the country. He liked to spend his summers in Guysborough County, just across the bay from my home. We would have plenty of time to build a friendship. We would share more jobs, more yarns, more drinks. We would meet one another's beloved wives, and our small sons would play together on the Atlantic beaches. With such images in our minds we shook hands and said goodbye. He walked out into the lean mountain air, bound for Calgary, and a jet plane, and a family in Dundas, Ontario.

He was 33 years old, and there were not 100 days left in his life.

I SHOULD NOT HAVE BEEN SURPRISED at how definite his moral views were—they *were* moral views, not just social ones—because his values are plain in his writing. In one song, he asks a groupie to leave him, saying, "I'm an old-fashioned guy/And I'd rather be lonely." He was indeed an old-fashioned guy, and he stood tall and strong for values too often dismissed as quaint: married love, honest speech, fidelity to friends, respect for one's elders (particularly one's elderly relatives), hard work, attention to duty, courage in adversity. My wheat-farming grandfather, 40 years in his grave, would have approved of every item on the list.

Properly so, too. For me, Stan Rogers rehabilitated the word "manly," which for 15 years has lain abandoned on the sexist junk pile. He was not sexist—the way he talked about men who exploit women would have done credit to the most militant feminist—but he was proudly and unabashedly male, and he made others feel good about being male. In a specific and admirably masculine way, he exuded strength, responsibility, honesty and the ability to love. Manly: We have no other word for that quality.

And he was in the full flower of his talent, still growing. The completely natural way he passes the ambiguities of truth and falsehood through the symbolic mirrors in "Lies," the complex imagery of oil and extinction in "Free in the Harbour," the bitter ironies of "Tiny Fish for Japan"—these mark a steady growth in perception and technique, just as the fuller orchestration of *From Fresh Water*, his last album, enhances and underlines his development in musical subtlety.

What he did in his short 33 years was just bloody marvellous. What he might have done in the next 33 years is wrenching to think about.

And when I reach that last big shoal
Where the ground swells break asunder
Where the wild sands roll to the surge's toll
Let me be a man, and take it
When my dory fails to make it....

Stan sings that exquisite Newfoundland ballad, "Let Me Fish Off Cape St. Mary's," on another posthumous album, *For the Family.* His dory failed to make it just a year ago, when Air Canada's flight 797 from Dallas to Toronto made a forced landing and burned on the runway at Cincinnati. Twenty-three people died. One woman survived, according to legend, because a big, bald man turned her around in the smoke-filled aisle of the plane and guided her to the door.

Let me be a man, and take it.

We in Nova Scotia have no exclusive claim to Stan Rogers: He spoke for all Canadians, he belongs to everyone. But his roots were here, and Nova Scotia's sorrow is both widespread and deep. Two nights after his death, a dozen people in my tiny village of D'Escousse gathered after a dance, and sat around a kitchen drinking rum, listening to his music and sharing their grief. A completely impromptu wake for a man we knew almost entirely through his music, but whose voice had become woven into the tapestry of our lives.

For the Family is a tribute to Stan's Guysborough County roots, just as its successor, *From Fresh Water*, celebrates the Great Lakes region where he lived. (*From Fresh Water* was required, he said, "to fill the gap on the map" bertween *Fogarty's Cove* and *Northwest Passage*.) *For the Family* consists of four songs written by his uncle and grandfather, with seven or more songs from traditional sources. The uncle, Lee Bushell, built Stan's first guitar, when Stan was five, out of birch plywood and welding rods. It was one of Stan's aunts in Canso, June Jarvis, who first suggested he write some songs about the area—which led to *Fogarty's Cove*. It was at his Uncle Prescott's house in Half Way Cove, where Stan had plans to make his own summer home, that he wrote the bittersweet love song to his future wife, Diane Ariel Rogers, which became the most popular of all his songs:

And I just want to hold you closer
Than I've ever held anyone before.
You say you've been twice a wife,
and you're through with life,
Ah, but honey, what the hell's it for?
After twenty-three years you'd think I could find
A way to let you know somehow
That I want to see your smiling face
Forty-five years from now.

When he loved, he loved for keeps. But Ariel sits now in the kitchen in Dundas, hearing with her inner ear "that familiar half-marching step on the back walk, and there are times when I could swear he'll fill the doorway with his arms and laughter. I get lost some nights in my own damn house searching for the reason why. I never knew there could be so much pain come from loving."

We all needed him—that giant of a man striding across our land singing like a mirror about marriages that endure, about men full of love and women full of courage, about the glory and pain of this land and its people. We needed that grand, blood-warm enthusiasm, that massive tenderness, that penetrating awareness of the dramas that everywhere surround us. We needed to be told, again, that human beings can be crushed and shattered, but never beaten.

In the days after his death, only one voice made sense: Stan's own. And only one song was worth singing, the greatest of all his songs, the lusty, rebellious, life-saving "Mary Ellen Carter," whose rousing chorus was screamed into the raging ocean night by Robert Cusick, a New England seaman dumped into the North Atlantic when his ship foundered in February 1983. For two freezing, terrible hours, Cusick screamed it out, and it kept him alive to be rescued:

And you, to whom adversity has dealt the final blow,
With smiling bastards lying to you everywhere you go;
Turn to, and put out all your strength
of arm and heart and brain
And, like the Mary Ellen Carter, *rise again!*

Rise again! Rise again!
Though your heart it be broken and life about to end,
No matter what you've lost—be it a home, a love, a friend—
Like the Mary Ellen Carter, *rise again!*

[1984]

Tim Crawford Meets the Mind Police

"A TEEPEE," SAID TIM, "is a very practical form of shelter. There's good ventilation, the fire is inside, and there's a lot of room in it."

In the seafood restaurant on the Restigouche River at Point à la Croix, Quebec, twenty-nine-year-old Tim Crawford was explaining why he had chosen to spend his summer in a teepee. You might think that nobody's business but his. You would be quite wrong.

"I'd been teaching at New Options, a free school in Halifax, and I'd planned my summer so that I would have a lot of time to myself, to bring together the experiences I had at that school, try to put them into a perspective and sort out the course of my life from that point. In the past two years I've felt myself drawn more and more towards crafts and away from more public, social work, and I wanted time to contemplate how that course would go for me if I chose to follow it.

"The teepee itself stems out of my concern for, I guess, finding the roots of human experience on this continent, which of course relates back to the Indians. I've felt that in transplanting a mainly European civilization to this continent something has been lost in relation to man's contact with his environment. I think this shows up with oil refineries and hydro plants and the exhaust from automobiles, things I worry about very much because they concern my own life and the lives of people who come after me. So I attempted to explore a way of life which seemed to me much more in contact with the fundamental environment, and to experience the elements that go into the way of life that one could live in a teepee. I was very happy in that teepee."

Until one July day his brother drove up in the deputy sheriff's official car....

The New Brunswick Mental Health Service considered him mad, literally *mad*. On August 20, as we sat with Tim's woman, Laura, eating fish and chips by the Restigouche, Tim was still an involuntary patient at the provincial mental hospital across the river in Campbellton. He had been certified, in the words of the New Brunswick Mental Health Act (1969) to be suffering "from mental disorder of a nature or degree so as to require hospitalization in the interests of his own safety or the safety of others."

I met Tim Crawford during 1969-70, when he was teaching high school in Sackville, New Brunswick. When the Sackville RCMP fearlessly smashed a major local drug ring (two teenagers sold some hashish) Tim was one of the few adults to insist that the police respect the rights of the high school students being interrogated. That spring he applied for a job at Fredericton's free school, The School in the Barn, of which I was a director. We interviewed and discussed a number of applicants—and offered the job to Tim. He was—he is—an exceptionally creative, gentle and sensitive man, a teacher of rare gifts. But he decided to do youth work in Montreal instead.

The following autumn he was back in the Maritimes, at New Options, living with Laura. By coincidence, Laura's father is Mount Allison University professor Herbert Burke, and the Burkes are among my closest friends. From time to time I met Tim at their house, the same thoughtful, honest man he had always been. It was good to see him.

The next I heard, he was in Campbellton.

"IT GOES BACK FOR YEARS," recalled Tim, now officially sane, sitting at the Burkes' table, "the inability of family members to recognize each other's ways of life. I think that's the basis of it.

"The most recent events began when I was on the Miramichi at the cabin, on vacation. My mother and sister lived nearby, and they came down one morning—my mother was very upset, and my sister wanted to know what I was prepared to do to help. I suggested that perhaps my mother and I go to Campbellton to seek psychiatric help for my mother. I thought that was necessary, just from my opinion of the state my mother was in.

"My sister then suggested that there was a mental health clinic in Chatham, and asked if I would go with my mother. I agreed—I've known that my present way of life upsets my mother, and so in a sense I'm a cause of her problems. I thought that seeing a psychiatrist with her would show her that although my way of life was different, there was room in the human experience for what I was doing, and that a psychiatrist would be able to distinguish that from sickness.

"So my mother and I went, we saw Dr. Fathy Tadros, and we talked with him for twenty or thirty minutes. He asked my mother what was upsetting her, and she said that it was mainly me, that she was worried about me and about my health, and about the way my life was going. I was terribly thin—in her opinion—and I wasn't eating well—in her opinion—and that's what was upsetting her. He asked me what I thought about politics, and I explained that I wasn't really too interested in politics, that my life was more geared to an immediate world around me. I explained that the political system of having mainly two parties I felt was not true to human nature, and to the way that people should govern themselves—to have a good and a bad, a right and a wrong, one side and the other side. He asked me how many sides there were to questions, and I said, probably an infinite number.

"Then at one point he turned in his chair, rather abruptly, to me, and asked me to come to the Hôtel Dieu Hospital in Campbellton for observation. I was stunned; I asked if it was absolutely necessary. He said, 'Yes, it is.' I asked why? and he said, 'Because it's my duty.' I was absolutely floored, both by the abruptness of this and by his absolute decisiveness. So I agreed; I agreed to do that. He immediately phoned for a room for me.

"Then we went outside, and the minute I got out of his presence I sort of sprang back to myself and realized that this was silly; we just hadn't talked enough. Nothing had been said about my work in Halifax, which was very trying work, and which had left me somewhat mentally exhausted, mentally fatigued, working in the North End of the city with kids who were dropouts from society, from their families, from school, from almost everything. I felt that going to Campbellton would only serve the purpose of my explaining this and it being understood, and then I would be back on my own path. I offered to come back the following week to the clinic to explain this, and he declined.

"So I went down to the cabin and spent the evening there searching very deeply into myself, looking at all sides of my life, looking at all the problems that I have had and did have at that time, and looking at the stars, and the water, and the trees, and looking at the cabin which I had built, and deciding that no, I won't do that, because I have plans for my summer and I'm going to carry out my plans. So the next day, or the day after, I phoned him and told him this, and saw my family and told them that I had made this decision for my own life, that I did not seek his help and that I felt it was a waste of time to go up there and explain what I was about, and what I'd been through, and what I was doing. They were very upset, and I felt that this was a very critical point—I sensed that—and so I made it perfectly clear that they either looked closely at me and saw what was standing in front of them, and agreed with my decision, or they did not, and if they did not we would not be together.

"My mother suggested perhaps seeing another doctor in Moncton, and I said there was no need for that. Then I went back to the cabin, stayed a few more days on the Miramichi, and moved down here to Sackville, to the teepee.

"I was invited back for my birthday, when my brother would be down from Toronto. My mother and my brother and I went out for dinner, and went back to the cabin. My brother and my mother became embroiled in an argument which I took very little part in; I don't really remember what they were discussing at all. I spent a lot of time out walking on the beach and wondering what kind of a birthday this was. The next day I went back to Sackville, and a day later I was walking along the road on the way to my teepee, and the sheriff's car pulled up with my brother and the deputy sheriff for this county in it, and they said that I had been committed, and to get in the back and go to Campbellton. I got in and asked to phone a lawyer, asked to phone friends, asked to visit the teepee—no, no, no. We went straight to Campbellton."

After one night in a locked ward, Tim entered the open ward he was to inhabit for twenty-nine long days. At once he phoned his friends: Brad Slauenwhite, another New Options teacher; Herb Burke; John Shuh, director of New Options; and, of course, Laura.

"I told them where I was," he remembered, "told them that I was fine, and that I had the strength of character and the strength of mind to see this through on my own if I had to, but that I sought their help, and that if there was anything they could do I completely authorized them to do it, because I wanted the hell out of there."

Tim's friends confirm that he did exactly that. But Dr. Claudette Durand, Medical Superintendent of the hospital says flatly that he agreed to stay, presumably because Tim thought it "futile" to demand his release. Silence is consent.

But how does one resist such arbitrary power? Protest vigorously? *The patient shows symptoms of paranoia.* Insist that one is sane? *Patients often find it difficult to accept the reality of their own illness.* Use outside channels and maintain a low profile inside the hospital? *The patient submitting willingly to treatment; we find it hard to understand why you people are so upset.* After one of John Shuh's visits, indeed, a hospital psychiatrist made the chilling comment that Shuh also showed signs of mental disturbance and perhaps would benefit from treatment.

THOUGH JOHN SHUH WAS HARDLY mentally ill, he was certainly disturbed. A stocky twenty-eight-year-old ordained minister who sports a beard, long hair and granny glasses, Shuh had known Tim Crawford since the two were undergraduates at Mount Allison. In 1971 he had convinced Tim to come to New Options, and during the next year the two had become very close friends. When Tim phoned, Shuh at once set out on the four-hundred-mile drive to Campbellton, stopping for talks with the Burkes in Sackville.

"By the time I started up the North Shore of New Brunswick," Shuh reflects, "I really began to wonder just what in hell I was going to be able to do. I had a vision of how the thing was going to work out; I thought that if I were going to make a movie about the whole thing, I'd make it in these terms, you know, that I saw myself walking into the office of a faceless psychiatrist, and pulling four balls out of my pocket, facing off to him, and then starting to juggle them. He sort of nodded his head, and took out *five* balls and started to juggle them. Then I took off a silk hat and pulled out a rabbit: He took off his silk hat and pulled out a chicken, and so on. The sense was that what was really going to be involved was working out of your bags of tricks, to see who could spring the definitive trick, the trick that would turn the whole thing. And that, in a very real sense, was the way things went."

Reaching Campbellton in the evening, Shuh went to see Tim. "He was on that occasion—as he was each time I saw him in the hospital—tremendously serene, very calm." Together they decided that Shuh would try to see both Dr. Tadros and a Dr. O'Callaghan, Tim's attending physician in the hospital. Next day Shuh found O'Callaghan at the Bathurst courthouse, seventy miles away.

"One of the things that struck me was that there seemed to be no way I could make any contact with O'Callaghan," Shuh says now. "He seemed to be tremendously threatened by the fact that I was snooping around and meddling. Furthermore—this was something that continued to amaze me—none of the psychiatrists could really understand why I was involved. I'd explain that I was there because Tim asked me to be there, and because I was his friend. They'd say, but the family has participated in the committal: Don't you just trust that what the family is doing is in Tim's best interests? And I'd say, well, I know that the family is very concerned for Tim and that they've done what they've done out of that concern, but I just don't feel that Tim is sick; and I think that perhaps at this stage I know Tim better than his family does.

"Whenever I'd say that I didn't really feel that Tim was sick, they'd say, 'Well, are you a psychiatrist?' There was so much feeling expressed both by the psychiatrists and by Tim's family that the only person who could really judge Tim's sanity or insanity was a professional. That's one of the really disturbing aspects of the whole business. Tim's brother even told me at one point that he didn't feel that Tim was mentally ill, but because a psychiatrist hung a label on him he'd obviously taken that man's judgment over his own. It's really amazing that professionals have so usurped the expertise of friends and families that a psychiatrist, after a twenty-minute interview, can make a pronouncement which completely outweighs all the best knowledge and understanding of people who've known a person for years.

"So I didn't get very far with O'Callaghan. But the funny thing was that all he talked about was really that Tim was not sort of straightening up and taking a regular job, that he was out there living in the wilderness and not eating his green vegetables and all sorts of stuff like that—but he didn't really put any *psychiatric* tag on the thing. I kept saying to him, yeah, that's okay, people *should* eat their green vegetables, I agree with that, a balanced diet is very important. But if somebody is not eating a balanced diet it doesn't mean that you have the right to put him into a mental hospital. Finally, in frustration, I just said that I thought this whole thing was unconscionable, and that a number of people agreed with that, and that we were willing to make a public issue out of it. And at that point he got up and walked away."

Shuh went on to see Tadros at the clinic in Chatham.

"Tadros was the one who laid the diagnosis of schizophrenia on Tim, and we went through his reasons in some detail. He talked of Tim's withdrawing from the world and from all people—this had obviously come from Tim's family, because when he went to Sackville to set up his teepee Tim didn't tell his family exactly where he was going. Now the reason he *didn't* should be quite obvious: He didn't want them hounding him and interfering with his life. He did let me know; the Burkes knew; I had been to see him and his teepee was next door to a number of other kids who were in a commune. A lot of friends in Sackville knew where he was, and most of his friends in Halifax knew where he was.

"Tadros also had a thing about Tim moving from a practical area—his background and training had been in science, and he had had some work in meteorology—into abstract, poetic and philosophical considerations. This is quite true: This is what has happened to Tim. But it's far more indicative of a very broad cultural movement, the kinds of things that have been going on in the last ten years all across North America. One of the difficulties that I sensed was that of the three psychiatrists, one was French, one was Irish and one was Egyptian, and I really didn't have the sense that they had a tremendously acute perception of the cultural situation in North America at this point in our history.

"However, my conversation with Tadros, even though we disagreed on just about every point, was far more affable and open than it had been with O'Callaghan, and when I left Tadros suggested two things: first, that if Tim was currently out of a locked ward—which he was—I could get a psychiatrist in Halifax to write and say that he would take Tim under his care if he were released from the hospital. Tadros said that he suspected the hospital would release him on that basis. He also suggested that, failing that, it would be possible to get an independent psychiatric assessment—but suggested as well that an ordinary private practice psychiatrist wouldn't pull any weight. As he said, 'It's just his word against mine, so you've got to go into the big leagues and get a psychiatrist who is teaching at a university.' As it turned out, that was pretty astute political advice."

Talking by phone, Crawford and Shuh agreed that the diagnosis "explained," as Shuh puts it, "his family's involvement, to a great extent. I was convinced at the time—and still am—that Tim's family was really operating out of a genuine concern for Tim. The whole process of diagnosis, I think, had been a vicious circle of misunderstanding, with the misunderstandings of Tim's family informing the misunderstandings of Tadros informing the family misunderstandings.... What had basically happened was that when Tadros said, 'This man's schizophrenic,' the family really got spooked. I don't think they would have wanted to go that route, of involuntary commitment, but they were scared, and when Tadros suggested that he be committed they went along. And in a very real sense, I can understand that. If I were really convinced that somebody needed to be hospitalized, particularly someone for whom I had love and concern—well, what do you do? One time Tim mentioned to me that his family talked to him about the parable of the Good Samaritan, and I think they really saw themselves as stopping to help when others had passed by on the other side."

DR. LESLIE KOVACS, A HALIFAX PSYCHIATRIST who has worked with New Options, sent a night letter to hospital Medical Superintendent Dr. Durand, agreeing to take Tim under his care. Next day Shuh sat in Dr. Durand's office as Kovacs followed up with a phone call. But Durand refused to release Tim without the family's consent. O'Callaghan refused to see Shuh at all. Shuh headed for Chatham to talk again with the family—and arrived just as Dr. Durand was speaking by phone to Tim's brother.

"From what I could judge," says Shuh, "she was basically telling him that any attempt to move Tim from the hospital at this time would be very bad for Tim, and should be resisted at all costs. When his brother got off the phone, he came out to the dining room where his mother was making me a cup of coffee, and I really felt that if it hadn't been for the presence of Tim's mother, his brother would have gotten into physical force to chuck me out of the house.

"He finally fumed out, and his mother and I talked. She very obviously perceived the whole thing as a kind of private family embarrassment which no one else had a right to become involved in, and she generally put across the sense that Tim's friends in Halifax were trying to manipulate Tim to achieve a political critique of mental health conditions in the north of New Brunswick.

Now I think such a critique is necessary, and very important, but the north of New Brunswick is generally outside my range of both action and knowledge, and the reason I was there was because Tim had asked that I come. At every point—I tried to make this very clear to Tim's mother—I always phoned and talked with Tim about what I was doing, who I had talked to, what they had said, so that Tim was really on top of the whole thing. Nothing was done without his approval.

"In some ways I think Mrs. Crawford viewed herself as the central figure in a tragedy. She kept saying, 'Wouldn't you come to the person who is most involved?' and I'd say, 'Yes, I would; I just happen to disagree with your perception of who that person is, and my feeling is that Tim is it.' She'd say, 'Tim is not well,' and I'd say, 'Well, I disagree with your perception on that, too.' You'd go round and round in rings and never communicate."

FOR A PERSUASIVE INDEPENDENT ASSESSMENT, Tadros had said, you have to go into the big leagues. You need someone like, say, Lionel Solursh.

Dr. Lionel P. Solursh, that is, M.D., D. Psych., M.R.C.P.(C), F.R.C.P.(C), of Toronto Western Hospital and the University of Toronto medical school. Apple-cheeked and precocious at thirty-six, Solursh has a string of qualifications that fills a typewritten page; his publications cover two more. He advises governments, chairs committees of the Canadian Medical Association, the Canadian Mental Health Association and the World Medical Assembly; he is the only Canadian consultant to the U.S. National Commission on Marijuana and Drug Abuse.

And so, on the sunny afternoon of August 20, we converged on Campbellton—John Shuh and two other friends from Halifax; Solursh and a social worker from Toronto; the Crawfords from Chatham; Laura from Campbellton itself, where she had stayed throughout Tim's confinement; and your humble narrator, from Fredericton.

By now the hospital, the Minister of Health, the Minister of Justice, the Ombudsman and the Premier had all been peppered by letters and phone calls. Tim's friends had considered—and rejected—the cumbersome process of a Review Board under the Mental Health Act. Shuh's probing had led the family to ask that Tim be denied both visitors and incoming phone calls, and the hospital had agreed. Since Tim and Laura were not married, his committal made his family legally responsible for him and thus cancelled his existence as an independent adult.

We sat on the low brick guard rail talking with one another, with Tim, with other patients. The afternoon ground on. Inside, Solursh was reviewing the case history, talking with Tim and his family and with Durand and O'Callaghan. A group of patients sang, accompanied by a rather good guitarist. The afternoon ground on. Tim showed us the wooden puzzles and the hooked rug he had made in occupational therapy. We asked one another what was going on inside. The afternoon ground on, interminably.

Mrs. Crawford emerged with her daughter Joan, and spoke to John Shuh. Then she asked to speak to me. What was my interest in this private family matter? Well, Tim was a citizen confined under law in a public institution, so the matter wasn't purely private. Who had asked me to write the story? It had been my initiative, undertaken in consultation with Tim and others. What protection did she have against what I might say? If what I wrote was not both true and in the public interest, she could sue for libel. *I am not interested in seeing my son used, I am interested in his welfare.* So am I, Mrs. Crawford. *Before you write anything, I think you should have a talk with me.* I'd very much like to do that. *Well, I certainly think you should.* But when I did visit her, she chose not to discuss it.

She turned to Shuh again, a tall, slim woman with silvery hair and fine features, a handsome woman in her trim tweed suit. *Now look here, John Shuh, if I hear any more of this business about Tim being imprisoned for his style of life, do you understand?* I could not hear what Shuh was saying. *I will not have my son used. I don't know whose idea it was to bring the press in. My only concern is for the welfare of my son.*

Mother, said Joan quietly, *Mother*. They got in their car and drove away.

The Halifax and Toronto contingents headed for home via the Moncton airport. Tim asked permission to have dinner with Laura and me, and we crossed the bridge to Quebec. Had I been Tim, I am not sure I would have had the courage to go back into New Brunswick. But he did, and I left him with Laura, two brave and weary young people.

"Thomas (Tim) Crawford," wrote Solursh in his report, "is a bright warm young man who, at most, is a borderline schizophrenic, who is not now psychotic, and who has been playing the mental hospital game (meeting expectations, not taking medication, etc.) in a frustrating situation which he wished to leave. He (and history from his family) provides no evidence of his currently being any danger to his life or property or that of others."

"What's interesting," John Shuh points out, "is that the hospital waited another week before releasing Tim. I think Durand wanted to emphasize that she wasn't about to be pushed around and that she wasn't going to release Tim before the thirty-day observation period was up. It's really rather a strange thing, because the agreement had been reached—in essence—that Sunday, that there was no reason for Tim to be hospitalized. And yet they kept him for another five days."

A borderline schizophrenic, Solursh explained two weeks later in his cramped office at Toronto Western Hospital, is someone who doesn't have "those classic symptoms of autism and affective disorder and ambivalence and the loosening of associations, that kind of stuff, but their history is such as to indicate that they've either been in and out of schizophrenic breaks or that they're close to one and could have it given sufficient stress—of almost any sort that's meaningful to the person. But what we were really seeing—and it's fairly typical—were symptoms of a family disorder."

And, Solursh pointed out, the question of lifestyle is really a pretext; if the family were not squabbling about that, it would be squabbling about something else.

No doubt. But in fact that is what they were squabbling about, and Solursh himself considered Tim's "unconventional social adjustment" to be a "symptom." The British psychiatrist R. D. Laing describes his fellow psychiatrists as "mind police," all the more dangerous for being well-intentioned. They only want to help people adjust, just as they do in the Soviet Union—and if that means subjecting them to imprisonment, electric shocks, lobotomies, aversive conditioning and psychotropic drugs, well, it's all done in their own best interests, eh?

And if the "patients" don't like these things, or, like Tim, object even to gentle jails?

Dr. Richard Short, Director of New Brunswick's Mental Health Services, smiles indulgently. "A patient's thinking," he says, "is not all that logical."

I WILL SPARE YOU AN ACCOUNT of my three days on the North Shore wading through the evasions and other defence mechanisms of three psychiatrists determined not to talk to me—though I will not soon forget the pinched expression on an angry O'Callaghan's red face; or the agitated Egyptian tones of Tadros offering yet another reason that we could not meet; or the clipped smile of Dr. Durand telling me she didn't understand my question (and she didn't; her English is at best uncertain) while trying to light a cigarette filter-first.

All roads led to Fredericton, to Dr. Short, a lean, stooped Scot with thinning hair who looks like a combination of doctor and bureaucrat—which, of course, he is. He couldn't discuss Tim without Tim's permission. I showed him a letter from Tim. "Well," said Short, "if he really wanted us to discuss it he should have approached us directly." Did Short think the letter was not genuine, then? "No, no, but there was no way of knowing the circumstances in which it was written. In any case you should really talk to the doctors who were directly involved." "I'd be delighted," I replied, "but I haven't even been able to get the correct spelling of their names, let alone their views."

Short later provided the correct spellings, but literally nothing more. "All that the public is entitled to know," he argued, "is that the relevant authorities are satisfied of their competence. Who are you, Don, to judge their qualifications, or to judge whether a person is sane or not? Three psychiatrists saw the lad, and they agreed, even the consultant from Toronto." "But Dr. Short," I said, "if the New Brunswick psychiatrists were of Dr. Solursh's opinion, namely that Tim was no threat to anyone, why was he kept in hospital for a month?"

"Well," Short conceded, "perhaps the diagnoses differed in some details. And when Solursh saw him, he had been under treatment for two weeks." I had seen no startling change, though, and neither had Tim, his woman, his closest friends, his colleagues. "Well," Short smiled soothingly, "for people without professional qualifications, Don, these things are often difficult to see." "But look here," I protested, "your staff claims Tim had some pretty gross disorder which has now vanished, that he was dangerous in July...."

"Not necessarily dangerous, but in need of care and treatment."

But if he *wasn't* threatening "his own safety or the safety of others," the whole affair, surely, was entirely illegal?

Short thought we were getting off the track. "Would you," he demanded, "challenge your family doctor's opinion about a *physical* illness." "Certainly," I said, "when I don't trust a doctor, I *do* challenge him." Such impertinence in a mere patient momentarily reduced Short to speechlessness.

Short is very touchy about medical prestige. Transferring Tim to Halifax, he believes, would have been to concede that "our" psychiatrists were wrong. He told me he had been attacked for allowing Solursh to see Tim: That, too, threatened his staff. "I am perfectly satisfied," he said, "that we did what was correct." And he summed up with an astonishing claim. "Our only interest," he maintained, "is in seeing that the patient received the treatment he needs."

Mental Health Services, in short, has none of the instincts for self-preservation that characterize virtually every other bureaucracy under the sun. No interest, for instance, in upholding the status of psychiatrists, or in proving its staff was not "wrong." Evidently it is an even more remarkable organization than I had suspected.

DESPITE A FURTHER MEETING with Short and Health Minister Lawrence Garvie, I discovered little more about the Campbellton Three. A Department of Health report admits that Fathy Tadros came from the University of Oran, Algeria, in December, 1970. Claudette Durand is rumoured to be Haitian, and O'Callaghan Irish. Other psychiatrists in the division come from Germany, India, and elsewhere. Some have enviable reputations—but there is a well-known anecdote about an Indian psychiatrist who believed an American was hallucinating because he reported "butterflies in his stomach." Language and culture are not irrelevant to psychiatry, and I would be happier if I had discovered at least one dull grey Canadian somewhere on the staff.

To work in Mental Health Services, a psychiatrist must satisfy both the Department of Health and the Medical Council of New Brunswick that he has trained in recognized institutions. For private practice among the middle classes, however, he must also pass the relevant Canadian examinations. The 1968 report of a Department of Health Study Committee on the provincial mental health services recorded that by December, 1967, only four of the division's twenty-three psychiatrists had passed them. And the division's psychiatrists were paid between $11,000 and $15,000, as opposed to Ontario's $18,000 to $22,000. Consequently, said the Study Committee, the division had "a poor reputation throughout the country. In particular, the marked shortage of qualified personnel poses the biggest single problem in the treatment and care of mental illness in the Province of New Brunswick today." If that devastating judgment is not still true, why are Dr. Short and his colleagues so defensive?

But the competence of the psychiatrists is not, finally, so important as the question of insanity itself and its relation to liberty. On one man's authority, Tim Crawford was imprisoned for twenty-nine days. He had no opportunity to dispute the judgment before an impartial third party. He had not committed or threatened any illegal or violent action—and if he had, he could have been committed through the courts. If he was threatening his own well-being—and I doubt that he was—does that entitle us to force our good intentions on him? Under New Brunswick law—and it is not radically different elsewhere—*any* physician may commit anyone he thinks should be committed, at any time. Considering the social attitudes of doctors, how confident can we be that they will not use that power on any harmless eccentric, any hippie, any radical? *Just who are they, those eight hundred and seventy-one New Brunswickers involuntarily committed last year?*

Back in Sackville, I told Tim that Dr. Short had asked me how I would like it if someone challenged my credentials as a journalist. I was going to say that people do that all the time, and rightly so, when Tim cut me off.

"How would *he* like it," asked Tim Crawford, soft-spoken but passionate, "if someone challenged his credentials as a human being? Because that's what happened to me."

[1972]

Snapshot: the Third Drunk

A SHORT STORY

THE MAN ON THE LEFT is Phonse. The man on the right is Wilf. The man in the centre appears to be drunk.

Falling down drunk. Head lolling, hair lank. Slumping between Phonse and Wilf. His knees loosely bent. Held up by an arm over Phonse's shoulders, another over Wilf's, each of them grasping his hand to keep him from falling. The drunk wears a dark suit. Phonse and Wilf in shirt-sleeves are grinning, grinning too heartily. Even in this dog-eared wrinkled old photograph, the well-dressed drunk looks pale.

•

PHONSE STAMPS ON THE PLANK FLOOR of the Anchor Tavern roaring for another.

"See 'im," grunts Jud. "Says it's dear, but he's havin' another."

"Didn't make beer money today anyways," Phonse says. "Got just about enough for a chowder, that's all."

"Them scales is wrong," Jud repeats. "We had that old box full up last week and they said it was two thousand pounds. Now we get half-filled and they say fifteen hunnert."

And the smell: the pungent, malty tavern, the sour reek of the fishmeal plant, sweat and tobacco, and beneath all, like a bass figure in an old song, the salt nip of the beaches and kelp, and cold spray over the stones....

"What the Jesus you gonna do?" Phonse shrugged. "Not like the old days. Didn't need no money in the old days." He winks at me. "You should of been here then, boy. By the Jesus, we had some right roarin' times in them days."

"Need money now," Jud said.

"You can't starve a fisherman, though," Phonse insisted. "Old Wilf Rattray used to say that all the time, ye can't starve a fisherman. D'you mind old Wilf, Jud?"

"Can't really say so. I was just a kid."

"He must have drowned in—let's think now. In the big storm in 'sixty-three, just before Christmas. He was on a wooden side dragger out o' North Sydney."

"I was about ten then."

"Must of been that 'sixty-three storm. Wilf was at Reg Munroe's wake in 'sixty-two, and there wasn't anyone from here drowned off a dragger for a couple of years after 'sixty-three, I don't believe."

"I got a sort of vague recollection of him."

"Oh, Jesus, he was a great old boy. Your old dad there, he'd mind him, don't you, Alfred?"

"Great old boy?" Alfred rumbled. "He was a god-damn Jonah, was Rattray. Black Foot Rattray, we used to call him."

Phonse winked at me again. "Call 'em Black Foot when they're so god-damn unlucky their feet get dirty in the bath."

"Black Foot Rattray," muttered Alfred, shaking his head.

"Great old fellow all the same," Phonse insisted. "He wa'n't so much unlucky as stupid. Sign him on as engineer, he'd go down and tinker with the engine. A tinkerer, that's what he was. No matter how sweet she'd been runnin', Rattray'd have her bustin' head gaskets and burnin' out bearings the first day at sea."

"I shipped along of him once," Alfred declared. "Never again. That was the trip he cut off his finger in the winch, an' Jesus, he'd *already* had us back home once with engine trouble."

Phonse started to laugh. "He was a Jonah, right enough. But

he was a barrel of fun at a party. We had good parties in them days."

Alfred chuckled. "We did so," he murmured. "We had some parties, all right."

•

NO BULLSHIT: THERE IS NO BULLSHIT in Widow's Harbour. Drifting along the coast with a little money and no plans, all my futures behind me, I followed the back roads off the back roads and discovered Widow's Harbour at the dead end of a rocky peninsula thrusting into the Atlantic like an arthritic finger. In Toronto, someone else was editing manuscripts. Someone else was meeting the Senator for lunch at the Westbury. Someone else was agreeing to be at the television studio a little before 3:00 for makeup. Someone else.

As for me, I was sitting on a precarious lobster trap at the end of a sagging wharf, sharing a bottle of Abbey Rich Canadian port ($1.40) with Phonse and Alfred Nickerson. After that there was a dozen of Tenpenny and some talk about gill-netting and long-lining and the lobster season, and then there was some Captain Morgan rum, and then there must have been something resembling a decision not to drive on that night. Around noon the next day I found myself surrounded by clean flannelette sheets with the threads showing, in a small, white, slant-ceilinged room, and when I stumbled downstairs I discovered Phonse's wife Laura making lunch for the kids who would soon be coming home from school. Laura snickered at my headache and poured some black coffee. Phonse had gone fishing at 4:00 A.M.

"He's usually away by three," she said, "but I guess you fellows really tied one on last night. Phonse, he was some full."

There seemed no reason to leave the next day, or the next, and when I found the shack across the road was for rent, I took it. I could make enough to get by on if I were to run into Halifax ever week or so with some radio talks, and I had friends in Widow's Harbour. It was a good place to read, talk, drink, and grow strong. In the scrubby woods, mushrooms erupted from the spruce needles underfoot. I combed the beaches for driftwood to be converted to lamps for the shack. There were deer and rabbits to be hunted with Purvis, my landlord; nets to be mended with Phonse and Alfred; and radio talks to be written about these things and others. I found I was living comfortably on about a sixth of my Toronto salary, and at that I was making a good thousand dollars a year more than Phonse or any of the others.

Widow's Harbour can afford no bullshit: It lives too near the bedrock of health and illness, shelter and food, death and tax sales. No one can hide: The snow-filled easterlies and the neighbors' tongues scour every cranny. Toronto's bruises soon fade. They are not, after all, catastrophes: On this bare rock, along this open coast, where even death is contemptibly familiar, the loss of a salary or a lover stands revealed as a petty misfortune at most.

•

"COME ON OVER FOR SOME BREAKFAST," says Phonse, shaking my shoulder, "and get a wiggle on. Supposed to be a blow coming up tonight, but we'll make a few sets before she hits."

Two shirts, heavy sweater, pea jacket; long johns, two pairs of pants; extra socks, rubber boots. Crossing the road in the coal-black night, slithering on ice, yawning and blinking. Phonse frying bacon and eggs. The kitchen clock: 2:15.

"You usually have bacon and eggs?"

"Me? Naw, just bread and molasses and away I go. Don't usually have company for breakfast, though."

"For Christ's sake, Phonse."

"Stop bitchin' and eat."

Down the snowy road to Alfred's, plastic bags of bread and molasses in our hands. Grunts of greeting, and down to the wharf. Fluffy snow on the *Harvey and Sisters*, a sweet, forty-foot Cape Islander with a high flaring bow. The Buick V-8 sends a throaty purr through the big hot stack spearing up through the wheelhouse. Frost on the windshield. A light chill wind ruffles the harbour.

The purr turns to a heavy burble as we clear the harbour

mouth, line up the yellow leading lights, and make an hour's straight steaming to the fishing grounds on Widow's Bank. Desultory talk. Phonse pisses over the side, back in the wide cockpit among the waiting tubs of trawl.

Then overboard go the highflyers, buoys with tall flagstaffs, easy to see even in the eerie predawn, and the trawl pays out, the baited hooks every fathom or so, and a highflyer at the end. Steaming back up the long lines for an hour and a half at sunrise, and hauling in fish.

"Another taxi driver, Jud."

"Why do you call pollack taxi drivers?"

"Dunno. We just do, that's all. Oho! Them big steakers is what we like to see."

Monkeyfish and dogfish to be thrown back. Cod and flounder. A day of heavy hauling, icy water everywhere, with one coffee break, bobbing around in the fo'c'sle with the engine shut off. As the short day closes in, Alfred spins the wheel, heads *Harvey and Sisters* toward shore.

And Phonse with a deft slash rips each fish from vent to gill and throws it to Jud, who scoops the guts out and overboard in one swift motion, tossing the fish into the bin in the centre of the cockpit. They gut a fish every six seconds. Every forty feet, regular as dripping blood, the guts hit the ocean, and the gulls come, a few at first, then a crowd, finally a swarm, dropping like dive bombers on the livers and intestines and half-digested mackerel. Ten minutes ago there wasn't a gull in sight; now hundreds hover over *Harvey and Sisters*.

The wind is rising, the whitecaps multiply, the promised blow is coming. Numb with cold already, I hunch in the wheelhouse, watching the first flakes of snow fly over the black water. Alfred has swung a hinged bench into place, and sits high behind the windshield, holding her steady by the compass now, back to Widow's Harbour. Phonse and Jud stamp in, shaking like wet dogs.

"Son of a bitch," Jud observes.

"Yessir," Phonse agrees. "Yessir, she's all of that."

Just outside the harbour, the storm hits: The sea begins boiling, the shriek of the wind sails in above the throb of the V-8. A whitecap foams into the cockpit.

"Self-bailing," Phonse reassures me. Another whitecap froths over the stern.

"Runnin' her a little close, Alfred," says Alfred.

"Save us some scrubbin'," Jud philosophizes. And we are in, inside the harbour, with the wind down to nothing and the sea no more than a chop. The motor dies down, and *Harvey and Sisters* idles over to the fish buyers' dock. After Jud and Phonse fork the fish into the crates for weighing, we will scour the boat clean and bait the trawl for the next day, coiling it carefully in the tubs so it will pay out smoothly.

"What's the time gettin' to be, there?" Phonse asks me.

"Two-fifteen."

"Good enough," Jud nods. "Be home by seven-thirty, quarter to eight."

"Might even be time for a beer," Phonse reflects for a moment. "Do you think, Alfred?"

"Might be," says Alfred.

•

YOU CAN'T STARVE A FISHERMAN. In the old days you didn't need money.

"Why, sure," says Phonse, draining a beer glass. "Look now, everyone had his own cow, so there was your milk and butter and cheese. Everybody had a few chickens, so there was your eggs and some of your meat. Everybody had a kitchen garden, so there was your vegetables, and the women got enough in preserves—well, you seen Laura's preserves even now, ain't you? We got enough there for two years even if we never *ever* got anything out of the garden this year. And there was always deer in the woods, more 'n now, and rabbits and ducks, sometimes a moose. You didn't have to be any too fussy about the season then, either. Then you had your wild berries—blueberries and cranberries and blackberries and bakeapples—you ever see bakeapples growin' wild? They look like a little orange hat on a green spike, just one to a bush, the swamps was full of ’em. Some folks had pigs and sheep, and the sea was always full of fish and lobsters, and we wa’n’t too upset about the season on them, neither.”

“You still aren’t,” I said, remembering an evening with a dozen of the biggest, reddest, juiciest out-of-season lobsters I ever saw.

“So they say,” Phonse countered, with a huge grin. “’Course I wouldn’t know. You take a chance now, you can lose your boat and your car and pay a big fine. I wouldn’t fool around with that sort of stuff.”

“Christ, no,” I said shaking my head. “Wouldn’t be worth it.”

Alfred burst out laughing.

In the old days, the cows were put out to summer pasture on Meadow Island, in the harbour mouth. You took a rowboat and two men: One rowed, and the other held the cow’s head up, and the cow swam over to the island. Horses will swim without coaxing, but you have to help a cow.

“I mind one time,” said Phonse, “I had to go get the cow at the end of the summer. Well, Jesus! Spent two days on that goddamn island and do you think I could catch that old son of a whore? No sir, couldn’t get near it. ’Course I always hated that Christly cow. I’m not a goddamn farmer, I’m a fisherman. But my old mom, she hadda have a cow, so of course I hadda get it out to the island in the spring and back in the fall. But I couldn’t even catch the bastard.

“So I come back with six other fellows and a motorboat, and we cornered the bugger and put a rope around her neck and led her down to the beach, but when we got her there do you think she’d go in the water? Not on your Jesus life she wouldn’t. We all got in the boat and sagged on the rope, and she wouldn’t budge an inch. Just dug her old hooves down in the sand and that was that.

“Well, I got mad. I said to myself, I don’t care if I kill that cow or break its neck or whatever the hell happens I don’t care. So I cracked the old throttle full out, and I let out all the slack and went roarin' out into the harbour, and that rope come taut and 'bout jerked that cow's head right off. She drove her hooves down in the sand to the knees and then she buckled, just come a-flyin' up in the air like a cork out of a bottle and hit the water about thirty feet out. I never let up on the throttle one bit till I got to the other side, I like to *drowned* that fuckin' cow, and she was comin' up and down and sideways and wallowin' around, her eyes buggin' out, you never saw anything like it. Jesus, I said to myself, that's the last time I ever have anything at all to do with that cow; and it was. Vet killed her before the next spring come around."

I was laughing too hard to speak.

"It's true, honest to God. And we had some parties, too."

"We did," sighed Alfred. "Oh, I guess we did."

"Remember that time Muriel Naugler and Loretta O'Leary got loaded at the beach party?"

"Lord, Lord," said Alfred.

"Jesus, that was some funny. The two of them got lit, and Loretta, she'd been foolin' around with Harry Naugler, and Muriel started to come onto her about it. So Loretta gave *her* a scandalizin', said if she was any kind of a wife to him there wouldn't be nothin' anyone could do about it, and Muriel—well, I guess she got right savage wild then. So she starts screamin' about how she's got a dose of clap from Harry bringin' it home from Loretta, and Loretta says it was Harry give it to her in the first place, so who'd he get it from, that's what she wants to know, and before anybody can say Boo they're clawin' at each other and tearin' off each other's clothes and pullin' hair and I don't know what all, and they're practically bareass to the weather—and all the guys standin' around, you know, and cheerin' and watchin' and havin' the finest kind of a time."

"What a night," sighed Alfred.

"'Twas the women broke it up, but it must of took 'em a good half hour. Those days," Phonse explained, "used to have parties someplace or other every night, practically. Nothin' else to do. There wa'n't no television, and you couldn't get nothin' on the radio, and the movies was a travelin' affair, used to come here once every two weeks, so what else could ye do?"

"The wakes was the best," Alfred opined. "D'ye mind Reg Munroe's wake?"

"Guess I do," declared Phonse. "'Twas me picked up the coffin."

•

THE CABLE FROM HALIFAX was very specific: TRAWLER ATLANTIC STAR RAMMED AND SUNK BY FREIGHTER HALIFAX HARBOUR, it said, REGINALD MUNROE KILLED STOP REMAINS SHIPPED CNR MONKSTOWN CHARGES COLLECT STOP PLEASE ARRANGE COLLECTION REMAINS YOUR END STOP SINCEREST REGRETS DEEPEST CONDOLENCES THIS TRAGEDY STOP CORONER CITY OF HALIFAX.

Phonse had been living with Reg's sister Alice, and while Alice comforted her mother, Phonse offered to take his pickup truck the fifty miles to Monkstown and bring Reg's corpse home.

"Lord dyin' Jesus, I'll never forget it," said Phonse. "I got down there about noon, and didn't they have him standing on his head in the freight shed? They had boxes of stuff and bales and rolls of linoleum and bicycles, and tucked away right in the middle of it was old Reg, standin' on his head. I said to the agent he might at least let the fellow lie down, but he said he was stuck for space, it was just before Christmas, you know, and the shed was right jammed. It looked some strange, though, that coffin standin' on its head in all that pile of stuff." Phonse waved his glass in the air. "I b'lieve I'll have another."

"Me too," said Jud. "Phonse, I been wondering if there ain't some way we can get them scales checked."

"Dunno," said Phonse. "We could try, I guess."

•

I TRIED TO IMAGINE THAT TRIP HOME over the twisting road to Widow's Harbour with the corpse of your woman's brother behind you in the truck. Tried to imagine how you would secure it against the swings and bounces of that unkempt gravel road. What would the coffin look like? Plain, no doubt; would there be places to tie ropes?

The road winds through fifteen miles of forest with hardly a house to be seen, nothing but scrubby evergreens in low, folding country. Perhaps it would have been snowing, isolating Phonse and the corpse in a moving dome filled with drifting white flakes, settling a coating of fluff on the coffin so that in the truck's lights it would seem, as you looked over your shoulder through the rearview mirror, as though the coffin were becoming vague in outline, but alarmingly larger. The truck would be slipping and slithering around rock outcroppings, over little wooden bridges, past the entrances to abandoned logging roads. The coffin growing and fading.

Reg Munroe, fisherman. Alice's brother. Dead, as you could be dead yourself any day of your working life. Drowned. Lying back there in the box of the truck, cold and bloodless, chewed up by the big blade of some freighter.

The road comes down to the shore at Owl's Cove, a handful of houses clustered around a gas pump. The winter night comes down, and nothing shows but a scattered light; and after that, darkness, and surf beside the shore road, flying cloud and wind.

Phonse would have remembered, surely, all the ghost stories: the Spanish galleon in flames that enters one little cove every seventh year, the woman in white seen in the bows of a sinking windship just before a shipwreck, the tales of jealousy, torment, and murder recalled in minor-key folk songs as common as rocks along this shore. Once, fishing in a dragger on the Grand Banks, Phonse had found a human skull and a thigh bone in the nets: some poor sailor or fisherman drowned God knows how many decades or even centuries before, one of those lost at sea whose bodies were never found, nibbled clean by the codfish and sand fleas. The crew had gathered around on the afterdeck, passing the skull from hand to hand, uncertain what to do with it, and finally they had cast it back into the heaving sea whence it had come, to continue its long rest without further disturbance.

Reg Munroe, Alice's brother, fisherman, in a coffin in the back of the truck, a coffin growing larger as the snow continued to fall and the truck ground along the foaming edge of a cold sea....

•

"JESUS, PHONSE!" I said. "That must have been some spooky ride."

"What's that?"

"Down from Monkstown with that coffin."

"Nah, shit, there wa'n't nothin' spooky about that. There was three of us went and we took a bottle o' rum and got right polluted. Nah, somebody had to do it, an' I had the truck, that's all." He pulled at his beer and then wiped his lips on his checked shirt-sleeve. "But I tell you somethin' that wa'n't too canny when we got here."

A mile before Widow's Harbour they nearly went off the road, swerving to avoid a snow-shrouded figure trudging along. Stopping the truck to give the fellow a proper old scandalizing, Phonse was greeted by a cheery, "Evenin', Phonse, thanks a lot," and Jack Kavanaugh climbed into the crowded cab. "What's in the back?"

"That's Reg Munroe's corpse."

"No," said Jack. "It ain't."

"It *is*," Phonse protested. "I picked him up in Monkstown. I got signed papers and everythin'."

"You look inside?"

"Hell, no."

"Well, it ain't Reg."

"How come you're so Jesus sure?"

"Well," said Jack, "Reg's body come in by sea this afternoon. I seen it. I'm just goin' in to the wake."

"Go away."

"It's *true*, Phonse."

"Snappin' Jesus Christ," said Phonse reverently. "Then who

the hell have I got in the back of the truck?"

"It ain't Reg; that I do know."

"Well, Jesus," said Phonse grimly. "Soon's we get to town I think we better have a look at you, stranger."

Under a streetlight they stopped and opened the coffin. A man's face stared out at the sky. Snowflakes fell on his eyes: They did not melt. Phonse whistled low.

"My God, it's Teddy Lundrigan."

"I didn't even know Teddy was dead," Jack marveled.

"Nor I," Phonse agreed. "But I'd say he is, all right."

•

"THAT WAS SOME WAKE," Phonse chuckled. "By the Jesus, I was half cut already. I went right wild that night."

"I'll never forget you runnin' down them stairs with your trousers around your ankles," said Alfred.

"Oh my God, yes. Jesus, Ma Munroe was some savage when she come up and found all four couples ridin' together in them two beds. Didn't she take the broom to us, though?"

"Didn't she?"

"And Alice, she was right owly when she found out about me being up there with Stella."

"But she wa'n't nobody to talk. She was married to Buzz when you were livin' with her, wa'n't she, and him off workin' the lake boats in Upper Canada?"

"He always wanted to get me for a divorce," Phonse said. "But he never did." He turned to me. "But that ain't the best of it, or the worse, dependin' how you look at it."

"No?"

"Hell, no. See. Later on that night we was just right out of our trees, you know? I don't think I was ever so full, never ever in my life. And old Wilf Rattray, him that drowned on that dragger, him and I heard that old Reg was cut up some when that freighter run them down. So what d'ye suppose we did?"

"What'd you do, Phonse?"

"We went into the room where the two corpses war, see,

'cause it was one big wake for the two of them, and we took old Reg out of his box and stripped him down. There was nothin' on his face, but his chest and legs was cut up pretty bad, all black and blue and the chest crushed in. Funny thing to see, all them cuts and him not bleedin'."

"Jesus, Phonse!"

"Well, hell, we didn't think old Reg'd mind. *I* wouldn't have minded, if it had of been me instead of him in that box. I mean, shit, we was old friends. Anyways, what d'ye suppose we did then?"

"Christ, Phonse, I hate to think."

"Why, we dressed him all up again, just like he was, and then old Wilf and me, we put one of his arms around each of our necks and had our pictures took."

"That's right," said Alfred, shaking his head. "That's right. God save us, you did that."

"Sure," said Phonse. "Sure we did. I still got the picture." He drew out his wallet.

•

THE MAN ON THE LEFT is Phonse. The man on the right is Wilf. The man in the centre appears to be drunk.

[1974]

Us Rustic Red Adairs

YOU SEE IT AS YOU RUN: smoke in oily rolls bursting from the back windows, sooty smoke streaming with hard determination from the eaves. You're running to the hydrant, then back to the pumper truck because the hydrant is dry. Scrambling and stumbling with Leo Martell, carrying the portable gasoline-driven pump to the beach. Laying out the four-inch black rubber suction line into the cold Atlantic water, screwing on the strainer which keeps out the pebbles and the yellow rockweed. Leo starts the motor.

It's bad. It's midday, and all the other volunteer firemen are at jobs, as much as thirty miles away. The old pool hall, once a sea captain's noble shoreside home, is well kindled. Along Arichat Harbour the houses stand jammed together like books on a library shelf, and the cold June wind rakes the smoke into shreds and stokes the fire. Prudent neighbours are carrying boxes and lamps and TV sets out to their cars. We could lose half the centre of Arichat.

Hook up the two-and-a-half-inch pressure line, with a Y connection to one-and-a-half-inch lines and nozzles. Here's Neil Smith, carpenter, and Jack Ouellette, potter, they've been fighting this thing alone, with no equipment, till a phone call snatched Leo and me from our work and hurled us seven miles down the road to the fire hall. *Give us the hose clamp, there. Got a wrench? Yeah, right here.*

More firemen coming with the little truck and the other pump. Bernie Fougère and Wilfred Boudreau, in high boots, patch coats and hard, black fire hats. Twenty-five minutes after the phone call we've got four lines spraying water on the pool hall.

The fire is on the second floor, at the back on the west side. No more than a foot separates that eave from the eave of Wilfred Sampson's house: Thank God the wind blows from the west. It was like this when the huge wooden church burned in West Arichat, spangling the night with sparks and cinders and threatening to take half the parish with it. It blew like this that frigid day when we clambered all over the old building at the end of the fish plant wharf in Petit-de-Grat. The wind screeched all night while we fought that trailer fire in Little Anse. The mind slides back over countless earlier fires, rummaging for procedures, precedents, predictions. Fires all over Isle Madame, which measures 14 miles by eight, from tip to tip, a little kingdom tucked into a notch in Nova Scotia's tattered coast. Six thousand people, scattered around the island in a dozen communities. They rely on 14 men. Fourteen carpenters, contractors, electricians, truckers, teachers: volunteer firemen.

YOU'RE RUNNING WHILE YOU THINK. Running for tools and couplings and hose. Running for a pike pole to break a window and let the water in. Running for a ladder. Running for an axe to break in the back door. Dragging hoses around the building.

The first decisions were yours: You were there first. Should you have strapped on the air tanks, taken the first hose and marched right into the building, taking a chance on killing the fire in its infancy? No: Nobody was in the building, it might have been dangerous. The power wasn't even shut off—look, here come Bobby DeWolfe and Johnny MacDonald now, in the white and orange Power Commission truck.

So you didn't go in because it would have been bad practice? No: I didn't go in because I was nervous and indecisive. I'm not a well-drilled fireman. I'm a writer.

"Louisdale's coming!" calls Jack Ouellette. You're running past him with a nozzle. You nod. Good news. Louisdale, a dozen miles away, has a well-equipped, well-trained department. If this blaze gets away, we'll need all their help and then some. We'll be hard-pressed to save Wilfred's house. Lucky that old house of Paul Doyle's, downwind, is 20 feet away. We'll keep it wet. By the end of the day, the high pressure hoses will have scoured all the paint off its shingles.

A mob of spectators. A Mountie's car, light flashing, the cop warning people away, rerouting traffic. Wilfred's furniture piling up outside Emile Benoit's house. *How did it start?* asks a bystander, as you race for the truck, tossing your salt-blinded spectacles on the dashboard. You shake your head. Don't know. Who cares? Let's get it out.

Getting worse. Firemen keep arriving. Bob Harris, truck driver. Leonard Marchand, cook from the motel. Lloyd Pettipas, from the heavy water plant. Listen: a crackle in the framing of the dormer on the side. The voice of the fire.

The chief, Ed Robichaud, is in the hospital 60 miles away, felled by a stroke. The acting chief, John O'Hearn, is on a construction job. Another veteran, Billy Diggdon, is making deliveries in Sydney. No officers today, and no commands. Everyone just pitches in where needed.

It takes four men—who are they, anyway?—to hold a two-and-a-half-inch hose on the narrow slot between the pool hall and Wilfred's house. The afternoon becomes a blur. Somehow you're on a ladder spraying a hose into the upstairs apartment, soaked to the skin by stray bursts of hose streams. The salt water stings your eyes. You hold them closed, winking them open from time to time to check where your spray is going.

You could get the stream up higher inside if that pane of glass were broken. You haul back your nozzle, strike quickly, and shatter it. Shards of glass pile up around the foundation like ice in winter. An hour later you notice that your hand is all bloody.

THE PUMPER TRUCK IS EMPTY. Leo moves it. The truck from Louisdale wails in. More hoses, water shooting in through every upstairs window. Shingles rip and fly. Water jetting, streaming, dripping. Choking smoke. You crouch down on the ladder, letting the smoke roll in dark clouds over your head. You cough and gasp as the wind blows it across your face. Tomorrow you'll wake up with a sore chest, as you do after most house fires.

Nothing in an old building is as bad, though, as that plastic foam insulation in the house trailers. Smoke from that stuff chokes you like mustard gas. A trailer is little more than plastic foam sandwiched between a sheet of aluminum and a sheet of panelling. Cheap, sure: but they burn like toxic matches.

A FLASH OF ORANGE AND BLACK in the smoke. With savage joy, you swing the hose, blast the flame into black cinders. In three years of house fires, grass fires, chimney fires, forest fires, car fires, trailer fires, you've learned to loathe that orange flicker in a strangely personal way. War must be like this: the adrenaline, the uniforms, the danger, the teamwork, the fierce concentration of will.

In the well-kept suburbs of your boyhood, fire is a decorator feature, an affair of hearths and barbecues. But in the country, you come to understand that, like Prometheus himself, who stole flames from the gods, fire can be a trickster, a deceiver, a shape-changer. In stove and furnace, fire keeps you alive in the vicious winters. But outside these cages, far from water mains and professional firefighters, that orange flicker is the most dangerous and wily of all man's necessities.

David Britten arrives with a long T-shaped wrench. Someone turned the hydrants off during the winter to keep them from freezing, and failed to turn them on again in the spring. David uses the wrench, and the hydrants flow. That's a break.

THE AFTERNOON RUSHES PAST. Not very much pressure in the mains. Hook up the pumper trucks to the hydrants, that'll give you pressure. By now St. Peter's, 20 miles away, has sent its pumper too, and 13 hoses are pouring hundreds of gallons of water into the pool hall. The back half of the roof has buckled and fallen in, but the fire still burrows under what's left and lies in under the debris. Gusts of seawater carom through the slot between the buildings. Four hoses appear on Wilfred's roof. Hey, there's Cline Bourinot and Bernie LeBlanc. They must have heard it on the radio, must have raced home from the plants in Port Hawkesbury.

STEAM AND SPRAY AND CHARRED WOOD flying. A river of water rushing over the grass to the harbour. *You've got hip boots, Don, go clear the strainers on the Hale pumps.* All right.

My house bristles with fire extinguishers. A smoke alarm and a water hose always stand at the ready. They arrived after I saw the night sky through the smouldering roof of little Remy's house, beat out grass fires with green boughs and shovels, watched spruce trees go up like signal flares. I am in the market for another smoke alarm and a couple more extinguishers. As I write this, the pungent odour of the pool hall's smoky dying clings to my clothes and rises in my nostrils.

EVEN IN YOUR FIRE GEAR, you're drenched and cold. But here's a bystander who's been putting his all into the fight, and he's only wearing a soggy T-shirt. Use my coat, buddy, I've got a sweater on. If you see Bernie Fougère, he's got my hat. Neil Smith stands in the lee of the pumper, water running off his clothing, shivering uncontrollably, trying to let the still air and sunlight warm him.

That wind makes it cold and miserable, despite the clear sky. Is someone getting some water on Paul Doyle's house? Yeah, there's Jack Ouellette, giving it another soaking. The hell, I'm having a smoke, there's enough guys now for a moment.

Look at the cant of that back chimney, there! *Hey, you guys! Stand clear of the back of the house!* They can't see the chimney. Okay, little fellow, go tell them why.

We've pulled even with the fire. It's not going to burst out into a crackling orange runaway licking at the sky. The outside of the building ripples with flowing water, huge feathers of spume arc into the fallen centre of the roof. Flame spews out under the eave; a hose drives it back inside.

"It's looking better for your place, Wilfred."

"I'd hate to lose that house. It's old, maybe 150 years, it's really historic. I spent $18,000 to put it in shape, you know, it's all done over inside."

"How come those asphalt shingles are all buckled on the front of your dormer?"

"That's from when the hotel burned. That was before your time. Even across the road it was hot enough to melt those shingles."

Stamp out the cigarette. Down to the back of the building, get a dry hose this time, upwind from the spray. It's only a one-and-a-half-inch hose, but the pressure in it! It takes two men to hold it. It's one of the St. Peter's lines, what a pumper that truck must be. Look, just over the back door, a tongue of fire thrusting through the shingles. Just to the left, that's it. You aim the hose like a gun.

Okay, I'll have a look at that strainer again. Here, give this man a hand with the hose. Look, if you stand with one leg back and lean the hose against that, you can brace yourself better against the pressure. Or squat down on the ground, let the earth take the thrust. That's it.

Seaweed and pebbles clog the strainer once more. Prop it up on a rock, keep it off the bottom. How are we doing now?

By God, we're getting it. All that water is smashing the fire down. A guy from Louisdale scrambles up on Wilfred's roof, reaching for a chimney with a pike pole, pulling it—there it goes! But the other chimney is the dangerous one. He can't reach it. *Stand well back, you can't see that chimney but it's leaning way over this way.*

Around to the front. Somebody going into the building through the front door. Bobby Stone! Even though he's hardly out of his teens, Bobby's president of our association, and he's organizing a fundraising fair for next month. He's forever checking out the equipment, taking weekend courses at the firefighters' school down near Halifax. We could use ten more just like him.

Hey, where's my coat? That's it. Gimme that hat, buddy. Bobby! Hang on, I'll come with you.

Bobby grins. "Hi there, Red Adair!"

INSIDE, THE POOL HALL is like a huge, cold shower. Sooty water pours through the crack in the ceiling. Ruined pool tables, deep-fry vats full of water, water brimming in the open drawer of the cash register. The diner at the front is in fair shape, but look at the sag in the ceiling back over the pool tables! *Don't go any farther*, says Bobby, *I don't trust those beams.*

But a stocky, merry, middle-aged Louisdaler marches past us, kicks open the washroom doors, peers up the waterfall which is the staircase, and—the ruby tip of his cigarette glowing in the aqueous gloom—pulls down a pool cue from the wall and mimes a shot at the pool table.

The firefighting game is not without its humour. Get the boys talking some time. *Lord, remember that day we went to that car fire in West Arichat, and the fire wasn't started yet? Yeah, guy was still standing outside the car with a pan of gas in his hand.*

What about the time you soaked the new Mountie? Served him right, he shouldn't have been in there. Still see the water drippin' off his moustache....

The fire's retreating. Still burning, but it's licked. Let's have a ladder up at one of those front windows, there, Jack, get out of there, I've got the protective clothing, I'll go. Mittens on, up the ladder, and smash what's left of the window. A leg over the still. Test the floor. It seems solid. A step inside. Shouts of alarm from below. Don't worry, this floor isn't even burned.

Six inches of soot and water lying on it, though. Fire an axe up here, will you? Chop away the wall covering, douse the fire where it gnaws into the rafters and sneaks along the roofing boards. Go in a little further. Still burning in this middle room. Soak it down.

What a mess. A TV set half melted in the corner. The hose strikes an overstuffed chair and blows stuffing all around the room. Blackened boards overhead, swinging dangerously loose. Pull 'em down. A spinning wheel, half drowned. A cast iron parlour stove, uniquely undamaged in the ruins, ashes and charcoal piled halfway up its height. A doll's carriage full of water. Fire under that bit of collapsed roofing. A jet of water underneath it flushes out smouldering socks and underwear. An empty picture frame swings vacantly against the remnants of a wall.

Jack—hey, how come you're here—gimme that pike pole. You reach the hook over the teetering back chimney. A pull, and you fall backwards; only one brick came loose. Try again. Pull, pull, pull, and the rhythm brings it down with a horrifying crash. It doesn't go through the floor, though. The floor must be sound right to the back of the house.

Louisdale and St. Peter's are packing up. They want your hose. You'll get another one. And still the water pours down from the clear blue sky where the ceiling once was, the Hale pumps still roar and sputter on the beach, the hoses on Wilfred's roof are still belching water. A smoking chest of drawers, glowing coals in a back rafter. Shoot them dead with seawater.

OUTSIDE AT LAST. Still a few embers in there, maybe, but we'll go in again later. Got a cigarette? Thanks. People in cars, the fire's out, they're anxious to drive down the street. Sorry, you can't drive over those hoses. I don't care how light your car is, the answer is *No*. Go around the block, chowderhead, is that so much to ask?

Peggy Ouellette has coffee and sandwiches, Bobby announces. Don't all go at once. Sounds wonderful. You've been working flat out for six hours.

In front of the Ouellette house are boxes of books, silverware, toys, the important possessions of the Collins family, who rent Paul Doyle's house. Their home wasn't damaged at all, and Wilfred's house only suffered one broken pane of glass, kicked in by a fireman heaving a hose up onto the roof. "Look," says Peggy, "we're all grateful to have houses to sleep in tonight."

Two chicken sandwiches, two cups of coffee, and you're renewed. With the adrenaline slowing down, though, you feel the ache in your smoke-filled lungs, the soreness in arms and back, the legs that will object to rising in the morning. Back to work.

It's near 7:00 in the evening. The pool hall stands blackened and ruinous, with only half a ragged roof, but it no longer smokes. Curious children form a crescent at the roadside. Old men and mothers with children stroll by, peer into the blackness, walk on. The owner's nephew and four firemen emerge from the wreckage carrying pool cues, the cash register, and other portable salvage.

The windows should be boarded up, to prevent looting and kids' exploring. We've had buildings like this flare up again as late as three days afterwards; we'll have to mount a guard tonight. The two trucks are gone, but one hose remains coupled to a hydrant. Cline Bourinot stands on watch with you.

We're going to have to go to the hall and coil up all those miles of hose, make sure the trucks are full of water, get someone to go into Port Hawkesbury to refill the breathing apparatus with compressed air, rinse the salt out of the Hale pumps and hoses. We're going to have to check out all the gear, make sure we've got hydrant wrenches and hose wrenches, adaptors and Y's, starting cords for the Hale pumps, hats and coats and mittens back to their owners. Some of the boys will be there until 10:00 tonight, and there's no delaying it: If we get a call at 2:00 this morning, the trucks had better be ready. I've seen the same men racing to fires every day for a week. I've seen five homes saved in a two-week period, just a year ago.

But people notice, instead, the times that the pump doesn't work, the times that only one man can answer the call, the times we foul up orders, the times our equipment fails. We drive too fast—and we take too long to arrive. When we succeed, we're lucky.

Perhaps we are, too.

As Cline Bourinot and I stand guard over the cold, wet ruins, eight hours after the call came in, an old man totters over. He's had a few drinks.

"Well, boys," he says, conversationally, but with a bit of an edge to his voice. "I guess you get overtime for this part of it?"

Cline looks at him and smiles.

"We don't get paid for this at all," he says. "It cost me $75 to book off work for the afternoon and come to fight this fire."

The old man peers at Cline, thunderstruck, unbelieving.

"You don't get paid for this *at all*?" he cries.

Hard to believe? Maybe. But think: Across this country there are thousands like us.

Washed by fiery colours of the setting sun, our comrades are trudging back toward us, full of sandwiches and coffee. Gaze at Wilfred Sampson's house, touched on its western eaves by the same crimson light. That fire only destroyed part of one building, when it was primed to gut this lovely village.

That fine old house looks even better than overtime.

[1980]

Ambrose Pottie Gets His House

ONE CALM MORNING LAST OCTOBER the villagers of Poirierville, D'Escousse and Poulamon, Nova Scotia, woke up to see a white, shingled house calmly proceeding across the waters of Lennox Passage, which separates Isle Madame from Cape Breton Island. It was a small house, 20 by 24 feet, with little dormers poking up through its roof, and it was floating high in the water. It had cleared the harbor mouth at River Bourgeois, on the Cape Breton side, and was making good progress toward Poulamon.

Everyone knew it. It was not just a house. It was Ambrose Pottie's moment of triumph.

AT 39, AMBROSE POTTIE IS A FIXTURE in the communities collectively known as "the North Side," on the northern shore of Isle Madame. Like many of his neighbors Ambrose puts a living together as best he can, cooking on the offshore draggers, painting houses, dabbling in the retail trade. A dozen years ago, he was a roistering bachelor who struck terror into the hearts of mothers all over the country. Then, 10 years back, he began going with Karen Boudreau. At 17, Karen was already more capable and astute than many a 30-year-old. Eventually, Karen and Ambrose were married. They have three children—Brandie, nine, Daphne, seven, and Dean, four.

The Potties live by the mouth of a creek in Poulamon. Their house had been gutted by fire before Ambrose took it over. With a little help from his friends, Ambrose rebuilt the interior and made it livable. But the house remains cramped, crooked and inconvenient. It rests not on a foundation but on four concrete blocks. It is drafty, the roof leaks, the floors sag.

Ambrose and Karen knew they needed another house. They also knew they couldn't afford one. Then, last spring, Ambrose's niece and her husband told him there was a little house for sale in River Bourgeois. It was appraised at $6,000, and the price was just $1,000—but it would have to be moved.

In keeping with a well-established local tradition, Ambrose and Karen decided to buy the house, tear it down and use the materials to start building. But when they examined it, they found it completely solid—sills and joists all sound, walls straight and true. Why tear it down? Why not just bring it home?

They consulted a contractor, who said he could move it for roughly $3,000. But the house is higher than the legal limit for highway travel. They would either have to remove the roof or disconnect and reconnect all the overhead wires across the 20 miles of road between the old site and the new one. The telephone company and the power corporation each required a $1,000 deposit, in cash, with no guarantee that the final bill would not be higher.

Their $1,000 house would cost at least $6,000 by the time they got it home. Impossible.

"Why not float it?" suggested Blackie Forgeron.

Why not indeed? In Cape Breton, buildings are often moved by water or over the midwinter ice. Claude Poirier's three sheds once adorned offshore islands as outbuildings for manned lighthouses. Glenn Marchand recently floated the lightkeeper's home from Jerseyman's Island to Arichat. My own home is composed of two tiny houses rammed together, and one of them was hauled over the ice by oxen from a former location at the opposite end of the harbour.

So why not?

Jackie Doiron had done this kind of thing before. Ambrose enlisted him. Jackie said they'd need eighteen 200-gallon oil tanks and nine 30-foot logs. With his brother-in-law, Carl Boudreau, and a couple of other friends, Ambrose scoured the island.

By the end of July his yard was piled high with tanks and logs. They sealed the tanks and hired a flatbed truck to take the whole pile to River Bourgeois.

"And then Jackie landed in the hospital with pneumonia," Ambrose sighs. "So I had all that stuff and no engineer. That's when we got Skipper Al."

Allan Savoury is a Newfoundland-born fisherman who plays a mean country-and-western guitar. He had just received his third-class fishing master's ticket, he wasn't working, and he had already opined that he'd like a crack at the project.

"I couldn't figure out how Jackie was going to do it," Allan remembers. "I figured we needed more tanks and more logs. I didn't want to get the house wet—you'd ruin all the drywall, and you'd have to rip out the whole interior and redo it. But the old fellows all said she'd float all right, but she'd sink as far as the ground-floor windows.

"I got out my books on stability and buoyancy, and I couldn't see where they were right. It worried me, because I usually listen pretty carefully to the old fellows. They've done these things before. They know. But this time I thought they were wrong."

Allan did some tests and found that if he loaded 900 pounds on an oil tank, it sank only nine inches. With an additional nine 45-gallon drums, he figured the raft he was designing would support nine tons—"and that house don't go more than seven or eight."

The summer became a long bout of backbreaking labor. They cut another 20 logs. One fell on Ambrose's pickup, smashing the windshield. They assembled the materials in River Bourgeois and carefully built an immense cage of logs 30 feet square, spiked and bolted together, lashed every which way with heavy steel cable, with all the tanks captured inside it. By early September, they had their raft.

River Bourgeois rejoiced, Allan says. All summer long, as the temperature rose and fell, the sealed oil tanks had been expanding and contracting—with a loud *boink* each time. "One fellow told me they'd be able to get some sleep after we got them tanks out of there," Allan grins. "Said he was kept awake for weeks by them tanks bing-banging all night long."

They jacked up the house and put skids under it. Ambrose and Carl tore down the chimney. Harold Martell's bulldozer cleared a path and hauled both raft and house to the water's edge.

"I was worried when we were getting her off the foundation," Allan says. "There was only about a foot of ground each side for the skids. I thought what if she slips sideways and drops down in the hole? It could happen."

But it didn't. She did hook a skid on a big rock and stick fast—"and that was about the only time I saw Ambrose right disgusted," Allan remembers. "I think he would have walked away from it right then, gone home and never looked at it again. But we jacked her up and got her free and she went down all right after that."

Imagine a raw, cold, rainy afternoon in October. The raft has been manoeuvred into the water by hand. One corner of the house is on the raft. Ambrose, Allan and Harold Christie are all soaked, floundering around in three or four feet of water, trying to lift the second corner with jacks set in greasy mud. The raft is held to the shore with heavy ropes and cables. Ambrose slips and cuts his hand.

"Look at that," he says grimly, holding the hand in the air. "Too damn muddy even to *bleed* properly."

They broke two portable winches and two chain tackles. They "snapped off wire left, right and centre." Harold stepped into the muck and sank right down to his chest. Allan and Ambrose pulled him out but his boots stayed behind. Ambrose wound up pawing at the mud to recover them.

It took them two days to get the house onto the raft. They called in all their buddies—Paul and Peter Fougere, Carl Boudreau, Clifford Marchand. Grunting and heaving, prying and pulling, they finally moved it aboard. When the tide came up, the house floated, high and dry, a clear foot above the water level. The harbour echoed with happy whoops.

Once afloat, the house was the plaything of the elements, rolling on the waves, tacking slowly to and fro in the wind. Harold stood in the water, physically holding the house in place as the tide rose around his body. By the end of the night, he "felt like a prune."

Ambrose and Allan raced home to get a towboat. First, they borrowed Bob Nichols's boat, but it broke down. It was almost midnight when they got back to Isle Madame, looking for another. Clarence David was just in from a fishing trip, and he was willing to help. The team, augmented by Paul Fougere, met at the wharf in D'Escousse at three in the morning. The six-cylinder Chev roared into life. The *Star of David* was underway to River Bourgeois.

In the eerie predawn light, they fastened the towline again. The *Star of David* strained, and the house slipped away from the beach and out toward the harbour mouth. River Bourgeois has a large harbour with a narrow entrance, which makes a strong tidal current. When they got to the gut, Allan Savoury remembers, they went more and more slowly—"and then the house stopped, and the boat stopped, and then the house started going backwards and the boat started going backwards." They were tide-bound for half an hour.

"There was a damned good ground swell outside," Allan says. "She'd roll away over one way, then back the other way. I didn't know how stable she was. I stood there in the stern of the boat watching that old house like a hawk with an ax in my hand ready to cut her loose."

Hour after hour, *Star of David* plunged forward, down the line plotted on Allan's chart—over to Bernard Island, up to the lighthouse at Eagle Island, in through Poulamon Bay to Ambrose's creek. At low tide, the creek is practically dry. But there is a channel in it, and Leonard LeBlanc led them up it in his boat, sounding the depths ahead. The house finally ran aground behind Beaton's General Store, a quarter of a mile from Ambrose's property. Nobody thought she'd get that far.

On the following tides they brought her right up to Ambrose's back door, where she lies tethered on the beach. In the spring Ambrose plans to pour a foundation in front of his present house and move the new house onto it.

"WE'D NEVER GET INTO IT AGAIN," Karen sighs, reviewing the costs. The cash expenditures so far total $1,314.60, and the last bill for the bulldozer hasn't come in yet. There's also the truck's windshield, the ruined battery in that old car, the chain saw crunched under the 'dozer's treads, the four broken come-alongs and chain falls Ambrose had borrowed from friends.

"And when you take into account all the hours," Karen points out, "two and a half months, working as much as 16 hours a day...."

"I wouldn't mind doing it again, if I had the time," Ambrose agrees. "There's lots of guys sitting around doing nothing that could be doing a lot of things, if they'd just put their minds to it."

[1984]

Confessions of a Cape Breton Moonshiner

IT LOOKED LIKE WATER dripping out of the end of the copper tube, but it wasn't: It was alcohol, 12 overproof, pure moonshine that burns in the spoon with a pretty blue flame. Mine. I had made it myself, in my own little still.

"Aaaah!" said Red Angus, approvingly. "*That's* good stuff."

Cape Breton, you must understand, is quite possibly the moonshine capital of Canada, and the centre of Cape Breton moonshining is the industrial area around Sydney. The core of the moonshining in industrial Cape Breton is New Waterford, and about ten years ago Red Angus MacGregor was the biggest moonshiner in New Waterford.

Red Angus, my tutor.

"We were into it on a commercial basis, you know? We had fellows working for us, and we had six stills running more or less around the clock, producing thirty or forty gallons a day.

"Mister Man, we had some great times. The winters was the best, after the first snowfall. You know the way the ploughs heap up the snow along the side of the streets? We'd just hollow out the snowbanks from behind and stick the shine in there in gallon jugs. Great place for it, eh? Cold, shine won't freeze. Half the Mounties in Cape Breton looking for it, and there it was right under their noses, right on the main street.

"But we didn't handle it ourselves very much. Oh, I don't say we wouldn't sell a gallon to a friend, you know, and we were on the stuff ourselves. But we sold it in drums, and then we had other fellows that sold it to the public. We had a sedan delivery—you don't see them much any more, sort of a station wagon with no windows—and we knew they were watchin' us, see? So Skinny'd get them watchin' him, acting suspicious and driving along, and then he'd head for Glace Bay with all the Mounties hot behind him. Soon's he got out of Waterford, why that's when we'd move."

He was never caught.

"I think there was only one half-gallon from our stills ever was seized, anywhere. They knew we were doing it, you know, but they couldn't catch us. But those Mounties were no better'n what we were. You remember that fire we had, Peggy?"

His wife laughed out loud.

"You tell him about that, now."

"Skinny's brother-in-law was a Mountie, see? And he had stashed all these blankets that he'd stole from the force over at Skinny's place. Well, one day we were down in Skinny's basement running some shine—we had five stills going, thirty gallons of mash in each of them—and my old uncle had converted a bicycle pump that it would pump naphtha into the Coleman stoves. That's what we used for to boil the mash, Coleman stoves. After a while Skinny looked down, and he said, *Hey, that tube on that pump's on fire!* So I went over to stamp it out, and right then, Mister Man, is when lightning hit that basement. It had got into the naphtha, see, and the room was full of flames. The stoves were burning and the furniture was burning, and then we were burning, our pants and stuff. So we jumped right into the barrels of mash to put it out. Then we tried pouring water on it, but that burning naphtha just floated on the water, and it went everywhere. Well, Skinny started calling out for his wife, the silly bastard, she was at work at Eaton's; and I said, *Shut up, you fool, we're going to lose the house if we don't get moving*—it was burning the sills by then, you see. So I said, *Grab them blankets of Pete's*, and after a while we smothered the fire.

"Course the blankets was pretty well ruined by it, so we took them over to my uncle's house and he let on that he'd had a fire in his chesterfield, and the insurance replaced the blankets."

"And they were stolen from the RCMP in the first place?"

"That's *right*, b'y. Oh, I liked that!"

Drip, drip, drip from the still. I hummed a Bob Dylan song:

My daddy, he made whisky;
My grandad, he did too.
We ain't paid no whisky tax
Since seventeen ninety-two....

"Look, there's nothin' to it, just nothin' at all. All you need is—what did we use, Peggy? Three to one? Five to one?"

"Three to one."

"I thought it was five—no, by God, you're right, it was six gallons of molasses to eighteen gallons of water, and sixteen yeast-cakes. You mix that up, and let it brew for—oh, ten days is pretty good. Then you run it in the still, and that's it."

"Could I get to see a still?"

"Yeah, I could probably get you in. But the best way would be to run a few gallons yourself. That way you'll understand everything about it, y'know, the proper way. If a fellow lets you into a real commercial still, why he's taking an awful chance. He could get six months and $500.00, and that's no joke for a coal miner in Waterford. Have a drink."

He poured a tot of rum. I drank it, and the idea no longer seemed quite so bizarre.

"I don't think we'd get caught," I said cheerfully.

"Have a drink," said Angus, pouring one.

"If I did get caught," I said, feeling the rum scald its way down, "I could always plead that I only did it in the interests of art, science, and folklore."

"Have a drink," said Angus. "Sure and I'll help you make the still. By the Jesus, it's a long time since I ran a batch of shine. It's like old times. Have a drink."

And so it befell that, one warm summer evening, I mixed up

four gallons of mash in a plastic bucket in my bathtub. Making shine with molasses, I discovered, produces a kind of rum; if you make it with sugar, it's whisky. Either way it's a clear fluid with a good kick in it. I left the mash to brew for a week.

"This is good stuff," said Angus, licking his lips over a glass of shine the next day in New Waterford. "You can drink it all night, and the next morning you won't even have a hangover. It's pure, eh? There's none of that crud you get in liquor from the government store. We call it Triple H, because you wake up in the morning healthy, hungry and horny. But don't drink water in the morning; one glass of water then, b'y, and you'll be drunk all over again. Drink up, now, and we'll go out and see my Da."

Alex the Dancer, Red Angus' father, is an old moonshiner too. You may think these names are invented, and I admit they are, well, adapted. But among the Scots of Cape Breton there are a limited number of surnames and a restricted pool of acceptable given names. There are dozens of MacDonalds in the New Waterford phone book, including three Alexes, six Anguses, four Archies and ten Johns. They're kept straight by their nicknames and second names: Alex Boo and John Hugh, Duddie and Sharkey, Spoonbill and Black Joe. One entire family is known as "the Farts"—Allan the Fart, John the Fart and so forth.

Alex the Dancer, who lives in one remodelled side of an old coal company duplex, was jailed once for shining. The man over the road was raided, and cut his own sentence by ratting on Alex. "Great God A'mighty, yes, Donnie," Alex laughs. "And the joke of the thing was, when the Mounties were in my basement seizing me still, the fellow on the other side of the basement wall was running off a batch right then.

"Let me get ye a drink, now. I won't drink meself, I'm on these queer pills, antabuse. The doctor gave them, y'see, for to help me untangle meself; I'm just after coming off a four-month binge, God help us, and I'm in hard shape. I'm on the keg now since a week, and I'm prayin' I'll never go back to it. But Great God, Great God A'mighty, it is a delight to me to get a copious swig of that dark rum in me mouth and swish it around and swallow it down; I do enjoy that, God help me. It's a terrible thing what it does to you, the booze; a man should stay clear of it. But if ye'd take a drink of me own rum, now, it'd be a thing I'd give ye from the bottom of me heart."

At sixty-six, Alex is still a big powerful man who takes your hand in a fist like a cottage roll, entirely self-educated, a great reader, a man of exceptional intelligence and warmth whose broken body speaks eloquently of his thirty-three years underground. The coal mines have broken his feet and arms, smashed his back, squashed his head. Once, Red Angus remembers, he was called to the mine because Alex the Dancer had had an accident. Struck by a coal car and catapulted against the mine roof, he had a broken nose and a mouth torn wide apart. His shattered shin bone was sticking out through the flesh of his leg and his foot was pointing behind him. "You know what he did?" demands Red Angus, who loves his father with ferocious devotion. "He sat up on the stretcher and started a conversation with the doctor about the best way to treat the leg, y'know, talking about each of the bones by its proper name." Alex was laid up for seventeen months that time.

To understand the moonshiners of New Waterford, you need to understand that this is a coal-mining town—and no Canadian workers have less reason to respect the law than the miners who worked for the British Empire Steel Company, later Dominion Steel and Coal. The miners were obliged to live in company houses, burn company coal, buy company power and get their supplies at a company store, known as a "pluck-me." Paying company prices, a miner would often receive no pay at all after deductions. Alex the Dancer went to work in 1925, when he was seventeen, for $2.89 a day. That year BESCO was asking the miners to accept a 20% pay cut, the second such cut in three years. The miners were already desperately poor, clothing their children in flour sacks and boiling soup from potato peelings. When they balked, the company reduced their hours and cut off credit at the pluck-me's.

The Great Strike of 1925 lasted 155 days. "It was a hard, hard time, Donnie," sighs Alex. "Lord sufferin' Moses, a hard, hard time. They cut off our power, so we had to steal that, and they cut off our coal, so we had to steal to keep warm. But we survived, what with robbing a few hens and raiding some gardens, making a little shine and buying fish from the fishermen—you could get a dozen mackerel for seven cents or so—ah, yes, b'y, we survived."

Three thousand on relief in Waterford alone "and the relief Donnie, 'twas nothing but a codfish and a bun of bread a day for each family, families of twelve and fifteen." Troops of company police armed with chains and iron bars riding down unarmed crowds on Plummer Avenue. Company water and power cut off from the entire town. Scabs, goons and special police recruited from the brothels and taverns of Halifax. Three miners shot, one fatally, on June 11, a date which is still a public holiday in Cape Breton. Martial law in New Waterford enforced by 1500 troops with fixed bayonets. All to help BESCO make poor men *even* poorer.

In New Waterford, you see, the law is not considered impartial. In 1925, the Chief Justice of Nova Scotia was the former president of a BESCO subsidiary. A man who obeyed the law in 1925 would quite literally have starved or frozen to death. The law is owned by the same people that own the industries, the newspapers, the Grits and Tories, and the distilleries.

So the men of the pit towns make moonshine, fight roosters, drink hard and vote NDP. And when you ask them why moonshining is illegal, their answers are crisp. "Excise tax," snaps Red Angus. "The government ain't makin' anything off shine," grins another. "The way it is now, they got a monopoly," explains a third.

After talking to half a dozen moonshiners and innumerable of their clients I had found no evidence at all that moonshine is any more dangerous than any other strong liquor. A few years ago a boy died after drinking a quart on a dare—but a quart of good rum would probably have killed him just as efficiently. Bad shine, the consensus has it, shine which has been distilled too fast, or made in a galvanized still, or bottled with impurities—that kind of shine will make you desperately ill, and you'll throw it up. But it won't blind you or kill you. Or so they say in Waterford.

My molasses cost $3.19, my yeast cost 39¢. A forty-ounce bottle of my shine costs about 90¢ to make, compared with a bottle of much weaker rum at the liquor store for $10.45. That legal bottle of rum includes excise tax at $14.25 per proof gallon, onto which is added a 12% federal sales tax, a freight charge of perhaps 40¢ a case, a markup by the provincial liquor commission and, finally, a provincial sales tax of 7% in Nova Scotia. Nobody wants to give precise figures, but about two-thirds of that $10.45 is tax. If Seagram's or Acadia Distilleries can't produce 40 oz. of liquor for less than I can, there's something wrong with them; and if they produce at the same price they must be making something like a 35% profit. No wonder the governments and distillers want to protect their monopoly; as Roy Thomson once said of his television license, it's like a license to print money.

Meanwhile the game of cops and robbers goes on.

"When you come to run your shine, Donnie," confided Alex the Dancer, "use hardwood to boil the brew. You want a nice steady heat, nothing too strong, and hardwood don't make any smoke. The Mounties today has planes and helicopters, and when they see a smoke, why they got you then."

Bob Dylan:

Build you a fire with hickory,
Hickory, ash and oak,
Don't use no green or rotten wood;
They'll get you by the smoke....

"We used to make our stills out of 45-gallon drums," Alex recalled, "or two drums welded together, that made a nice still. Or if you could get hold of one of those big puncheons, yah, that molasses came in, fifty gallons I think they were."

What was the biggest still he ever saw?

"Well, now, I remember when I was seventeen going through the woods and I took a short cut—Lord God, I came on a still must have held a hundred and twenty gallons, specially made by a tinsmith. Two fellows there, both of them half-drunk, and one had a rifle. Oh, it was a big still, that. 'Course I was only a schoolboy, they weren't bothered. They offered me a drink, but I wouldn't take it; I didn't start drinking till I was nineteen.

"The woods was full of stills. Thirty years ago you could go up to Waterford Lake in the winter and see a fire every couple of hundred feet along the shore—all stills, you know. You don't see that today."

How would a moonshiner get caught?

"Oh, some woman'd get all upset with her husband coming home drunk, and she'd tip off the police. Or there's always someone jealous of the money you're making. There's good money in shine, b'y. Used to get fifteen dollars a gallon, they get twenty now, and it didn't cost more'n a dollar or two to make it. You take forty or fifty gallons of shine, now, that's quite a profit. Yes sir, quite a profit. And it's still a better buy than the government store."

Get you a copper kettle,
Get you a copper coil,
Fill it with new-made corn mash,
Never more you'll toil.....

Where was I going to get a copper kettle? If need be, said Red Angus, we'd make one. But I went to see the Drummer, another experienced moonshiner. The Drummer poured glasses of clear alcohol smuggled in from St. Pierre, stuff that reams out your innards the way a blowtorch lifts paint, and he gave me a flask to treat my friends. He told me stories, and he asked about my article.

He told me about the moonshiner in Reserve who had reared a dozen or so children on the proceeds of shine, and whose wife distributed the products from her baby carriage, a couple of gallons cunningly concealed under the floorboards. He told me about the time his brother was coming out of the woods with two quarts and a gallon jug—and met the Mounties coming in. He smashed the quarts together and threw the jug high in the air over the road—but it hit a telephone pole and bounced off, hit the roadside grass and bounced again, then rolled along the road where the Mounties stooped down and picked it up.

He told me about the Mounties who used to come and buy shine from him after hours, and about the fellow who kept his private stock of shine in an old car battery, which the police dutifully shifted around as they searched the house, never suspecting they had shine in their hands. The Drummer remembered the Mounties raiding him once when he had a pitcher of shine on the table; he handed it to his wife, who washed the dishes in it while the liquor squad prowled the house.

Once, working in the loft of his barn, he saw a Mountie sneaking up on him. "I picked up a two-by-four," he chuckled, "and when the Mountie's head came up the trapdoor I took a swing with it—not to hit him, just to whack the wall over his head, and I shouted, *Now I got you, you son of a bitch that's been stealing my rabbits!* He dropped on the floor like a sack of scratch feed, squealing *Mounted Police! Mounted Police! Don't hit me!* Scared the be-jesus right out of him."

And when I told the Drummer that I thought I'd run a gallon of shine myself, he beamed. "You got a still?" he demanded. No, I said, I thought we'd have to make one. "You just sit right here, b'y. I'll be right back."

Twenty minutes later, soaked to the knees from wading in a swamp, he was back with a copper drum perhaps sixteen inches in diameter, with two tubes leading into its top and a drain cock at the bottom. "This here," he said, "is as nice a little still as you're ever going to see, and it's just the rig for you. I couldn't find the worm for it; that you'll have to make yourself."

Three nights later, while my mash bubbled, Red Angus fitted the necessary reducers and wound a 25-foot coil of 3/8 inch copper tubing inside a tin lubricant bucket. Alex the Dancer forms the tubing around the outside of an electric motor; that, he says, makes "the most beautiful helix you ever saw. When I done my last one it was that pretty it should have been photographed." But ours worked just fine.

A day or two later, nine of us went for a picnic on one of the islands off Cape Breton, and while we ate hamburgers on the beach a propane stove burned behind us in the woods, under the Drummer's copper boiler. The tubing ran through cold water in the lubricant bucket, to condense the steam, and out of the end of the tubing ran the shine.

Ah, it was good stuff, me son, good shine, strong as brandy, with a rich flavour like rum. We ate and sang, drank and told stories—and then, as the evening came on, we wobbled back onto the boat and, out in the channel, we threw the still overboard because we can't any of us afford six months and $500.00.

So, if you're a Mountie, this whole story is a fiction. There is no still, nobody named Red Angus or Alex the Dancer or The Drummer. There is, I assure you, no moonshine left lying around. We are all law-abiding citizens who drink only government booze.

If you're not a Mountie, of course, you can believe anything you want.

[1974]

Going down the Road with the Atlantic Symphony

IT IS A CURIOUS SCENE: forty-five adults in full evening dress entering a technical school gymnasium in Sydney, Nova Scotia, carrying various quite lovely objects made of brass, gut, hair, wood, and skin. They sit up front and make a wild caterwauling. Five hundred or 600 assorted persons face them—schoolchildren, priests, pensioners, mechanics, housewives, surveyors, professors.

Who are all these people?

Who, for instance, is that blondish fellow with the beard and the rimless glasses, holding a metal tube to his face and blowing across it? How did he get there, and for what purpose?

Who is that woman, and why is she embracing that large, strangely curved box, caressing it with horsehairs stretched along a stick?

THE WOMAN IS BETTY PEDERSEN, the man is her husband Stephen, and they play the double bass and the flute in the Atlantic Symphony Orchestra, which is just tuning up. Eleven hours ago, as the symphony's big Trailways bus rolled out of Halifax,

Steve Pedersen told me that when he first joined the symphony he found the whole thing so strange that he took to reading books about the psychology of small groups.

Making music, he explained, was in a fanciful way like making love, and being in the symphony was a bit like being in a marriage. The relationships between people were oddly intimate, petty and profound at the same time. Attuned to one another, deeply committed to a common enterprise, the musicians could still be angrier with one another than with virtually any outsider.

At 8:30 a.m. the bus had been parked in front of the Lord Nelson Hotel in Halifax, the driver stowing bags, violinists and percussionists scrambling into Murray's Restaurant for a coffee to go. Cellists awkwardly lugged their instruments between the high seats, clarinetists and trumpeters tucked their little cases on the hat rack. Really large instruments—harp, tympani, four double basses—were already en route in the orchestra's panel truck, driven by stage manager Jimmy Tasco and his assistant, and in a rented van driven by horn player Phil Myers and percussionist Jim Farady, who earn a few extra dollars that way. By nine-fifteen we were making our way through the woods to Highway 102 and distant Sydney.

A large family car, I thought, listening to the buzz of conversation. The musicians are men and women of all shapes and sizes, long-haired and short-haired, young and old, natives of Basle and Prague, Dallas, and Dartmouth. Some are settled in Nova Scotia, others dream of playing in Berlin, Montreal, Philadelphia. They are connected by their careers in music, and often by little else. But in the seat behind the Pedersens, Wolfgang Flebbe was reading *Der Stern* while his wife, Loredana, clicked her knitting needles. Both violinists, both German, the Flebbes met and married in Halifax. Ten of the orchestra's 45 players are married to one another.

Around us people drank beer, played bridge, peered out the window. Betty was knitting too, and Steve was saying that many musicians really distrust words. Some therefore distrust Steve himself, a one-time English teacher at Toronto's Danforth Tech and Centennial College. His room in the Pedersens' snug little seaside house at Portuguese Cove, 10 or 12 miles down the shore from Halifax, is lined to the ceiling with books; by contrast, Betty's practice room is sparsely furnished, almost bare.

AS A GIRL IN REGINA, Betty wanted to play the violin, but by the time she could begin she was in Hamilton, going to high school—too old to begin the violin. She switched to the double bass, finished her commercial course, and took an office job, traveling every weekend to Buffalo for music lessons, and winning a chair in the National Youth Orchestra. Then a bassist who taught in the Toronto public schools got a one-year symphony job, and she filled in for him.

"There I was," she remembered, "teaching bass, and I hardly knew how to hold it. Then I got a job in the Atlantic Symphony for two years, but still just a rank student. I wonder how I ever managed to play parts."

One evening just before she left Halifax, a fellow bassist dropped in with a friend, Steve Pedersen, who was challenged by Betty's example.

"When I was maybe 10," Steve grins, "I got a hold of a little plastic trumpet with four notes on it, and I ran around the farm back in Alberta playing what I thought was Beethoven's Fifth. Well, my mother could just make out enough of it that she could see what I was trying to do, and it drove her crazy. So she got me a tonette, a plastic affair very much like a recorder."

A high-school band in Calgary College in Alberta; a job in Toronto. A year in Europe; teaching in Toronto. All the while gradually moving from English to music. Then Betty's example. Steve quit his job, became a full-time flute student and stayed alive by supply teaching. Later he went back to teaching, but kept right on with the flute.

"But eventually I just had to make a decision. I found I could give up teaching, but I couldn't give up music." The Atlantic Symphony was looking for both bass and flute. The Pedersens auditioned and got the jobs. Steve was thirty-three.

TRURO: THE BUS SWUNG ONTO the Trans-Canada, up over the hills toward New Glasgow and Antigonish, past Bible Hill, through Kemptown and Salt Springs and past the turnoff for Garden of Eden. Garden of Eden, Nova Scotia.

Steve is 37 now, and he has a good life. A grand piano dominates the Pedersens' long, low living room. Sunlight filtering through the pine trees. At home the Pedersens often take their morning coffee down to the shore and watch the ships enter Halifax harbour. Would they move? Well....

"Moving becomes less and less attractive the more involved we become here." With other ASO members, Steve plays both in a chamber group, the Halifax Woodwind Quintet, and in inNOVAtions in MUSIC, an ensemble devoted entirely to modern works. He composes music, gives some CBC radio talks, and teaches flute in several cities the ASO visits.

Betty has a few students, but she would as soon not teach. "Really, I just want to become a very good bass player." She studies with Gary Karr, the great bass player who lives in Halifax and teaches at Dalhousie University—and two years ago taught at the Juilliard School of Music in New York, and the New England Conservatory as well—while still maintaining an international concert career.

Gary Karr will be the guest soloist tonight in Sydney. He's a showman, a tireless promoter of himself and his instrument, and he is one of only four virtuosi in the whole history of the double bass, the kind of musician for whom composers write special works. To the Pedersens he is both friend and inspiration. Betty works part-time as his secretary. As a member of his International Institute for the String Bass she wears a lapel button—BASS IS BEAUTIFUL. Steve illustrates his points with quotations from Karr. Betty admires his work with Halifax schoolchildren.

As we talked, I wondered whether at some level they weren't thinking about the Sydney concert. True, Steve admitted, "For instance, there's a very tricky entry in Swan Lake. I have to put my flute down and come in again with the piccolo after eight very fast bars. If the piccolo is too warm or too cold it'd be out of pitch: If it doesn't seat on my chin exactly right, or if my embouchure is wrong, the way I hold my mouth, or if I don't count properly, I'll come in at the wrong time, or just not crisply and firmly, but a little tentatively. I don't exactly worry about it, but from time to time my mind wanders to that kind of thing."

At noon the bus turned left down Church Street into Antigonish, pulling up in front of Wong's Restaurant, stopping an hour for lunch.

IN SYDNEY, 137 MILES AHEAD, Gordon LeDrew scuttled up and down steel ladders, repairing fans and conveyors in the Kaiser Minerals plant at the Point Edward Industrial Park. His mind ran ahead to the concert tonight: Gordon had been playing the double bass for 30 years, in dance bands like the Acadian Orchestra and in a back-up group for the Cape Breton male choir, the Men of the Deeps. He would take his sons Kevin and Paul. Kevin was starting to play the double bass, and this Gary Karr had quite a reputation. He would fire Kevin's interest. When Gordon first began playing the double bass, there was no teacher in Sydney—still isn't, in fact. He smiled to himself. It would be good to see the whole orchestra playing second fiddle to his big clumsy bass.

Pat Cormier was driving to a property he would survey, thinking that, dammit, tonight was the last symphony concert of the season. Pat's father led an orchestra that played for the old silent movies, and he taught Pat to play the violin. It must be wonderful to play for a living: Pat can only play for his own enjoyment. There aren't enough good string players in Sydney to form a chamber group. Pat smiled, remembering the time he played with some ASO musicians in Antigonish, and they told him he was good enough to audition for the orchestra. He never did, though. Never got to Halifax. The only live music he and Irene hear is these concerts in Sydney. Wonderful. Records aren't the same thing at all.

At Xavier College, a fighting Irishman named Father Luke Dempsey was lecturing in theology when it occurred to him that tonight was the symphony which certainly added a touch of grace to this tough industrial area. We'd be much the poorer without it, he thought. It was a thing to look forward to.

LEAVING ANTIGONISH, we crossed the Canso Causeway into Cape Breton, 103 miles from Sydney, still talking about the orchestra which was sleeping around us. You don't get rich playing in an orchestra, Steve remarked; he's still only making about half a teacher's salary. The musician's basic pay is $150 a week plus $53 from the CBC for that 34-week season: about $6,900 a year.

Lionel Smith worries a lot about money, too.

Tall, trim, suave, Smith wears evening dress as though to the manor born. Originally English, he had a varied business career before dropping out in 1958 to raise chickens in Nasonworth, New Brunswick. His wife became interested in the semiprofessional New Brunswick Symphony, which merged with the Halifax Symphony in 1968. Lionel had joined the Fredericton symphony committee, found he had a taste and a talent for arts administration, and eventually moved to Halifax as the new orchestra's executive director.

Despite all the grand talk about Maritime union, Lionel said, the symphony was the first significant regional venture and is still the only regional symphony in North America. It gave 122 concerts and broadcasts this season, in 18 centres scattered along a base line stretching from Edmundston 1,600 miles to St. John's. Last year Smith, Mizerit and Leone Wilcox made 12 attempts just to come up with a workable schedule.

The ASO budget of $712,559 makes it a pretty substantial industry. With the office staff and stage crew its payroll totals 52, about a third of that of the Halifax container port. Every time it visits a city, it leaves up to $1,500 behind.

The symphony is supported by the Canada Council, the CBC, the various municipal governments, and the governments of New Brunswick and Nova Scotia. The box office provides about 40% of the revenue, and six local committees raise the remainder.

"Our organizational structure," Smith explained, "is unique.

Our board is made up of representatives elected from the local committees. When they meet as a board, they are in effect telling themselves what they are going to do, and they have to go home and implement their own decisions. It's a lot of damned hard work for practically no recognition."

Why do they do it, then?

"People used to say it was for social reasons, but I don't think that's true any more. Today the arts must literally be for everyone, and we notice a real democratization of the audience. People feel they can come as they are and just enjoy the music. I think our volunteers probably begin with an interest in the art form, and later find the committee work itself a real challenge."

The audience has grown enormously, especially in the past two years—in Fredericton and Saint John, for instance, the concerts are completely sold out. In Halifax, the orchestra now gives two subscription series: The two nights combined are 95% sold out. When the orchestra brought guest conductors such as Arthur Fiedler, Mitch Miller and Skitch Henderson to Halifax last season for its first series of pop concerts, every seat was taken.

What about support from industry? Smith frowned. "In Canada," he said, "we're far behind the United States in the degree of support we get from industry." Examples? Smith flatly refused to give any, but other sources reveal that National Sea Products, Nova Scotia's giant fishing company, last year gave a paltry $100. K.C. Irving Ltd., which virtually owns New Brunswick, has never given a cent.

The symphony is an industry, an educational resource, a kind of family, a traveling museum of music. The symphony is a group of people snoozing and quiet, tired by their trip as the bus pulls up in front of the Isle Royale Hotel in Sydney in the middle of the afternoon.

IN THE LIVING ROOM OF THE HIGHRISE apartment, Gary Karr, thoroughly Jewish and a native of Los Angeles, talked with the Pedersens, myself, and his friend, Harmen Lewis, who is also his colleague in the Karr-Lewis Duo. We talked casually, and dined, but hadn't time to linger over coffee. Leaving for the gym, I looked at Steve.

"Still thinking about that entry in Swan Lake?"

"Yeah, a little. I've been thinking about it a little all day."

JIMMY TASCO HAS THE BASSES LINED UP in a hall outside the gym. In their fibre glass traveling cases, they look like coffins for monsters. The musicians trickle in, sporting evening dress now. Slowly they gather in the hall, instruments wailing and blasting.

There, on the right, that's Gordon LeDrew and his sons. Ten rows back, that priest is Luke Dempsey. And look. Back a bit, that's Pat and Irene Cormier.

And here comes Jan Bobak, the concertmaster, calling for the ritual A from the oboe, and the orchestra tunes up by sections. It is a piece of theatre, and a spectacle, the lights bouncing off the brass, the musicians drawn up in a semi-circle.

In a moment Klaro Mizerit will mount the podium at the centre. A charming man, Mizerit—"Maestro," most people call him—has been the orchestra's conductor and music director since its inception in 1968. Though nobody suggests he is another Toscanini, more than one member of the ASO will say flatly that he is head and shoulders above anyone who could conceivably be asked to replace him.

The ASO, like most Canadian symphonies, grew out of amateur and semiprofessional orchestras, and some of its veterans have to work furiously to keep up. I am told one or two probably don't belong in a professional orchestra at all. What does Mizerit think? Tactfully, he shrugs and smiles, but he admits that the ASO only now, after six years, begins to sound like "a normal symphony."

Mizerit concedes that Maritime audiences are not as sophisticated as European audiences but, he smiles, they have a compensating "hunger for the music." In Fredericton a couple of years ago, Mizerit was walking across the dark lobby of the Playhouse when a stranger appeared from the shadows. "Klaro!" he cried.

"Klaro!" He was a millhand from a town 30 miles off, he never missed a concert.

"Thank you," he said, pumping Mizerit's hand. "Thank you!" He plunged out into the night, and when Mizerit opened his hand he found a crumpled dollar bill.

You don't tip the conductor, it's just not done. But Mizerit looks up at me, obviously very moved. "What you can expect," he says softly, spreading his hands, "more than this?"

And here he comes now, after Ljubljana and Vienna, Koblenz and Dubrovnik, smiling at the audience of Sydney, Nova Scotia. Ceremoniously, he shakes Jan Bobak's hand in the traditional greeting to the musicians, turns and bows to the audience, turns back, raises his baton, and calls forth the great wave of sound which is the essential sensuous delight of a live orchestra.

In his head he is "singing" the music a half second ahead of the orchestra, trying to induce a sound as full and clear and rich as that ideal performance going on in there behind his eyes. His stocky body, with its sweeping baton, becomes one with his mind, one with the orchestra. Perhaps tonight he can "sing" especially well, for after Shubert overture the orchestra plays "Variations On A Theme Of Handel," by Klaro Mizerit. Charmed by the piece, the critic of the *Cape Breton Post* will describe Mizerit's performance as "sensational" and "inspired."

And Gary Karr is bowing now to the applause, addressing his instrument, playing a rare bass concerto by Domenico Dragonetti. The bass hums, sobs, roars, sparkles. Even I, who scarcely know an allegro from an avocado, am astounded. Karr is simply dazzling.

Finally, astonishingly, Karr offers comedy—Paganini's "Moses Fantasy," treated with a wit so pointed the audience laughs out loud. The wit is in the music, not in Karr's facial expressions or his occasional cheery foot-swinging. Those musicians who aren't offended by Karr's lighthearted showmanship are breaking up too, as Karr waits till the last split-second before picking up a theme from the orchestra, dallies with it, passes it back. Pat Cormier is craning to see. Later, queuing up to congratulate the soloist, he will be utterly floored by Karr's spontaneous comment: "You have the neatest little eyebrows I ever saw!"

On the closing selections from Tschaikovsky's "Swan Lake" the orchestra lets go, the gym pulses, swirling blasts of sound, you never heard anything like it on your stereo, a rich driving wash of music, 45 people releasing torrents of music to an audience now strangely cemented into a single listener, 500, 600 people still as the fixed core of the spinning earth, hear it build now.... And as the music soars and crashes, Steve Pedersen sets his flute down, takes his piccolo from his vest pocket, counts eight bars, and makes his entry....

They have heard that entry, the LeDrews and the Cormiers and the Dempseys, whether or not they even noticed it they have heard Steve do that; and hearing that, you see, is the thing, the whole point; those little notes adding up to one vast music—that is what this exotic occasion in the steelmilling city of Sydney is all about.

[1974]

Underground in China with the Men of the Deeps

YOU LEAVE THE TANGSHAN HOTEL through large stone gates, turn right, and walk down a walled side street. A woman with a baby comes to an entryway, and stares at you.

"Knee-hah," you say, nodding and smiling. They smile back.

Across the street another wall is set back behind grass and shrubbery. In the bushes a couple is engaged in low-voiced talk, the first such couple you have seen in a week in the People's Republic.

"Ha!" says Jack O'Donnell. "So it does happen in China!"

Young men cycle past, one or two at a time, smiling and nodding at your greeting. You feel your heart pumping, and your face feels as though it has frozen into a smile. *Knee-hah!*

"What's that you're saying?" asks Jack.

"Knee-hah," you answer. "It means hello, more or less."

"Ah!" says Jack. A girl rides past, ringing her bell. "Knee-hah! Is that right? Knee-hah?"

At the corner you join a wide main street. A mob of people are buying vegetables; they turn, one after another, and gaze at you. To your right, a huge statue of Mao Tse-tung extends an arm in greeting. Over his shoulder, small in the distance, a pagoda crowns the hill behind the hotel.

Around the plaza, perhaps 150 sets of eyes are fixed on these two Westerners who have materialized like apparitions on a street corner in Tangshan. They are not hostile. They are curious and reserved.

You clap your hands to them, and suddenly everyone smiles and claps back, an agreeable Chinese custom you have picked up in Peking and Tientsin. You smile, and clap, and call "knee-hah!" and small boys gather around you, cocking their heads curiously, grinning and uncertain.

"Jahnada!" you say, fingering the maple leaf pin in your lapel. "Jahnada!" Everyone grins some more.

You walk along the wide street, rimmed with trees and high walls, filled with carts and bicycles. The children follow. *Knee-hah! Jahnada!* You tousle a kid's head, and he wrinkles his nose and giggles. Overhead a loudspeaker blares a woman's voice ceaselessly into the street.

It is time for supper. You turn, and walk back to the corner. The entire entourage follows. When you turn up the street to the hotel, you look back.

A crowd of perhaps 300 people has assembled, all smiling and nodding. "Tsai dien!" you cry, and clap again. They all clap and wave.

"What does that mean?" asks Jack.

"Good-bye. I've been reading my phrase book."

"What do you think would happen," says Jack slowly, "if we came back with the whole chorus after supper, and sang for these people?"

Six weeks later the radio reported that two severe earthquakes had demolished Tangshan, killing thousands and trapping an unknown number of coal miners in the Kai-luan mines. I would like to tell you everything about that whirling three weeks we spent in China, about how we went to the Forbidden City, the Summer Palace, the North Tombs, about how we belted out *O Canada* at the top of the Great Wall. I can hardly fail to mention Dr. Norman

Bethune, the Canadian surgeon who fought and died with the Chinese Communist army in the 1930s, and whose reputation—second only to that of Mao himself—watches over Canadians in China like the benevolent presence of a patron saint.

But the July earthquakes in Tangshan overshadow everything. To most Canadians, no doubt, Tangshan's anguish is only another gruesome item of distant disaster. For 28 Cape Bretoners who make up the Men of the Deeps, North America's only coal mining choir, it means we have almost certainly lost some friends. Last June, the Men of the Deeps became the first Canadian cultural ensemble ever to tour mainland China. In China, the Chinese boast, the workers are the masters—and we were their brothers, workers from Canada.

"Enjoy it, boys!" called Yogi Muise, as our bus crept through yet another swarm of clapping, smiling Chinese workers. "Coal miners don't get treated like this anywhere else in the world!"

Tangshan in the evening, the air gilt with dust in the falling sun, impassive crowds observing us file into our bus. We clapped, and the faces broke into smiles, hundreds of hands replied. Through streets crammed with carts and bicycles, past courtyards and unpaved alleys, through underpasses with slogans painted in white characters on red billboards. Learn from the working people! A salute to the working people! A smoky, grimy industrial town, with brick apartment buildings rising no more than four stories, for the Chinese do not believe in wasting electricity on elevators. With all the buildings so low, it is hard to realize that as many people live in Tangshan as in Montreal or Toronto—and there are 22 Chinese cities larger than Tangshan.

Up a narrow side street between stone walls, to the Tangshan Hotel. The hotel was a four-story yellow brick building, still unfinished; the Men of the Deeps were the first foreigners ever to stay in it. On the second floor, a large reception room, plum carpets and handsome bamboo furniture. A greeting and a briefing from the local guides. Expressions of friendship and welcome.

Jack O'Donnell replied. O'Donnell is chairman of the music department at St. Francis Xavier University in Antigonish, Nova

Scotia, and musical director of the chorus; he had been largely responsible for arranging the tour in the first place, and most of the diplomatic duties fell on his shoulders. We were especially pleased to be in Tangshan, said O'Donnell, having traveled so far to this mining town in China; it was "our great hope that warm friendships will develop in the next few days."

We crowded into the cage like commuters on a subway, elbows snug to our sides, pit helmets clacking together, a mass of blue-clad Chinese and Canadians, miners, guides and officials. With a hardly perceptible jerk the cage dropped towards the mine roads 1,300 feet below. Jack O'Donnell struck up a song:

Down deep in a coal mine, underneath the ground
Where a gleam of sunshine never can be found,
Digging dusky diamonds, all the seasons round,
Down deep in a coal miiiiine!
underneath the grou-ou-ound!

The mine officials and the handful of Canadians who had stayed on the surface heard it floating up from the mine shaft, softer and softer as the cage dropped, four-part harmony, a driving, cheerful sound.

One chorus, and we reached the level. Miners greeted us, ushered us into the micro-railway that would take us a mile to the coal face, huddled together, our passage marked by occasional dim lights. When no one has a light on, a coal mine is the most inconceivably velvet, inky black you can imagine. The coal, the black dust, the dark uniforms: You can almost feel the environment soaking up light.

The little train stopped, and we scrambled out. Billy Copeland, who is 69 and on the silicosis pension designed to compensate him for the loss of 90 percent of his lung function, grinned and loped off uphill towards the coal face. Wayne Scheller, at 30 the youngest member of the chorus, walked along beside me, showing the German jacks that hold the roof up, the power lines, the pumping systems that inject air and remove water, the tools cast aside along the tunnel walls. A hard climb, a sharp turn, and we found ourselves in a large open area, where a clanking chain conveyor remorselessly carried coal down to the level and away.

Now the tunnel narrowed and lowered dramatically, and we moved in a crouch, helmets banging on the roof: Miners in England, working nearly naked in such tunnels, used to scrape their spines so frequently that the row of scabs along their vertebrae were known as "buttons down the back." The tunnel was perhaps four feet high and eight feet wide, with a conveyor running along its floor, the air close and dusty and hotter all the time.

And now lights and faces began to appear in nooks behind the props, men tucked out of the way to allow our passage. Chinese miners, black but for their eyes, reached out of the darkness to shake our hands in greeting, and suddenly it was a magic moment, for there was no mistaking the delight in those smiling faces, the warmth of the greeting, the flowing current of fellowship as the Tangshan miners, a quarter of a mile under the ground, grasped your hand in both of theirs and held it. Knee-hah! *Knee-hah!*

LONG LIVE THE UNITY OF ALL THE WORLD'S PEOPLE!

Wump! The coal face: an awful concussion, a scream of heavy machinery, black dust like a charcoal fog in the narrow beam of the pit lamp. Yogi Muise yelling that the machine travelling slowly along the wall beside you was a coal cutter, that the water spraying down over the face was to keep down the dust, that the coal cutter was essentially a giant saw which would slice off the face of the coal, then advance by its own width and take another slice, cutting 250 tons per hour. As it advanced, the stone would be allowed to cave in behind it, removing the seam of coal as though you were extracting the centre layer from a gigantic block of Neapolitan ice cream.

Back again, past the smiling white eyes and reaching black hands. The mini-railway, and back into the cage. And on the ground above, they heard the song rising from the shaft, growing in strength as the cage drew nearer:

We're all jolly wee miner men, and miner men are we!
We have traveled through China for many a long day.

We have traveled east and traveled west,
this country round and round,
For to find out the treasure that lies below the ground!

On that last line, we marched out of the cage into the sunlight.

A hot shower, a nap in an armchair—surprisingly tired, considering we did nothing but travel up and down—and a splendid lunch, fish and poultry, and vegetables from the mine's own garden: The waste water from the pits is used to irrigate the fields. In Fushun, the dangerous methane gas which is pumped out of coal mines to minimize the risk of an explosion provides fuel for the city's stoves and furnaces. "We could be doing that," said Tommy Tighe, "but we just waste it. These people don't waste *anything*."

Then a discussion about mining, led by Ya Yu-kun, vice-chairman of the mine's Revolutionary Committee. Afterwards the mine workers gave us an impromptu concert, playing traditional instruments and singing. The traditions of Peking opera go back a thousand years, but the young woman now sang a selection from the Peking opera, *The Red Lantern*, entitled "You Should Learn From Your Father's Skill and Determination in Making Rcvolu tion." To a Western ear, Peking opera sounds shrill, abrasive and chaotic—"like a castrated cat with a power saw," muttered a Cape Bretoner—but by now many of us were developing a taste for it: the singer with her formal postures and quavering melody, the mallet-like Chinese fiddles wailing in the background, the occasional rippling statement from the *pï-p'a*, the pear-shaped lute.

Small chorus: "By playing ping pong we will spread friendship." More operatic selections. A *pï-p'a* solo, a plaintive minor key number, easily appreciated by Westerners. A male solo:

Sailing the seas depends on the helmsman,
Life and growth depend on the sun.
Rain and dewdrops nourish the crops,
Making revolution depends on Mao Tse-tung's thought.

We saw and heard many such performances, by workers in factories, by school children and college faculty, by hotel staff members and dock workers. "Make the past serve the present," Chairman Mao had said, and so the ancient traditions of China in painting music, theatre and other arts have been preserved, but turned to the service of the revolution.

"Shall I sing a song for you?" asked Chou Song-pai, and the room filled with applause. Chou (pronounced ("Joe") was our chief interpreter, and at first he had seemed stern and reserved; as the tour continued, he became more and more meshed with the chorus. By the time we returned to Peking he was singing first tenor and making plans for our next visit.

"I will sing a song from Peking opera, *Taking High Mountains by Strategy*. It is entitled, 'Communists Are Always Ready at the Call of the Party.' Just try it, uh? Don't laugh at me."

He sang lustily, nothing tentative about it, and unaccompanied. He faltered once, laughed, and drove on to a firm conclusion, among cheers and applause.

Then it was our turn. We sang work songs, and songs about the mines: Those are the Men of the Deeps' stock in trade, and the Chinese had made it clear they did not want to hear songs about religion, love, superstition, or drinking. Music is, they say, an international language—and though that is not entirely true, the music made this trip splendidly rich and human. We ended, as we often did, with our only Chinese song, a great crowd pleaser even though it must have sounded very odd with English words, a slow tempo, and four-part harmonies:

I love Peking's Tien An Men
There the red sun rises high;
Our great leader, Chairman Mao,
He leads us marching on.

And so home on the bus, through paddy fields and stands of grain, along tree-lined lanes choked with rubber-tired carts pulled by oxen, horses, burros, donkeys. The carts are everywhere in China, loaded with brick, cabbages, bamboo matting, stone, baskets, soil. China makes its own cars and trucks, handsome ones, too, in a somewhat utilitarian style, but not enough to meet the need, and the carts still carry the loads of the country. We jolted past generating plants and farmyards, the horn blowing incessantly as we forged a path through the swarms of bicycles.

In the smoky air over Tangshan's industries, the pagoda shone on the hilltop. Under the hill waited our supper, and a round of jokes with the cook, a jolly barrel of a man who seemed to regard his outsize guests as a special challenge to his art. What we would eat, we never knew: fish and chicken with the heads still attached, moth larvae soup, jellyfish, preserved eggs. By and large we didn't ask: We just enjoyed it. You'd be surprised just how good a crisp, deep-fried jellyfish can taste after you've put in a day touring the coal mines.

Next day we visited the Tangshan Municipal Exhibition of Class Education, a large building devoted to showing the lives of the miners down through the ages, the horrors of mining in the old days when Japanese troops guarded the mines and the price of a meal underground was double a man's daily earnings, when naked miners hauled baskets of coal by straps around their foreheads, when the manager earned $43,000 a year and the miner $15—before deductions. Recorded deaths of miners by 1936: 5,397. Disabled: 200,000. Total profit earned from the miners: "over 300 million silver dollars."

Never forget the past, said Mao. The exhibits, made by the miners themselves, showed life-size mockups of these conditions, and of the changes since the armed risings of July 15, 1938, which ultimately delivered the area to the People's Liberation Army. Conditions in Cape Breton at the same period weren't so very different, the Men of the Deeps remarked, and there were plenty of communists in New Waterford and Glace Bay in the 1920s and 1930s for the same excellent reasons.

All the same, when the time came to sing for the museum guides, the Canadians had a statement to make: We too were proud of our country, and in this temple of the new China it was time to assert that pride. So we stood under a vast mural showing the workers, soldiers and peasants putting their oppressors to flight, red flags and bayonets held high, and we sang a song that nearly made some of us weep:

O Canada! Our home and native land!
True patriot love in all thy sons command....

The Chinese beamed. Love of one's country is a sentiment they understand perfectly.

En route to the porcelain factory I sat with Li Tsun-ying. She was, she told me proudly, a peasant girl who had finished middle school—high school, more or less—and then worked five years in the countryside. Marxist theory has always maintained that socialism will produce people who can do anything: China is—especially since the Cultural Revolution—actively trying to shift its people from one role to another, so that one person may be a factory worker, an intellectual, a farmer, a soldier, a bureaucrat and so forth, at different times in his or her life. If today's manager may be tomorrow's farm hand, no system of social class can develop, and the complete eradication of the class system is a chief goal of the Communist Party.

From the fields, Li Tsun-ying had gone to university for two years, having been nominated by her fellow workers as eager and capable and politically advanced. She had taken English, from Chinese teachers only, and she hoped to become an interpreter "if my Yinglish is good enough." She wanted to be a "cadre," a "core element" in the Party, but she was doubtful whether she could qualify for such honorable work; after two years, her English was still uncertain.

Strangely touching, that conversation, not so much for its substance as its style, for Li Tsun-ying chatted about her dreams in much the same tones that a comparable Canadian might reveal very different ambitions. I hope her dreams come true.

We had seen a good many factories and we would see many more: It would be easy to be cynical. Yet the Chinese have grasped a basic truth we commonly ignore: Places of work are *interesting*, and the skills of the human hand and mind are fascinating. Here is a woman at a ratty old workbench by a grimy window, deftly painting in by hand the colours of the flowers on a saucer. Here is another, dipping unfired cups in a glaze. Here is a toothless, skinny old bundle of bones briskly wrapping them up for their long, safe journey to Amsterdam, or Angola, or Alberta. And though the managers always spoke proudly about the improvements, they were forthright about the inefficiencies still remaining, about the modernizations that remained for the future.

And again the choir made friends, singing to the workers, plunging into the assembly line to shake hands and try to do the job the worker was at—usually with great laughter and shaking of heads—giving away maple leaf pins, clapping their greetings and smiling their friendship. Back in Peking, Canadian staffers would tell us our tour was unprecedented because we did not come on official business and we did not merely observe; with the miners' music and laughter, their jokes and their audacity, their utter lack of snobbery—who else would sing for the kitchen staff in every hotel along the way?—they touched the Chinese in a way foreigners rarely manage, they made friends for Canada among people who scarcely know where the country is located.

WE HAVE FRIENDS ALL OVER THE WORLD!

The night which lives most vibrantly in memory is that night in Tangshan when Jack and I came back from our stroll and suggested we all wander downtown after dinner and sing for the people in the streets. We asked Chou to come along to explain who we were. He gathered the other interpreters, and we set out in the twilight.

Down the long, walled street to the gate of the park, and along a wide thoroughfare in the gathering darkness, curious people trailing behind us. We lined up on the concrete steps of what seemed to be a workers' club and asked Chou to explain. He shouted in Chinese, nodded, and we began.

We looked out on a semicircle of bewildered, tentative faces, and launched into "The Man with the Torch in His Cap." The perplexity turned to smiles, to pleasure, to applause. We sang "Tien An Men," and the crowd laughed aloud: so *funny*, these Canadians who appear from nowhere and sing one of our songs in their queer, exotic language. And yet—one of *our* songs! Beaming approval, the crowd began clapping in rhythm.

We ended, and walked on down the street. The crowd followed, perhaps four or five hundred, swelling as people came from the alleys and courtyards: There's something going on in the street. Around a corner onto an enormous avenue, 50 yards wide, perhaps more, with the Chinese pressing up against us, children grinning at us, hands shaking, *knee-hah!* Under a street light we stopped again, gathered on the curb, the last light fading behind the half-finished apartment block across the road, the mass of grinning, excited faces melting into the dark distances, a thousand people, fifteen hundred, willing us to sing:

And many a miner has laid his head
In death on the coal's black lap;
So don't forget he's a hero too:
The man with the torch in his cap.

And again that passport to Chinese hearts, their song, "Tien An Men":

Our great leader, Chairman Mao,
He leads us marching on.

And suddenly it burst, that membrane of reserve which keeps strangers apart burst, and the people of Tangshan surged into our midst and we into theirs, the distance dissolved, the barriers swept away, the language conquered. Al Provoe walked down the centre of the street with a Chinese child holding each hand, capering and squalling. Alex MacDonald shot by on a bicycle while its owner held his jacket and roared his enjoyment. Then everyone seemed to be on bicycles, Bob McLeod wobbling along, his first bike ride in 40 years, Sid Forgeron vanishing into the dusk. Chou clutched Jack O'Donnell by the arm, telling him, "You have made that song much more beautiful. Really. *Really*." And Donnie Matheson walked beside me and said, in an awed whisper, "Look behind you."

I looked, and as far as I could see that immense street was choked with people: mothers with baby carriages, old people, young people, children, people on bicycles, people on foot, people running, people walking, people clapping. And here and there a tall stout figure surrounded and smiling: a Cape Breton coal miner, in the warm Chinese evening, in the warm Chinese crowd.

We sang again and turned up a side street making for the hotel, the crowd thinning as we went, though a good part of it followed us right to the door. Alex MacDonald came by. "I can't find that kid," he said. "I don't know where he went."

What kid? "He came up beside me," said Alex, moved almost beyond speaking, "and I saw him tugging at his jacket. I didn't know what he was doing. He was tugging away so hard, and it took him quite a while, and then he came running up and pushed this in my hand. I wanted to give him a maple leaf, but when I turned around he was gone."

He held out his hand. In it was a tiny metal badge—a merit badge of the Young Communists, someone said later, a thing so precious the boy should never have given it away.

"I don't know what it is," said Alex. "But I'll tell you, b'y, I'll treasure that little jigger for the rest of me life."

Hundreds of thousands dead in Tangshan. My God, can you wonder that we grieve?

[1976]

Down Home No More

ON A BRILLIANT JULY MORNING, two cars swept along the Trans-Canada Highway where the green hills of Cape Breton roll down into the Bras d'Or Lake. Edison Lumsden, a Canso fisherman who had recently become a full-time organizer for the United Fishermen and Allied Workers' Union, drove the red fastback. The green station wagon belonged to Con Mills, another UFAWU organizer. Their nine passengers were fishermen from Canso and Mulgrave, heading for Sydney and a plane to Vancouver.

Fifteen months of struggle to be represented by the union of their choice had ended. They had fought not only the international corporations that employed them but also the courts, the churches, the media and the government. Twice they brought Nova Scotia to the verge of a general strike. In the end, the companies had outflanked them by exploiting the divisions within the labour movement itself.

ERIC FITZPATRICK RENTS A BUNGALOW just outside the straggling bayside village of Mulgrave. The night before he flew west we talked in his kitchen about being a working man in Canada. A hefty blond-haired man of 37, Fitzpatrick has worked hard since he left his native Newfoundland at 18. "I used to think there was a halfway respect at least in this country for democratic rights," he told me, shaking his head. "I thought you had a democratic right to the union of your own choice. Now, when the politicians talk about democratic rights, why it just makes me sick to my stomach. There aren't any democratic rights in this country. Not for fellows like us."

As we talked, Eric watched Gail Fitzpatrick feed the six children he wouldn't see again before Christmas. Would the family head west eventually? "Well, right now we don't have any plans at all," Eric shrugged. "Just get some food for the kids, that's all. And clear off the debts."

ERIC'S STORY BEGINS IN 1947, when the Nova Scotia Labour Relations Board certified the Canadian Fishermen's Union as bargaining agent for Lunenburg's trawlermen. On appeal the courts held that the fishermen were *not* employees but "co-adventurers" who shared both risk and profit with Lunenburg Sea Products. The CFU organizing drive died. Twenty years later, Atlantic trawlermen were still unorganized.

On a trawler, wrote Catholic priest Thomas Morley, who spent eight days on one, "You can work steadily for 20 hours as long as the fish-finder needle keeps pointing out fish. And when the fish are slack and the boat changes course, even then rest is not assured. There are fish to be cleaned and put in the hatches, ice to be shoveled, bottom-damaged nets to be mended. One of our crew was on his feet for over 30 hours. Add to this the wind and the frost, the snow and the sleet of winter trawling, the open decks, the bare hands and the exposed machinery of running winch and speeding steel cables, and you get a faint idea of the hardest life by which men still earn their daily bread."

The boats carried only rudimentary medicine chests; when a cable ripped off three of Gerald Collins' fingers, he could only be given cotton batting to staunch the bleeding and a bottle of rum to ease the pain. A hydraulic hatch cover once pinned Eric, pressing down on his back till his leg broke in eight places. "When you get hurt on a dragger on the East Coast," he says, "it's, 'Oh, you're not hurt, it's just pinched.'" The dragger made another two-hour tow, and only 23 hours later did Eric arrive in Antigonish hospital. He was laid up seven months.

When a trawler docked, the company weighed and graded the catch and calculated its value. At Acadia Fisheries in Canso and Mulgrave, deckhands were paid four dollars a day, plus a share in 30% of the catch. At Booth Fisheries in Petit-de-Grat, the share was 37%, with no guarantees. A man might make $150 on an average 12-day trip. A trawlerman working steadily makes about $3,000 to $5,000 a year—but he works eight hours on and four off, putting in twice as many hours a year as the average industrial worker. In heavy fishing the men spend five days in six away from home.

ACADIA FISHERIES WAS ONE of more than 60 subsidiaries of the Boston Fishing Group of Hull, England. Booth Fisheries was a subsidiary of Chicago's Consolidated Foods, with 1969 sales of more than a billion dollars. Acadia had tapped the provincial treasury for loans totaling nine million dollars.

The Canadian Labor Congress has given jurisdiction over fisheries to the Canadian Food and Allied Workers' Union, chartered by Chicago's Amalgamated Meatcutters and Butcher Workmen. But in 1967, before the CFAWU—"the Meatpackers," as Eric scornfully calls them—started in Nova Scotia, the United Fishermen and Allied Workers, a militant non-CLC union which represents a large majority of West Coast fishermen, sent a two-man organizing team east. Soon the UF had members in Halifax, Lunenburg—and Canso Strait. By late 1969, 250 fishermen in the Strait locals were ready to ask the companies for recognition.

ACADIA FISHERIES' MANAGER A.L. Cadegan—"Donnie" Cadegan, as he is known in the industry—paces back and forth in his modern office in the six-million-dollar Canso fish plant. Canso smells of fish everywhere, but in the manager's office the reek is overpowering. "This plant doesn't smell bad," says Cadegan, surprised. "You ought to have smelled some of the old ones." Cadegan works hard, angers easily, and speaks bluntly.

He is saying that he knew from the beginning that the choice was recognition or a bitter strike. "I'm not anti-union," he snorts. "I thought they *should* have a union. But not the UF."

Why? In a huge advertisement, Booth Fisheries once described the UF as "irresponsible and unreliable." Moreover its president, Homer Stevens, is a Communist Party member. In May, 1970, the Canadian Labor Congress annual convention in Edmonton voted two-to-one against admitting the UF except by merger with a CLC affiliate—part of the Congress policy of creating fewer and bigger unions. Then CLC President Donald MacDonald attacked "sinister efforts to pervert the labour movement" particularly by "the Communist Party of Canada." As masses of delegates protested the smear, MacDonald roared, "If the mukluk fits, wear it!" In mid-strike, the Halifax *Chronicle-Herald* resurrected the story: BC UNION LACKS TOP CLC BLESSING: COMMUNIST LEADERSHIP IS FACTOR.

"This is another way they have of scaring the people," Eric shrugs. "There's lots of religious people around Nova Scotia, and if you're a Communist you're not supposed to believe in God or truth. They say in this country you got a right to be what you want to be—well, if Homer Stevens is a Communist, that's Homer Stevens' business. As long as he don't tell me what church to go to, that's okay."

In fact, Acadia's British parent company regularly bargains with Communist-led unions. "The UF would have demanded ruinous prices from the industry," Cadegan says. The issue was not Communism, but money and power.

IN EARLY APRIL, 1970, the fishermen polled the crew of each incoming trawler. The men voted overwhelmingly to strike. By mid-April picket lines surrounded the fish plants in all three ports. "You'll be out there till snow flies!" Cadegan predicted. They were.

On April 19, Booth used the companies' ultimate threat to industry-starved Nova Scotia: Either the union would pull out or Booth would. Since when, retorted Homer Stevens, putting the whole point of the strike in a capsule, did anyone but the fishermen have the right to choose their union? On May 11, a fish-laden Acadia truck drove through the Canso picket lines, headed for Halifax. Mulgrave fishermen intercepted it at Guysborough, and five were arrested. The incident publicized the strike, and the union stepped up its campaign for funds.

Meanwhile Booth Fisheries met its commitments from its numerous plants in Newfoundland and the eastern United States. For much weaker Acadia—the only Boston Group company in America, with no other plants than those in Canso Strait—members of the Nova Scotia Fish Packers' Association arranged to cover market commitments and raised a cash subsidy for the duration of the strike.

On May 21, Judge Nathan Green was appointed a one-man federal-provincial commission of inquiry into the strike. A week later the companies accepted his interim recommendation that the fishermen return on the old terms while the inquiry continued, but the fishermen overwhelmingly rejected it.

So, out at the eastern tip of mainland Canada, where the tiny shingled houses of Canso lie scattered among the boulders, the Lumsdens and the Gurneys and the Richardsons walked the picket line. Men and women whose ancestors had sailed out of the Maritimes' oldest fishing village for centuries would split a few bottles of beer in parked cars, banter among themselves and taunt company officials as they came and went. Cadegan says he's heard some rough language, but none rougher than some that the women hurled at him. When you ask the fishermen's wives about it, they just chuckle.

In all three ports, the fishermen had found the Mounties taking pictures, and on June 4, as the strike moved into its third month, they found out why. Supreme Court Justice D.J. Gillis awarded the companies *ex parte* injunctions—court orders based on the company's arguments only—prohibiting the UF and 37 of its members from picketing the three plants. The fishermen, their wives and supporters gathered in the union halls and decided to risk contempt of court charges by ignoring the injunctions.

For two weeks, the law was silent. Twelve UF members, including Stevens, Con Mills and Everett Richardson, went to Ottawa, where Tommy Douglas promised them support.

Back in Nova Scotia, the National Farmers' Union was sending truckloads of fruit and vegetables. Money came from pulp workers in BC, electrical workers in Amherst, firemen in Sydney. Houses, cars and clothes were plastered with UF stickers. Members of the Halifax New Democratic Youth joined the picketers, sleeping in the Mulgrave union hall. "There's no way I could describe what those young people did for us," marvels Eric. "It was really wonderful. They walked the picket line, they went to meetings with us, they went to negotiations with us, when we had to go to Halifax they kept us under their roofs. When I first heard about them, I figured that they were, you know, like the papers described them and television—they were just a bad bunch of people. Then I got to know them, and I think they're a *great* bunch of people."

But the courts had not forgotten, and on June 19, Eric and eleven of his comrades from Mulgrave found themselves in a Halifax courtroom, facing contempt charges. "I felt pretty nervous," Eric remembers, "looking at the old judge there. When he wanted us to apologize—well, really to apologize to the companies—and we said we wouldn't apologize, he broke off for a 15-minute session to give us time to talk about it. He figured that we didn't know what was going on, you know, he figured somebody got to explain it to us. The problem was a very very serious problem to *him*, I guess.

"Homer simply told us what we were up against, and the lawyer briefed us, and Homer said, 'Well, you're facing something now that I faced, and you could possibly wind up getting a year in jail. It's in this judge's hands now, and God knows how he'll judge you. But I don't want you to go in there feeling that you don't know all about it. I want you to understand it.' I don't know whether I was the first guy, or whether Jim Lundrigan was the first to say, 'Well, we'll take our chances.'

"When we went back in, I was kind of nerved up, but I was still going to go through with it. If it meant a year, well, I was going to take a year, and I think all the fishermen felt the same way. We never went into it ignorant or anything, we knew what was going to happen."

Chief Justice Gordon Cowan gave them 20 and 30 days each. Three days later 16 Canso fishermen came to trial. "I saw smiles and laughs over the sentences on Friday," Judge Cowan told them. "This is not going to continue. Picketing has got to stop." He asked Everett Richardson whether his defiant comments in Ottawa meant he would continue picketing. Richardson wouldn't say. Furious, Cowan sentenced him to nine months, holding the other Canso men over to see whether Richardson's sentence would stop the picketing.

In Port Hawkesbury, 2,400 pulp mill and construction workers walked off the job in protest. In Sydney, 3,000 miners wildcatted. Near Pictou, construction workers left the Scott Maritimes site. Hundreds of sympathizers descended on the Canso Strait ports to walk the picket lines with the fishermen's wives and children. The Rt. Rev. W.W. Davis, Anglican Bishop of Nova Scotia, "deeply regretted" the sentence.

The Nova Scotia Federation of Labour had been lukewarm to the strike, its fellow-feeling for the strikers countered by the official CLC hostility to the union. Now it slammed Attorney-General R.A. Donahoe, who had ordered the contempt proceedings, for his "open bias against all working Nova Scotians, in favour of foreign corporations who are exploiting our natural resources and who have clearly indicated their total irresponsibility to the people of this province." Halifax's opposition paper, *The Fourth Estate*, ran a full-page editorial headed CONTEMPT FOR THE LAW: WHAT ELSE COULD AN HONEST MAN HAVE? Jeremy Akerman, leader of the Nova Scotia NDP and the only politician to give the strikers full support, damned the government and the courts "which claim to be impartial yet continue to be the tools of the corporations." Labour Federation Secretary-Treasurer J.K. Bell suggested Acadia Fisheries be nationalized, and within three days of Richardson's sentencing, with over 7,000 workers still out, the federation president, John Lynk, was discussing the "strong possibility" of a general strike.

Faced with this unprecedented solidarity, the government put off the remaining contempt trials until October 27, and the fishermen already in jail were released on bail. Returning to Mulgrave, as calls for a special session of the legislature to amend the co-adventurer law echoed around the province, Eric Fitzpatrick was jubilant. "The people are 100% behind us," he said, "and we're going to win."

AS THE SUMMER ROLLED ON, Tory Labour Minister Thomas McKeough agreed with Judge Green's remark during a hearing that the fishermen's demand for a union was "fair and just," and opined that the law would be changed "within a year." In early August, the government got around to asking the Supreme Court for a ruling on whether it had the power to change the law. The companies remained obdurate; a union maybe, but not the UF. In late July, Booth Fisheries ran several large newspaper ads attacking the UF and threatening to leave Nova Scotia. Acadia bought similar ads, and Cadegan gave substance to the threats by declaring in August that Acadia's Mulgrave plant was permanently closed. "Fishing," he pronounced, "is finished in Mulgrave."

The Mulgrave fishermen were undaunted. "Let them pull out!" cried Reg Carter. "Let them get out and good riddance!" In Petit-de-Grat, however, Father Georges Arsenault was getting worried. Months had gone by; people were suffering, "After six months, it was getting too long," he frowns. "The one thing we couldn't stand was to see Booth leave. And the company was staying only if there was a CLC union." As Booth's August deadline approached, shore plant union president Albert Martell and others conducted a poll: Should Booth stay in Petit-de-Grat? Not surprisingly, only one of 273 employees voted No. Interpreting the poll as a repudiation of the UF, Martell began firing off telegrams to provincial and federal government demanding "positive action" to "remove Homer Stevens and his co-workers from our province."

For the moment Martell's work went for nothing. Strong as ever, the strikers held fish sales and rallies in Halifax and Sydney. The Mulgrave union hall was papered with letters of support. Wives took the story to construction workers in Cape Breton. Whole families turned out for demonstrations and marches. When you ask Eric what he especially remembers about the strike, he says he thinks a lot "about the women and the part they took in it, going down there when we were in jail. They went down and stood on the picket line there, and they defied the law and the courts and everything else. I feel kind of proud about them."

Gail Fitzpatrick put in 20-hour days for weeks on end, picketing and collecting money, baking bread and pies and cakes for sale in a nearby store until her health gave out and the doctor ordered her to rest. Eric pitched in around the house, somewhat clumsily at times, helping with the kids and the housework. Union men and women came and went in what they both recall as a warm glow of comradeship. Once Homer Stevens and Glenn McEachern, the UF business agent, were coming up for supper. The Fitzpatricks were living on $20 a week strike pay plus what Gail could earn, and there was nothing in the fridge when Gail went out to work. When she came back, "Homer and Glenn had filled the fridge." Her face lights up, and in the rich tones of her native Cape Breton she says, "I think it was the most wonderful thing that ever happened to me."

Having fought the companies and the law, Gail says she is less reluctant to tangle with Eric. "I used to be scared all the time. But now I'm not frightened of things. I stand up for myself." Eric feels the two are closer than ever. "Gail stood right by me," he muses. "I've got much respect for her."

On the eve of a general sympathy strike planned by the Cape Breton Trades and Labour Council for August 21, Judge Green brought down his report. His findings: The law gave the fishermen no right to a union, but the law should be changed. In the meantime the fishermen should form an ad hoc committee to negotiate with the companies, leaving the question of recognition until after the new legislation. At first the fishermen angrily rejected the report. Recognition was, after all, their main demand. But after consulting with the Federation of Labour, the fishermen agreed to elect an ad hoc committee of four fishermen from each of the ports. Under the chairmanship of Labour Minister McKeough, talks began in Halifax early in September. Everett Richardson was there and so was Eric Fitzpatrick, facing experienced top management. Not surprisingly, communication often broke down.

On one memorable occasion, Eric blew up. "We're here, I said, talking to a bunch of men that's got 20 years of negotiating these things, and you got 20 years of experience of screwing the rich and the poor. You got a bunch of fishermen in here now, I said, and you're tryin' to walk all over them. You should be ashamed of yourselves. This is a disgrace to the community, and it's a disgrace to the whole country." Everett recalls that when Eric was done "there wasn't a drop of blood left in any of their faces." The company men got up and walked out and had to be talked into returning.

Just before the provincial election in October the fishermen signed a contract which gained them higher fish prices, grievance procedures, some improvement in working conditions. Cadegan denies that the agreement contained anything new, aside from the fish prices. But the men sailed under the first collective agreement they had ever had. A few days later, Nova Scotia handed the Liberals a bare 23-21 victory—and gave two seats to Akerman's NDP. The fishermen's lawyer, Leonard Pace, became the new Attorney-General and Minister of Labour, and the Liberals were pledged to "seize jurisdiction," as Pace puts it, by changing the Trade Union Act. After that the trawlermen could have their union certified, whether the companies liked it or not. As Christmas approached the fishermen had things to celebrate.

"THE MEN WERE BACK TO WORK," says Pace in his lawyer's modulated bass, leaning back in his desk chair in the Attorney-General's cavernous office overlooking Halifax harbour. "No one was unduly handicapped by a delay, and the first opportunity we got to bring in the legislation in a responsible manner, we did." But by then it was March 18, and for the fishermen the delay had been catastrophic.

Welcomed by the companies, blessed by the CLC, the Canadian Food and Allied Workers had begun raiding the UF locals almost before the ink dried on the October agreement. "There is a community of interest," admits a CFAW official, "between the government, the companies, and our union." In Petit-de-Grat, the CFAW contacted sympathetic people like Albert Martell and Father Arsenault, and signed up not only trawlermen but shore plant workers as well. On December 23, 1970, Booth Fisheries granted CFAW voluntary recognition and a union shop. Anxious to keep Booth in Nova Scotia, most trawlermen fell into line.

In January, CFAW organizers Jim Bury and Jim Coles moved into the Acadia fleet. They avoided Canso and Mulgrave at first, signing up trawlermen who lived in Linwood, in Glace Bay, in Guysborough and elsewhere. "We did it rather quietly," recalls Bury, 55, smooth and assured, fully at home in his modern Don Mills office. "But we signed up a majority." On March 9, Acadia granted voluntary recognition to CFAW, and three days later signed a union-shop collective agreement for the trawlermen.

But who are the Acadia trawlermen? They come and go, making anywhere from one or two trips a year up to Eric's 27. The CFAW claimed 57 signed membership cards, but the UF fishermen insist that many of them were signed by men who had made only occasional trips, months or even years before. Before March 18, however, CFAW was under no legal obligation to prove to anyone that it represented anybody: It had only to satisfy Acadia.

Trawlermen landing in Canso were told to join CFAW or quit. About 80 of the 112 crewmen walked off, and 65 filed complaints of unfair labor practices with the Labor Relations Board. When Bill 11 was signed into law March 18, Acadia and CFAW lodged their agreements with the board; if the board accepted them, CFAW was automatically certified. Naturally the UF challenged the agreements, filing 87 signed cards. Over the next four months the board held several hearings on the disputes, while the adamant trawlermen stayed ashore.

"It had something to do with Homer," Eric concedes. "To think that for 20 years, the only man that had guts enough to come to Nova Scotia to try to organize the fishermen—well, you just *couldn't* turn coat on him. I'd rather starve than join the CF. I didn't like the principles of it, I didn't like the way they came in there. Another thing about the UF, it's an all-Canadian union. I don't see why we have to have the Meatpackers come up from Chicago to organize fishermen on the East Coast. I just couldn't join the CF, that's all there is to it. I don't think I could sleep at night—and I like my sleep."

Once again the fishermen were living on what they could raise themselves, and on donations from sympathizers. As seasonal workers, they could not draw unemployment insurance, and local officials were denying them welfare, despite threats and promises from the provincial cabinet. On May 21, Bishop Davis finally buckled to heavy pressure and announced that Father Ron Parsons, who had supported the fishermen all along, would be relieved of his job in Canso August 31. "I didn't think you could be fired from a church," Parsons muses, "but I have been, so I guess you can." Even the NDP, closely tied to the CLC, was emitting what Parsons calls "silences that could be heard across the province."

While the board deliberated, a citizens' Committee for a Free Vote for Fishermen appointed a five-man panel headed by three college presidents to supervise a vote of every available fisherman who had been employed by Acadia on March 9. On May 3, 69 of the 112 men voted. They chose the UF in a 66-3 landslide. Jim Bury and Donald MacDonald denounced the vote, with Bury charging election irregularities and UF intimidation. MacDonald went on to warn that "if people of Nova Scotia wish to usher in a decade of violence and confusion which could spell ruin for the fishermen, the way to do it is to permit the UF to grab control of the industry."

Homer Stevens had always said that temper was a luxury, and even now, as the desperate fishermen tried to dramatize their grievances, they remained nonviolent. On June 4, 14 UF members boarded the *Acadia Gull*, warped her out from the dock, and held her until five carloads of Mounties hauled them off and charged them with mischief, a charge later dismissed on a technicality.

On June 25, the Labour Relations Board came to its final conclusions. "The board couldn't hear evidence on anything that happened before the eighteenth of March," explains a source connected with it. "All it could do was see that the CFAW had a majority as of the nineteenth and after." A legalistic view, the board's critics retort; it could have held a vote had it wished to. In any case, the UF fishermen had already been ousted by the nineteenth, so the CFAW certainly did have a majority. As for the unfair labour practices, the board held that men were fired not for belonging to the UF but for failing to join the CFAW. It dismissed the complaints. Since there is no appeal from a board decision, the companies and the CFAW had their way.

Five days later, in a last flash of defiance, a handful of fishermen and a crowd of supporters shouted slogans from the gallery of the legislature and hurled abuse at the government, fading away before the police arrived.

Was it over? Several fishermen thought so, and signed CFAW cards to get back to sea. "It's going to hurt me more to sign that card than it did to sign my father's death certificate," one told Edison Lumsden. "But what the hell else can I do?"

But some of the UF's strongest supporters could not get jobs with Acadia anymore. Cadegan denied that there had ever been a blacklist, but he declared that "Acadia has the right to hire *who* it wants, *when* it wants, *where* it wants. And the boats are fully crewed. I admit there are men I wouldn't want back. But Eric Fitzpatrick is strong UF, and I'd hire him anytime."

Some of the men found fishing jobs elsewhere; others went to Ontario. A good many took the UF's offer to lend them air fare and find them berths in BC. Meanwhile, Acadia Fisheries itself was actually in trouble, looking for a buyer for its plant and trawlers. On July 21, a mimeographed letter informed plant workers that the company had gone into liquidation. A.W. Suddaby, one of Acadia's British directors, blamed "the disastrous financial effect" of the strike, and assailed the provincial government for not putting up more money. The government coolly replied that the Boston Group had left the company undercapitalized and badly managed for years. Cadegan says the Boston Group put four million dollars into Acadia and never took a nickel out. But, if Acadia couldn't survive the strike, why didn't it settle? In November the plant at last prepared to reopen under the management of H.B. Nickerson & Sons of North Sydney, subject to a federal grant through the Department of Regional Economic Expansion.

FROM MULGRAVE TO THE HOSPITAL in Antigonish is nearly 40 miles. Gail Fitzpatrick's health is still not good, and today she is to have a barium X-ray. Since the Fitzpatricks can't afford a car, she faces a $12 taxi ride. But I have a car and things to do in Antigonish, so we drive in together. The doctor has denied her morning tea, and she feels "right owly." All the same, she seems her usual outgoing and cheerful self. She needs a new washer, but the Fitzpatricks won't have any credit in Port Hawkesbury until Eric's money comes in. Meanwhile she'll try to get a job.

The strike was the best thing that ever happened, she says. It brought people together, showed them how things really worked, and made them feel they could do something about it. She says that if they have to move to BC, why they'll have to, that's all. But she wouldn't want to. Her family and Eric's are in Mulgrave, and so are all her friends. A Port Hawkesbury firm plans to build some new houses you could get on a low down payment, and maybe.... "A house of our own," she says. "Now that'd be something. Or one of them big trailers—I'd love to get one of them."

"IF YOU'RE GOING TO FISH, this is the only place to fish," Eric says, standing on a Vancouver dock. "You got so many opportunities for to make a dollar, you know?" He thinks of taking the whole family out this year. He likes BC, and Canso Strait families are arriving all the time. He wonders what Gail thinks, and says he thought of phoning a couple of times, but didn't want to run up the bill.

"I miss the kids an awful lot," he says wistfully. "I see kids sometimes, and I start to feel lonely then. I think about Jeanie an awful lot, you know—I suppose because she's the youngest in the family. I think of her smile and then I'd give anything, you know...." His voice trails off.

But he doesn't regret the strike. "When I tell some people I'd do it again they say, 'Oh no, Eric, you wouldn't'—but I *would*, because of what I *learned* through the strike. And standing up for something you believe in, and standing by it—this is one thing I'm happy about. During the strike Gail used to say, 'I know we're having it hard but you're standing up for something you believe in.' I got to give her a lot of credit.

"I don't think anybody can figure we lost, because we got bargaining rights, and the only place in North America where the law gives bargaining rights to fishermen is in Nova Scotia today. I guess a lot of things went on in that strike that'll go down in history and be talked about for years to come. It puts me in a kind of bad position, but I don't regret it, and I'd do it again.

"There's another thing I took into consideration," said Eric, pausing for a moment. "I think that when the kids grow up, they'd like to figure that their father stood up for something he believed in. I figured sometime the kids would say, 'Well, Christ, my old man stood up for something he believed in, one time. So maybe I'll do the same.'"

[1972]

O Atlantica! We Stand on Guard for Thee!

SAVE CONFEDERATION. JUST SIGN HERE.

It's Denis Smith, editor of the *Canadian Forum*, on the phone from Toronto. A group calling itself The Committee for a New Constitution will shortly issue a statement declaring "that English-speaking Canada exists as a viable national community. We have faith in its will to survive as an independent nation regardless of the choice that the people of Québec may make about their future." It goes on to make various sensible proposals: a constitutional commission, a constituent assembly, a new constitution.

Would I, Smith asks, care to endorse this?

No, I reply, gazing out over the wind-whipped Atlantic waters, the wet brown fields of a Cape Breton April. I like the committee's open and exploratory tone, and I'd like to see those mechanisms tried. But I'm sick to death of being the token Maritimer whose endorsement gives a bogus "national" patina to such ventures, I think the unity of English Canada is an Ontario fantasy, and I'm damned if I'll help manipulate the Atlantic provinces during the death of Confederation as they have been manipulated through its lifetime.

Look here, Denis, I continue, you have twenty-eight people signing your statement; twenty-four are from Ontario. That's the way this country works: Ontarians cook up schemes, and the rest of us are conned, cajoled, or bullied into going along. If we don't, we're pitied for our petty, provincial loyalties.

You want me to make a statement? Try this: If we can work out a just and equitable Confederation, I'm all for it. But if we can't, and Québec pulls out, I'm prepared to contemplate independence for the Atlantic provinces as well.

Your statement could have allowed for that, Denis, if you'd let us provincials play a part in formulating it. But Ontarians don't do that: They assume we'll simply buy their mythology along with their manufactures.

Well, says Smith apologetically, there wasn't time.

There never is.

An ironic footnote: One of the Ontarians who signed the statement is my brother.

1843 *Liverpool, England, is home port to 150 ships of more than 500 tons. Of these, all but thirteen come from Canada's East Coast—seventy-nine from New Brunswick alone. In Boston and London, the drawing-rooms are chuckling over the wicked satire of the Nova Scotian writer Thomas Haliburton. In Halifax, Joseph Howe is demanding democratic self-government within Nova Scotia.*

"We ask for nothing more than British subjects are entitled to," cries Howe, "but we shall be contented with nothing less." In 1848 he will succeed, setting a pattern for the entire British empire.

I live in an Acadian village. What about the Acadians? A significant minority throughout our region, a powerful minority in New Brunswick: Are they merely the Québec diaspora? Hardly.

The Acadians have no special love for the Québecois, or *canayens*, though they recognize that Québec pressure in Ottawa has often worked to their benefit. "When I started in business, my father told me, 'Watch out for the *canayens*,'" remarks Fernand

Nadeau, a businessman, a former New Brunswick cabinet minister, a former mayor of Edmundston. "If you're going to be screwed, you'll be screwed by a *canayen.*"

Gerald Forgeron, a Nova Scotia contractor, says that if Québec separates our best bet would be to join the United States. Michel Blanchard, a young radical in Caraquet, New Brunswick, has lived in Québec and could do so again, but he felt like a refugee there. He didn't belong. That's why he fights for Acadian rights: He belongs to French New Brunswick.

1860 *The shipping of the Atlantic colonies, the sale of vessels from their shipyards, has made each of them a commercial power in its own right. Nova Scotia and Newfoundland are among the most active trading nations on earth. One-fifth of Britain's imports come from New Brunswick.*

In 1858, memoranda were sent east from the Province of Canada, that sprawling, disunited, landlocked colony up the St. Lawrence: The Canadians proposed discussions of a possible confederation of the British North American colonies. Most Maritimers considered the idea absurd. The seaside provinces were prosperous, peaceful, and cosmopolitan; about a third of their trade involved the United States, and less than five per cent involved Canada. The Canadians were men of large ambitions and small means. What on earth could they offer the Atlantic colonies?

"Goddam Upper Canadians," snorted the sawyer. "Jesus Christ-son-of-a-bitchin' Upper Canadians. They're worse than the fuckin' Yanks." We sat in the autumn sunlight, sharing a beer while the sawmill lay silent, the air sharp with the smell of sawn spruce and ripe hay, the truck already loaded with lumber. The sawmill is one of those little one-man affairs powered by an unmuffled engine from a dead truck, tucked away at the end of a dirt road. Around it stand the ruins of a farm, the house caving in, the untended apple trees bowing low with masses of little apples, a forlorn symbol of our lost self-sufficiency.

Cape Breton is a vast forest, cut these days chiefly for the Swedish-owned pulp mill at Port Hawkesbury, some of its wood exported as peeled logs to mills in Europe. For generations, Cape Bretoners have built their houses by felling their own trees, hauling them to miniature mills such as this one, paying to have them sawn, and building the houses themselves, with whatever help their friends and family can provide.

Now the country is adopting the National Building Code, which means all building lumber will have to be "stamped"—kiln-dried and inspected. Cape Breton has no facilities for preparing such lumber: It is trucked to Cape Breton from Montreal.

The National Building Code is a colonial instrument, used by our Upper Canadian masters. So is the National Housing Act: In 1967, a study showed that thirty-nine percent of new Canadian homes were financed through NHA, but only seven percent of new homes in Cape Breton. To get an NHA mortgage, you required an income of more than $6,000—and in 1967 that eliminated about three Cape Breton families out of four.

The little sawmill is the last dying kick of what was once a great lumber industry. Its days are clearly numbered.

Bring in a regulation in Ottawa. Destroy a man's little livelihood. Boost the price of Cape Breton housing. Then complain about the lack of Maritime enterprise, the apparently endless welfare payments to the East Coast, the intractability of regional disparity. And blame the Maritimers for the poverty you organized.

1864 *"The Lower Provinces have all the elements of social, commercial, and political prosperity and greatness without respect to Canada," declared the Saint John* Globe. *But times are changing. Railways and steamships are gaining ground. The Americans are ending their civil war and muttering about ending the lucrative free trade under the Reciprocity Treaty. Indeed, the victorious North is making threatening noises about annexation, and the Irish fanatics, the Fenians, are preparing to raid the North American territories of the hated British Crown. An Intercolonial Railway from Halifax to Canada via the Gulf of St. Lawrence begins to look like a military necessity, and the British are increasingly reluctant to pay for colonial defences.*

Almost absent-mindedly, the Maritimes decide to hold a conference at Charlottetown to consider the possibilities of Maritime union. In Canada, Reform leader George Brown proposes to John A. Macdonald and his Conservative co-leader George-Étienne Cartier a coalition government to push for a confederation of all the British provinces. The Canadians ask to participate at Charlottetown—and there, aided by excellent food, copious drinks, sparkling oratory from the engaging Thomas D'Arcy McGee, "they carried the Lower Province delegates a little off their feet," as a Fredericton journal remarked. An October conference at Québec firms up the proposals. Confederation is on its way.

Regional disparity is not a problem: It's a policy. Regional disparity is the whole point of Confederation.

Subsidies to the Atlantic provinces are out in the open: equalization payments, regional economic expansion grants, and so forth. The much greater federal advantages to Ontario (and, to a lesser extent, Québec) are concealed. Who paid the enormous capital cost of the St. Lawrence Seaway, covers its perennial operating losses, keeps it open all winter with icebreakers, to the detriment of Saint John and Halifax? The government of Canada. And who benefits? Ontario. Who does the tariff serve? Ontario.

Ontario Hydro imports coal from Pennsylvania at the same time that coal mines are being shut down in Nova Scotia and New Brunswick. Not only that, it's paid a subsidy to do so. Does the Cape Breton coal miner, by the same token, get a subsidy for buying a car from Sweden rather than Ontario? Don't be foolish.

We can't compete, they say, because we're remote. From what? We're half an inch from New England, a short sail from Europe, New York, the Caribbean. We're only remote if the centre of the universe is in Ontario.

The Arabs raise oil prices, and suddenly it's an economic imperative for Alberta to follow suit. Virtually all the electricity in Nova Scotia and absolutely all of it in Prince Edward Island is produced by oil-fired generators. Taken as a whole, Canada is self-sufficient, for the moment, in oil. But Canada is not taken as a whole. The Maritimes get a bit of "transitional" assistance, and then an explosive rise in power rates: Nova Scotia's are now by far the highest in Canada. People with electrically heated homes face bi-monthly bills of $400, $500, $600. They have to move out: and their houses are unsalable.

Is this one country, or is it not?

1865 *The Confederation movement is well under way. It has vast support in Canada—but in New Brunswick, this spring, a general election defeats* every single delegate to the Québec conference who held a seat in the House. *The government of S.L. Tilley is replaced by a violently anti-Confederation government headed by Albert Smith. One new MLA describes Canada as "a bankrupt wanting to assume the debts of a rich man."*

"Forty-eight thousand men," exults Fredericton's Billy Needham, "have said we don't want Confederation, and that should be the end of it."

Late in 1967, Premier Alex Campbell of Prince Edward Island thought the Council of Maritime Premiers should initiate a study of Maritime options in the event of Québec's separation. Hatfield of New Brunswick and Regan of Nova Scotia declined: Québec separation was simply unthinkable, and thinking about it would somehow increase its likelihood. So we blunder on through the darkness, assuring one another we can see.

Politicians have always loved Confederation, which gives them a larger stage on which to play their roles. Its demise, they chorus, would be disastrous for the Atlantic provinces. Campbell says, "It would take us fifty years to get back to just where we are right now." Tory MP Elmer MacKay considers it "criminal."

Allan J. MacEachen, who represents my own area, invites his constituents "to think about...the fundamental question: 'Do I want Québec to remain within Confederation?'" Apparently he believes that warm thoughts in Inverness will somehow change opinions in Chicoutimi.

Listen to that delightful man, the Québec novelist Roch Carrier, saddened as long ago as 1971 by "that inevitable war between the French and the English." Why was it inevitable?

"You don't accept that somebody takes what's yours," Carrier explained. "I think that for an English Canadian Québec is his property, because it's part of his country; and nobody wants to lose what belongs to him. It's not possible to imagine Québec leaving smoothly."

He sounds chillingly correct. Listen to Elmer MacKay: "I just can't see how we can *allow* one-third of our country to secede."

Our country. You don't accept that somebody takes what's yours.

1866 *A bad Fenian scare, the end of Reciprocity, heavy pressure from England (where the Canadians have powerfully lobbied the Colonial Office), and a highly irregular use of the royal prerogative to dismiss Smith's anti-Confederation government. Reluctantly, New Brunswickers are becoming persuaded that Confederation is the best of a series of unpalatable alternatives. New elections, in which tens of thousands of Canadian dollars flow east, and in June a solid majority for Tilley and Confederation. But the Acadian counties remain firmly opposed.*

Joseph Howe tours western Nova Scotia and reports he "could not find 500 confederates" in eight counties. But the Tupper government was elected in 1863, before Confederation was even an issue; it does not need to go to the people again before the fall of 1867. Indeed, it doesn't dare.

Consider Irene's teeth. Better yet, consider her gums, since she has no teeth to speak of.

Irene is a pretty, good humoured thirty-year-old who has lived on welfare since her husband deserted her and her five children four years ago. One Saturday night five friends dropped in.

"Going to the dance, Irene?"

"Now how in the hell can I go to the dance? I got no teet'."

"Use mine," said George, pulling out his plate.

"Use mine," said Bernice, doing the same.

"Here's mine," said Freddy.

Five of them, none over thirty, and all with false teeth. The nearest dentists are thirty miles away, and they are taking no new patients; they're booked up for over a year. Regular check-ups? You're joking. Add in poor food, no money, no public transportation. Irene's teeth never had a chance.

Finally they abscessed. Her jaw bellied out, she gnawed on painkillers, and on an emergency basis the dentist pulled all her uppers. He proposed to pull the lowers as well. She appealed for a special allowance to get false teeth. The welfare committee in Arichat decided that she didn't actually *need* teeth; she only needed to deal with the abscess. False teeth, said the committee, are only "cosmetic."

Before Confederation, Arichat was a prosperous shipbuilding town, centre of an international trade, the seat of a college and a Catholic cathedral. In 1873, Arichat boasted 143 sailing ships and a steamer. Today it's little more than a couple of food and hardware stores, a consolidated high school, and a poignantly oversized church.

Regional disparity is a community so straitened it has to quibble about paying for a deserted mother's teeth.

May 22, 1867 *Tupper still has not submitted the Confederation plan to the Assembly. Joseph Howe speaks in Dartmouth: "A year ago Nova Scotia presented the aspect of a self-governed community, loyal to a man, attached to their institutions, cheerful, prosperous, and contented.... Now all this has been changed. We have been entrapped into a revolution.... The Canadians are to appoint our Governors, Judges, and Senators. They are to 'tax us by any and every mode' and spend the money. They are to regulate our trade, control our Post Offices, command the militia, fix the salaries, do what they like with our shipping and navigation, with our seacoast and river fisheries...."*

"I'm very glad you called," gushes the federal bureaucrat over the phone from Halifax. "Our department has funded several welfare rights groups in the past, and I'd like you to invite me to come down and tell you how to tailor your programme to fit our national priorities, and make you eligible for funding."

Your national priorities, buddy? Who is this group supposed to serve: the poor people who organized it, or the Master Planners of Ottawa?

June, 1867 *An obituary in the Saint John* Freeman*: "Died,—at her late residence in the city of Fredericton, on the 20th day of May last, from the effects of an accident which she received in April, 1866, and which she bore with a patient resignation to the will of Providence, the Province of New Brunswick, in the 83rd year of her age."*

July 1, 1867 *The first day of the new nation's existence. Newfoundland and P.E.I. are having no part of it. A front-page obituary in the Halifax* Morning Chronicle*, edged in black: "Died—Last Night at 12 o'clock, the Free and Enlightened Province of Nova Scotia."*

September 18, 1867 *Tupper at last faces his infuriated electors, in simultaneous provincial and federal elections. Of thirty-eight provincial victors, thirty-six are committed to the immediate repeal of Confederation. Of nineteen federal members, the only supporter of Confederation even to win a seat is Tupper himself.*

Consider the views of E.F. Schumacher in *Small is Beautiful: A Study of Economics As If People Mattered.* Large countries, he says, don't work: Most large countries are terribly poor; those that are rich are perpetually riven by gross disparities and social strains.

"Some people ask, 'What happens when a country, composed of one rich province and several poor ones, falls apart because the rich province secedes?' Most probably the answer is: 'Nothing very much happens.' The rich will continue to be rich and the poor will continue to be poor. 'But if, before secession, the rich province had subsidized the poor, what happens then?' Well then, of course, the subsidy might stop. But the rich rarely subsidize the poor; more often they exploit them. They may not do so directly so much as through the terms of trade. They may obscure the situation a little by a certain redistribution of tax revenue or small-scale charity, but the last thing they want to do is secede from the poor.

"The normal case is quite different, namely that the poor provinces wish to separate from the rich, and that the rich want to hold on because they know that exploitation of the poor within one's own frontiers is infinitely easier than exploitation of the poor beyond them."

After the Québec election, Canada was swept (I hear) by a wave of unity movements, One Canada organizations, and similar effusions. Oddly enough, the Atlantic provinces—which, all official voices claimed, had most to lose from Québec's separation—have shown no such patriotic panic. The popular agitation is an *Ontario* agitation, and to a lesser extent a Western agitation. The economic muscle of Canada is in Ontario, and to a lesser extent in the West.

The last thing the rich want to do is secede from the poor.

1868 *Two years earlier, Joseph Howe carried a petition to London with 31,000 signatures—from a province of 400,000 people—begging that Confederation be delayed until after an election. He failed. In 1868, now an MP in the federal House himself, and bearing a commission from the intransigently separatist government in Halifax, he tries again.*

"Nova Scotia," writes John A. Macdonald, "has declared, so far as she can, against Confederation; but she will be powerless to harm, although that pestilent fellow, Howe, may endeavour to give us some trouble in England."

Again Howe fails—and the next year Macdonald offers some financial adjustments to Nova Scotia. Howe considers all the alternatives, including armed insurrection, and concludes that further resistance would be futile. He accepts the improved terms, and a seat in the federal Cabinet for himself.

1886 *Premier W.S. Fielding fights a Nova Scotia election on the platform of Maritime separation, and Maritime indepen-*

dence. He wins handsomely. Again the federal government comes up with more money, and takes Fielding into the federal Cabinet. Saint John is still the fourth largest wooden-ship-owning port in the world, but the Maritimes have already become what they remain to this day: colonies of Upper Canada, captive Third World countries in a federation they never had reason to love.

1887 *Newfoundland again rejects Confederation.*

The Maritime public, as opposed to the politicians, seems distinctly cheerful about the prospect of Canada's disintegration. René Lévesque's case, people whisper, is the same as ours, and his solution is the proper one. "The separation of Québec," declares a Nova Scotia harbour pilot, "may be the best damn thing that ever happened to us." A Cape Breton historian, Terrence MacLean, agrees: "November 15, 1976, may well turn out to be a more significant date in our history than July 1, 1867."

The Halifax *Chronicle-Herald* runs speculative pieces about an independent Nova Scotia, and publishes huge ads throughout the region explaining Tupper's chicanery and the illegality of Nova Scotia's forced entry into Canada. New Democratic MLA Paul MacEwan publishes a book, *Confederation and the Maritimes* (Lancelot Press, 1976), concluding that "very soon after Québec independence, we in the Maritimes would have to follow suit." Nor does he seem reluctant: "In the next few years, Maritimers are going to be giving Confederation its one last chance. There is no great sentiment within these provinces to leave Canada; but *there will be* if Canada does not end its systematic injustice."

MacEwan points out that Canada's trade arrangements, notably the tariff, mean that Maritimers must *sell* in the international market, as we always have done, but cannot *buy* there. The tariff protects Upper Canadian manufactures, not Maritime raw materials. Of the Canadian jobs dependent on the protective tariff, forty-nine percent are in Ontario, thirty-seven percent in Québec, and only fourteen percent in all the other provinces together. And MacEwan warns Québec, rightly, that the vision of economic association between an independent Québec and the rest of Canada is probably pie-in-the-sky; the Maritimes, at least, "would have no desire whatever to participate in any such set-up."

1895 *Newfoundland again rejects Confederation.*

1911 *In London, one Beckles Willson publishes a book:* Nova Scotia: The Province That Has Been Passed By.

1936 Maclean's *publishes an article: "Will the Maritimes Secede?" by S. Leonard Tilley. A joke, or an irony? Samuel Leonard Tilley led New Brunswick into Confederation in the first place.*

1938 *Addressing the Canadian Club of Toronto, Nova Scotia's perennial premier, Angus L. Macdonald, reminds his audience of the arguments of the anti-Confederates, their claims that the union would wreck Nova Scotia's economy, and admits he finds them "well-founded." In economic terms, "it would have been distinctly to Nova Scotia's advantage to remain out of Confederation."*

I have a mother in Vancouver, relations strewn across the Prairies, two brothers in Ontario, children in New Brunswick. Yes, I'd prefer a united Canada. But not at *any* price—and the price the Maritimes have paid in political, economic, and human terms has been outrageous.

In May, when I spoke at the college in Sydney, I was interviewed by the *Cape Breton Post.* What did you say? asked my tablemates at lunch—young, bright people who are building one of the most interesting colleges in Canada.

I said I had told the *Post* reporter that Québec's separation might be a sovereign opportunity for us. That the four Atlantic provinces might make a nation comparable to Norway or Denmark. That if the Scandinavians can use similar resources to make cars, furniture, diesel engines, and surgical instruments for the markets of the world, so can the people of Atlantica. That if China, for generations the sick man of Asia, can pull itself together so that a mere twenty-five years after a crippling civil war it can export work shirts and teacups to Cape Breton, we can do it, too.

That Canada, in short, is an encumbrance, and that René Lévesque has done us all a favour by declaring that this corrupt, lopsided Confederation is finished. Things unthinkable a year ago can be thought about today.

Had we all been thinking these things in solitude? Suddenly the table was crackling with plans, prospects, and opportunities. Visions began to crystallize: farmland coming back into production, sawmills and woodworking plants springing up, the triangular trade with Europe and the Caribbean flourishing, films, publishing, boat-building, the liberation of Maritime vitality. Like a lightning rod, the very thought of independence seemed to concentrate energies that had been dissipated in a century of stagnation.

What was happening to us? I wondered, and then I saw it: the graphic demonstration of Confederation's failure. For these young people were electrified by the mere idea of a *country of their own*, a country in which their humanity would be respected and their labours needed, a country in which they might develop for the glory of their gods, and for the flowering of their people.

If Confederation had succeeded, they might have felt that way about Canada.

[1977]

The Gathering of the Sheep

THE GATHERING OF THE CLANS—in Nova Scotia? Is this history's bitter joke?

Here is the story of three Donald Camerons. The first was "the gentle Lochiel," 19th chief of the Camerons of Lochiel, a passionate Jacobite who led 800 Camerons into battle at Culloden. In 40 minutes, English grapeshot destroyed his ankles and his society. Lochiel spent the summer of 1746 hiding in the heather, watching the Duke of Cumberland's soldiers burn his house at Achnacarry, trying to rally the remains of the Highland army which had earlier borne Prince Charles Edward to Derby and shaken the throne of England. Now they were broken. More than 460 of Lochiel's 800 fighting men were dead. In September, the gentle Lochiel abandoned his forfeited lands and, with the Prince, sailed away to exile.

The Highland chief, writes John Prebble—whose trilogy *Fire and Sword: the Destruction of the Clans* should be required reading in Nova Scotia this absurd Scottish summer—was "a savage man who might speak French and Latin, who could distinguish between a good claret and a bad...who would bargain like an Edinburgh chandler to secure a profitable marriage for his daughter, who could sell his tenants to the plantations but who would touch his sword at the slightest reflection on his honour."

Technically, the clan lands belonged to the chief, the absolute ruler of his native glen, but he held them on behalf of his people. "If he had the right of life and death over his people, he was equally responsible for their welfare," says Prebble. Clan life was as harsh as it was intimate. Raising his regiment for the 1745 rising, the gentle Lochiel sent his gentle lieutenants to "intimate to all the Camerons that if they did not forthwith go with them they would instantly burn all their houses and (kill) their cattle." Some reluctant soldiers later testified that Lochiel himself gently "beat them severely with his whip." Accepted practice, says Prebble. "Within the context of the clan it was the reluctant Cameron who sinned and betrayed his ancestors."

But the gentle Lochiel was at least true to his code and his people. His grandson—Donald Cameron, the 22nd chief of Lochiel—was true to nothing but his own avarice. In 1784 the forfeited estates were returned to the young Lochiel, who was 15, foreign-educated, estranged from his clansmen. By 1792—The Year of the Sheep—he was deeply in debt. He began to evict his people and to rent or sell the clan lands for sheep farming. In 1793, a thousand men of his district swarmed into the army. Others ended up in hovels on the moors, in Glasgow slums, in the work camps along the Caledonian Canal, in Canada and Australia. And yet, when the 22nd Lochiel died in 1832, he was still buried in debt, and his new house at Achnacarry was only half-finished. His son, Prebble says, "held a banquet to celebrate his accession to the title, but could not find a single tenant of his own name" to attend it.

Young Lochiel was not unique. When the Macdonell chiefs were done, 20,000 of their people were in Canada and none in Glengarry. Between 1801 and 1803, the 24th chief of the Chisholms evicted 5,000 people. Many went to Antigonish, and are there yet. The MacNeils were swept from the isles of Mingulay and Barra. Their descendants live in Cape Breton, at the throat of water still called the Barra Strait. In 1831-32 alone, 124,000 Highlanders boarded festering ships bound for Canada. In 1854, the laird of Strathcarron ordered the eviction of the Rosses from their glen. When sixty-odd women resisted, 35 police charged them with batons. Afterwards the blood lay pooled on the ground, and the dogs licked it up.

GATHERING OF THE SHEEP

In 1956, Donald Cameron (your humble narrator) thought Billy Fisher eccentric; Billy wore a kilt and took his Scottish heritage seriously. Donald Cameron did not consider himself Scottish, but Western Canadian. His Highland heritage amounted to little more than a Harry Lauder song about meeting and treating MacKay. But when Donald Cameron came to Cape Breton he discovered that his tastes and emotions were surprisingly Scottish. And when official Nova Scotia had touristic orgasms about a Walt Disney fantasy called The International Gathering of the Clans—which would bring Highland chiefs to Nova Scotia—he felt a low, black, Celtic anger.

Why here? Why International? Because the forefathers of these honoured guests betrayed our families and scattered them like litter from here to New Zealand and Chile. Whatever we have to say to them should be in the spirit of the ruined men of Golspie, when the second Duke of Sutherland tried to enlist soldiers there for the Crimean War. His father, the first Duke, had begun the infamous Highland clearances, and now the men of Sutherland refused to go to war. "We have no country to fight for," they told him. "You robbed us of our country and gave it to the sheep. Therefore, since you have preferred sheep to men, let sheep defend you."

We will rejoice at the fiddles this summer here in Cape Breton, as we always do. We will stepdance and sing the mournful "Boat Song" of Mingulay. But let us not welcome the chiefs. Let the clan chiefs stay at home with those with whom they threw in their lot. Let those in Scotland have the Gathering of the Sheep.

Rocky Mountain High

IN WHICH THE WHEEZING AUTHOR is bamboozled into downhill skiing, and on the mountain loses dignity, meditates on knowledge, enriches his fatherhood, tumbles, swears, meets some challenges of love, and finds God.

DOWNHILL SKIING IS A CERTIFIABLY silly sport, I whimper to myself as the chairlift bears me inexorably over the treetops and gullies, like a slab of beef going around the overhead conveyors in an abattoir. I cling to the cold steel pipe of the chair with sweating hands.

I am terrified of heights.

Deposited on the frozen top of Mount Norquay near Banff, I turn my cumbersome slats downwards and slide to the bottom. There I wait in line for a chance to do it again, while my feet freeze, my nose runs and my glasses steam up. This may be all very well for the sex-maddened youths and maddeningly sexy maidens who mentally measure the pert and pertinent bodies in the skin-tight suits—but one can scarcely imagine an entertainment less well-suited to a round-shouldered, short-winded, tight-fisted 45-year-old author whose notion of strenuous exercise is opening his second daily package of cigarettes.

Why am I doing this, anyway?

I am doing it—sigh—for love. I am hopelessly in love with a bewitching woman who is passionately in love with skiing—and who yearns to share it with our four-year-old son. I believe in participation, if not Participaction, and Lulu has not had a chance to ski for six long years. For seven years before that, she sampled the great ski hills of Europe. She enjoyed spring skiing in shorts at Val Gardina, Italy, and hissed down 15-mile runs in the Swiss Alps. She was on intimate terms with the peaks of Bavaria and had fond memories of Les Trois Vallées, France. She had investigated the plummetting pinnacles of Norway and yodelled through clouds of powder snow on the alpine meadows of Austria.

Then she came home to Nova Scotia and married me. Nova Scotia is a province of small trees, small distances, small incomes and small mountains. Skiing in Nova Scotia is like sailing in Saskatchewan: One is surprised to find it done at all. Lulu languished.

And then a committee of the gods headed by W. O. Mitchell granted me the opportunity to spend six winter weeks working on a new novel in the splendid seclusion of the Banff School of Fine Arts. The heart of the ski country—at the height of the season.

Go to Banff—without Lulu?

Go with Lulu—and not ski?

Move over, Podborsky. That flash on the slopes is Cameron, making the best of it, a bizarre snowbird desperately acting out his mating ritual.

ONE DOES NOT COMPETE with a four-year-old. Still, comparisons are hard to resist if you start at the same time. And Mark Patrick was doing better than I was.

He took to skiing like a seal to a school of herring. Chirping and laughing with pleasure, he zipped from one side of the run to the other looking for bumps that would get him airborne. Innocent of fear, heedless of dignity, he roared down vertical headwalls faster than the eye could follow.

"Come on, Daddy, come on!"

If you looked back up the run, *far* back up the run, you might have made out a dumpy figure in blue, cautiously traversing the hill in long, slow, horizontal sweeps, concentrating fiercely on methods of slowing down. His one ambition, evidently, was to reach the bottom of the hill in one piece. Skis are wilful, recalcitrant instruments of the devil, far too slippery and far too long. Put them down on the snow, and they slither away at breakneck speeds, taking you with them. If you try to turn, they trip you. Eighteen-inch skis would be much better. If God had meant us to have fibreglass feet two metres long, He would have evolved toenails big enough for our needs, as He did with the moose.

Consider, for example, my first day on skis. A svelte young woman named Pat—whose suit revealed some of the leading attractions of Mount Norquay—showed three of us how to "snowplow," putting the ski tips together to slow down or turn. Then she led us to the rope tow, which was to haul us up the giddy heights of the bunny hill.

I grabbed the cable, and both my arms shot off towards the hilltop. Some time later the rest of my body followed, aching considerably at the shoulders, slipping under, over and beside the cable. I concentrated furiously, muscles locked rigid, slopping and clattering upwards. After a hundred feet or so, I felt confident enough to raise my head.

Far above me, on an awesomely steep run covered with huge round bumps called "moguls," a little figure was dancing elegantly downwards, soaring around turns, throwing up sprays of snow, skis perfectly parallel, poles tapping the snow—a little dancer, doing a winter ballet on the plunging mountain.

It was glorious. It was like visible music.

It was Lulu.

I gaped, utterly transfixed in admiration for my wife. I forgot what I was doing. My ski tips crossed, and my legs lost their bearing.

I tumbled out of control, a mad melee of orange skis, aluminum poles, blue nylon windbreaker and red face. A wipeout—going *upwards* on the bunny hill. Lulu waltzed and dipped down through the moguls, oblivious to the wobbling, trembling ruin snowplowing to the bottom of the rope tow. With a screech of delight, Mark Patrick sizzled past me.

Damn kid.

THAT VERY DAY, THOUGH, I faced an insurrection in my psyche.

I was coasting slowly across the bunny hill when I suddenly felt relaxed enough to stand straight and look around. I saw dazzling fields of snow interrupted by clumps of spruce and pine. The town of Banff lay in the valley bottom far below, overlooked by the Victorian splendour of the Banff Springs Hotel. All around me rose some of the world's most majestic peaks, fractured and serrated against the vast Alberta sky. Across the snowfields moved tiny figures dressed in crimson, royal blue, lemon yellow, skimming over the slopes, swooping and arcing their way to the bottom, having fun.

It was a novel and lovely experience, slipping lightly across the face of the hill, wafting along without effort, cruising like a glider in a thermal and entranced by the sensuous pleasure of the moment. I had to admit—and it felt like a betrayal—that I was having fun, too.

I smiled. The effort unbalanced me, and I pitched sideways and forward, wrenching an ankle and plowing a furrow in the snow with my nose.

A DAY OF MISERY. The hill is hard and icy, and a thin drizzle of rain weeps from the mist that hangs in the treetops. You slow down by "edging" the skis, turning them inward so that their metal edges bite into the snow—but today it's impossible, the hill is so hard that the edges skitter over the crust. So you fall, and slide helplessly down the run for 40 or 50 feet, looking up sorrowfully at those mocking orange skis against the steel-grey sky. You get up with your back and bottom soaking wet. Your glasses are running with water. You would gladly pack up the skis, drive down to town, and give up skiing forever.

The day drags on. First try at a T-bar, and I fall twice going up it. The second time I'm just a few feet from the top, and I have to inch and crawl and flail upward. Mark wants to go on the chairlift, and Lulu will take him. Will I come behind, carrying his ski poles and my own? What can I say, even though I'm still terrified of the wretched contraption? Mark insists on going to the top of the lift, to a run for intermediate-level skiers. He snowplows down, a sturdy little figure in puffy thermal clothing, but it's too steep for me. I deliberately dump, and slide down on my back until the hill flattens out a little.

Later on, I stall completely, standing rigid at the top of a short, steep, icy run. Lulu and Mark are at the bottom, waiting for me. It's still drizzling, the sky black, the hillside slick with ice and water. As I stand there, an instructor coasts up behind me with a dozen grade-school children following behind like ducklings. They meander down the run in wide, slow, snowplow turns, and stop midway for a lecture. The instructor is wearing a green garbage bag, which makes her look fairly silly. The way the garbage bag negotiates the hill, however, makes me feel silly.

Lulu and Mark are still waiting. I try to tell them, in sign language, that I am not going anywhere until the class gets off the hill. Otherwise there is a good chance that I will hurtle right into them, welding the whole class with me into a gigantic ball of protoplasm which will roll down the hill like an escaped blob of jello. The class stays on the hill for an interminable length of time. Lulu and Mark head for a T-bar and take another run. The class leaves, and I sidestep down the hill with water in my underwear and murder in my heart.

Mark Patrick concludes the day by skiing straight into a rope fence which peels the skin off his upper lip. This is highly satisfactory. At last there is someone else in the family as miserable as I am.

A GLORIOUS DAY, the very next time out.

Mark has a brand-new "brain basket"—a little hockey helmet to protect him from concussion, which is the usual skiing accident for children, a result of caroming into trees, buildings, fences, rocks and other people. He wore his helmet all night—"in case

I fall out of bed"—and today he looks The Compleat Skier, with his white plastic head, blue dacron body, and stubby little Rossignol skis. He reaches the top of the T-bar and shoots off, shouting, "Go, Rossignol, go!" Out of sheer joy, he stands upright in his skis, windmilling his arms as he flies downhill.

On this brilliant sunny day, I find myself learning so fast that my body almost tingles with consciousness, taking in knowledge through the pores and lungs and inner ears. It's a sensation almost impossible to describe, a state I've known only once before, when I was learning to sail. I come down hard on a ski, for instance. The ski turns uphill. Aha! I try things again and again, feeling the way more weight produces a sharper turn, the way a slight turn downhill yields instant speed. I don't look particularly graceful, I'm sure, but my nerves and muscles are soaking up information, storing knowledge. It's like riding a bicycle, or dancing—or log-rolling, no doubt. It's rhythm and balance, a matter of poise, timing and the kind of knowledge musicians mean when they talk about "getting the piece into your fingers."

I believe I am going to ski acceptably, sooner or later. And right this minute I am having the time of my life, completely submerged in learning. What does a ski do if you flatten it? If you flatten it pointing uphill? If I let the uphill ski float weightlessly around a turn, can I convert my dogged snowplow to a parallel turn? What happens if you try these evolutions twice as fast? Three times as fast? By God, it works just as well. Fancy that.

Away in the back of my head, a cynical voice whispers, *So what? Once you know how to do it, what can you do with it?* I'm not a jet setter, whisking off to taste glacier skiing in New Zealand or the latest resort in the French Alps. Am I going to spend my winters going up and down the brief runs of Nova Scotia's modest hills?

Well, time enough later for worries like that. And then it hits me—after 15 years of skiing, Lulu still tries to improve every single time she skis, still likes to take as many lessons as she can afford. What for? For the sheer joy of learning, for the pleasure of doing it well.

That's the heart of the matter. Skiing well doesn't earn you anything, isn't marketable, doesn't lead to anything else. Skiers learn to do it excellently simply for the pleasure of doing it excellently. And the urge to be excellent at something graceful, rhythmic and, in the narrow sense, pointless, is a performing artist's motive, a celebration of one's being in the world. It's not so much sport as art. And art, as E.F. Schumacher notes, is always about the Divine. Recreation becomes re-creation, an echo of the Great Creation.

Heavy thoughts, these. They unbalance me. As if by design, I take a spectacular tumble, and come up with snow in my hair and laughter in my throat.

I FALL BACK, OF COURSE. Learning is not a smooth, flowing curve. The next time out I am all knees and elbows, graceless and irrhythmic. My frustration is tamed by an astonishing demonstration of gumption and courage. Today the hill is speckled with disabled skiers. A Japanese man in his twenties passes under the chairlift, wearing a sign that says BLIND. Behind him is a companion calling out, "Left! Right! Traverse! Left!" While I watch him, feeling small, he swings nimbly down the mountain. A woman sweeps by, balancing her upper body with only her one remaining arm. A middle-aged man comes down with a single ski on his single leg. In his hands are special poles, each with a stubby ski on its end. The ski flips up, so the pole can be just a pole if he chooses.

Meanwhile, Mark Patrick has lost his nerve in a frightening fall. He's slow and stiff, creeping down the hill in a rigid snowplow. He says he wants to ski still, but he's ill-tempered and fretful, full of emotions too complex and contradictory for his vocabulary.

He and I learn differently, I realize, but we learn at the same overall pace. For him, skiing is a physical activity. He charges into it and mimics what he sees. With little experience, he has a limited imagination. So he goes too fast, too soon, and a disaster throws him far back down his learning curve.

For me, skiing is a mental activity first, a matter of thought and imagination and understanding. I could imagine a fall without having to fall. He could not. I was paralyzed with apprehension at the beginning. He is paralyzed with apprehension now. He had to learn fear. I only had to learn skiing. As he relaxes, we come out even.

So Mark and I become skiing buddies. We go without Lulu, we progress together. The three of us make a family excursion to Sunshine Village, a wonderland of fresh powder snow and cross-linked runs and chairlifts, a vast pleasure bowl above the treeline which easily digests thousands of skiers at a time. When Lulu goes with friends to try the expert runs, Mark and I roam around all afternoon, zipping between the trees, dipsy-doodling up and down the hollow walls of gullies, shooting straight down long open hills, weaving around the lumpy moguls on steep intermediate runs. It's delicious.

How often do we find ourselves on an equal footing with a small child, doing something we both love to do? One pays a price for the experience, feeling a clumsy fool and imagining oneself to be the laughing-stock of the lithe and youthful figures who make it look so easy. But look more closely. The people on the ski hill are *smiling*. A man having fun with his son as though there were *not* forty years between them has a rare and precious privilege.

The difference between us is that Mark has a future. He could conceivably become a world-class skier. I will never again have the reflexes and suppleness of a young man, though I am feeling better physically than I can remember ever feeling before. But I am slowly decaying, and Mark is just budding. We will not likely ski together when *he* is 45.

Still, I don't want to be young again. It hurt too much. I want to be as I am now—secure in my identity, loving my wife and my work, happy with my place in the world. And filled with delight at the snow-reddened cheeks, the toothy grin, the merry eyes that look at me from under the white plastic rim of the brain basket. It is not given to many men to have small children in their forties. It is not given to many fathers to have such moments of closeness with their infant sons, ever.

One of the secrets of happiness is to know it when you have it.

OUR LAST DAY OF SKIING, at Whistler, B.C., began badly. Mark fell getting off the chairlift and brought his mother down on top of him. Grumpy and ill-coordinated, we skied badly, straying into difficult corners and flat spots where we had to trudge wearily to the nearest slope. But then, at the end of the day, we got it.

Closing time, time to get off the mountain, and down we flew, the three of us, through moguls and around curves, between the trees and beneath the chairlifts, near the lips of cliffs and beside rock faces, joined by tributary rivulets of skiers from a dozen runs over the face of that great mountain, weaving and edging, slowing down and gathering speed, rushing for the valley far below. Lulu was leading, elegant and ethereal, while I charged recklessly behind her, the wind pushing tears from my eyes, and our racing dumpling of a son came speeding close on my heels.

We reached the gondola, throwing up sheets of coarse spring snow as we turned on our tracks to stop. We arrived there together, all three of us, at the end of the last run on the last day of our season, the middle-aged man and the pre-school boy, and the woman who loved them both.

I had left a cast-off shell of fears and inhibitions above the treeline.

I had found, once again, what my life was all about.

[1984]

Tossing the Torch

A SPEECH TO GRADUATES OF THE UNIVERSITY COLLEGE OF CAPE BRETON

THE OTHER DAY I WAS SITTING AT MY DESK lazily pondering what I might say to you today, when it occurred to me that I had nothing whatever to say to you. Nothing at all. Zero. I was suffering from what I've come to call "teacher's block."

You've all heard, of course, about *writer's* block: that condition in which a writer finds that his well has run completely dry and he's incapable of writing a word. I'm told it's a terrifying feeling, like being a scuba diver who suddenly finds himself sucking furiously at an empty tank. One friend of mine, a gifted poet, tells me he became a dope smuggler and went to jail for two years in a desperate attempt to break through a particularly bad writer's block. I don't mean to suggest that most drug smugglers are inspired by the muse, of course, though my friend says it was a pretty good way to finance a career as a poet. The royalties from his poetry paid for his toothpaste, and the mark-up on hashish sold at wholesale paid for everything else.

Actually, you might like to bear my friend in mind. You're graduating into a country so wracked and drained by stupidity and dishonesty that a million of its workers can't find jobs—though any of us could easily point out a dozen things within the borders of the town of Dominion, let's say, which need to be done. If you're interested in the welfare of humanity, you're probably better off as a dope smuggler or a moonshiner than as a builder of nuclear power plants or an aerospace worker. I'm not being entirely facetious. We do suffer from various collective insanities. If a farmer grows tobacco—which is unquestionably harmful stuff—he's eligible for various forms of government assistance. If he grows marijuana—which may or may not be harmful—he gets assisted straight into the penitentiary. If a distiller lives in Montreal, we send him to the Senate. If he lives in Scotchtown, we send him to Cape Breton County Correctional Centre. (Which, I suppose, corrects him.)

Anyway, now that you're graduating and you're fully qualified to become unemployed like everyone else, you might consider dope smuggling. We've sold most of the rest of our industries and our resources to the Americans, and the jobs have gone with them. Nova Scotia, for example, is North America's largest producer of gypsum. Does that mean you can get a job in one of our many sheetrock factories? Don't be foolish: The factories are in the States, which is where the owners of the gypsum live.

But dope smuggling is a growing industry, and one where a local kid with courage and cunning can still rise from nowhere to become a captain of the industry. There aren't many such industries, and we should make the most of our opportunities. Think about it.

Anyway, that's the kind of thing writer's block can lead to. It has been known to drive writers to drink. Actually, a good many things have been known to drive writers to drink; it's one of the things they're most easily driven to.

I myself have never suffered from writer's block. How could I? I live in Cape Breton. Cape Breton sometimes drives me to drink—or at least *induces* me to drink—but it even more frequently drives me to the typewriter. How can I have writer's block? I haven't written much about Louisbourg yet; I haven't written about St. Paul's Island, or about rooster fighting or about sheep farming or about steel or coal. I haven't written about the

Minglewood Band or Sam Moon or Buddy and the Boys. I haven't done a profile of Lee Cremo, Father Greg MacLeod, Fred Tomie, Newman Dubinsky or Gerry Doucet, just to name a few of the remarkable characters who thrive on this island. Look at the ethnic mix in that group, too: Indian, French, Scotch, Lebanese and Jewish. Is there any other community of 180,000 people which boasts *four* functioning languages?

Some day I want to write a singing little book about Isle Madame, the tiny perfect island where I make my permanent home. I want to write about cruising the Bras d'Or Lakes in autumn, when the scarlet and saffron leaves storm across the mountainside and the big boats have all gone back to Boston and Philadelphia. I want to figure out and explain just exactly *how* the Nickersons of North Sydney bought the North Atlantic Ocean. I'd like to write about the mournful abandonment of Creignish Rear, and I think I could write something very funny about Port Hawkesbury, the only suburb I've ever seen with no city attached to it.

And all this, of course, is superficial. When one writes fiction, poetry, drama, one moves *inside* the people. If we could lift off the tops of the skulls of everyone in this hall, what would we find? Here are some of the thoughts I suspect are going on *right now, right this instant*:

Imagine that: My stupid little son is actually graduating.

How can that character stand up there and make jokes about dope?

Ask me if I'm thirsty, just ask me if I'm thirsty.

I wonder can I slip out and take a leak?

Lord liftin', Donnie F. Campbell is a good-looking man. How come priests have to be celibate, anyways?

If that woman kicks me again I'll drive her one, I don't care if it *is* graduation.

I wonder what this building cost? What holds up the roof?

Phewey! what did that guy behind me have for dinner?

If I loan that kid the car tonight, is he going to get drunk and wreck it? It's not paid for.

I better not let the old lady catch me squintin' at that blonde.

I wish her father were living, he'd be some proud.

I can't think how I'm going to pay those bills.

I'd sure like a smoke.

That bugger up there thinks he's some smart, don't he?

Behind each of those lines there's a story. You could start with any of them and go on to write a novel. Occasionally we've had a writer who's given that kind of expression to our place and our people. Hugh MacLennan, in *Each Man's Son*. Ray Smith, from Mabou. Ray's first book was called *Cape Breton Is The Thought Control Centre of Canada*, and I won't soon forget what he did at a Writer's Union banquet one time. The dessert was chocolate mousse, and as I bent to eat it a beard tickled my ear and an Inverness County voice said, "Hey, b'y, what's a Cape Bretoner say when he sees a chocolate mousse?"

"Dunno, b'y," I said. "What's he say?"

"I'd sooner a strawberry Schooner."

The writer, I think, who has come closest to expressing the internal life of Cape Bretoners is Alistair MacLeod, from Dunvegan, near Inverness. Alistair's book, *The Lost Salt Gift of Blood*, will be re-issued in paperback this fall; if you haven't read it, I urge you to seek it out. His stories are so beautifully crafted, so truthful, so penetrating, that reading them is like an exquisite form of pain. Endurance and suffering, desire and rage, loyalty and escape, fear and love—the great human themes wrestle with one another in MacLeod's pages, and in the end you realize that though he is describing the life he has known on this island he is writing to anyone who can read English; he is describing the human spirit, the human condition, the human soul, and one comes out of his stories feeling stronger, more compassionate, and in awe of the human possibilities.

How does such a writer find his way into those crannies of experience? I think he does it by listening to people; listening very hard, even when he's not aware of it; listening to what is *not* said as well as to what *is* said; and then bridging the gaps in his knowledge with imaginary extensions of his own experience. We all know the meaning of lust and joy and hope and jealousy because we have experienced them. We know their sources and we can recognize them in others. That's how I guessed what some of you were probably thinking; I've listened to enough speeches and lectures, God knows, and I know what I felt like.

I said that the writer listens, that that's one of his basic sources. I think it's more rewarding to listen here than in most of the other communities I've known, because Cape Breton is a small intimate community in which the most fundamental and important human experiences are never very far away. The most fundamental experience of all is death—a point to which I'll return. On this island we live unusually near the prospect of death. If you're a fisherman, say, or a miner, you face the possibility every single day that sloppiness, incompetence or bad luck will kill you.

Incidentally, it's this fact that makes me furious when I'm told that capitalists deserve to make fortunes because they "take risks." What do they risk? Money: mere money. It seems to me obscene to mention the loss of a million dollars in the same breath with the loss suffered this winter by thirteen miners in Number 26 colliery. In this society, it's not the entrepreneur who takes the real risks.

The result of that risk of death, perhaps, is a different sense of life. People down here tend to be very blunt. When we want something, we go get it. When we party, we pull out all the stops; the party ends when it runs out of steam, which might take a week. When someone does something rotten, you puck him. Sometimes you puck him just because it'd be good sport to have a good ruckus.

For a writer, of course, this directness is pure gold. You actually *see* how human beings operate and interact; you know a dozen different aspects of the people around you, and they tell you very straightforwardly what they're feeling and why they act as they do. Now stockbrokers and deputy ministers operate *exactly the same way*—but they'll never tell you, and in the thickets of the city they're often able to hide it. How long did it take us to discover that Prime Minister Mackenzie King was as mad as a March hare? If he'd lived in Ashby, he'd have been known as

Batty Mac, and everyone would have known the details.

That same directness is reflected in the *language* of Cape Breton, a language coloured by borrowings from Micmac, French and Gaelic, a language which spins off metaphors, similes and comic analogies as fast as the steel plant ejaculates rails. He's deaf as a haddock, tough as a boiled owl, horny as a bag of sculpin. She was alive when Christ wore gumboots. He's so ugly that when he was a child they used to have to tie a pork chop around his neck to get the dog to play with him.

That vitality, that playfulness with language, is associated with storytelling, talking about people, describing them and their actions. And that completes the writer's central equipment: a clear and profound grasp of human nature, a fresh and entertaining approach to language, a love of storytelling: Those are the ingredients of great literature. This island has already produced some wonderful writers, but I suspect the best is yet to come. It wouldn't surprise me to see Cape Breton produce a writer comparable to Joyce, or Proust, or D.H. Lawrence. Maybe such a writer is sitting quietly among these graduates right this minute.

So much for writer's block: I don't have one. I don't see how *anyone* could have one, not in Cape Breton. Farley Mowat had a bad one, and he moved to River Bourgeois a couple of years ago; since then his typewriter has been going like a triphammer and his new book will be out in September. Writer's block is not a problem.

Teacher's block *is* a problem, and I've had it repeatedly. It's probably the main reason that I wouldn't want to teach full-time again. Teacher's block occurs when it strikes a teacher that he or she is supposed to manipulate and shape the students, to pump them full of ideas the way a balloon is pumped full of air, and then to let them go soaring off into the world as a balloon does when you release it. And the situation in which the teacher pumps in ideas more or less determines the ideas that can be pumped.

For example, I know pretty well what speakers at graduations are supposed to say. They're supposed to congratulate you on having passed the final hurdle into adulthood, like African kids who have killed their first antelope, or whatever. I should point out that you're heading out into a horrible mess of a world, and that it's up to you to shovel up the mess. I should imply that those of us who are older will now throw the torch to you, and go like senile cocker spaniels to our kennels, where we will whimper and whine a little in our sleep, as our dreams replace our memories. You should be told that you have had the finest preparation for your responsibilities of any generation in history, and at great public expense. We now hand this great country over to you. May you treat her with the dignity she deserves.

What the lazy slut actually deserves is a swift kick in the Aspy Bay, and the injunction to get the hell up and make something of herself before we all give up on her of sheer boredom. But suppose I *do* tell you that; then you'll go out into the world all wrong, you see? You'll have a Bad Attitude. You'll probably get athlete's foot, and you'll never get a job.

The problem with teaching is that the process insists that the student absorb what's being offered, be it Marxism, milk marketing or critical thinking. But is that good for the student? If you really think hard about that question, it gets more and more complicated, and the whole enterprise becomes more and more dubious; in the end you become silent, because what on earth do *you* have to say that's worth imposing, more or less forcibly, on the student? This past winter I taught—in a very gingerly fashion, often—a writing class. Was it good for the students? I have no idea. Some of them said it was, but they could be very wrong. Maybe I didn't help them to find their own voice. Maybe I simply insisted that they mimic mine.

That's why I realized, the other day, that I had nothing really to say to you. I don't want the responsibility. In this respect writing is fundamentally different. You can buy my book or not buy it. (I point out that it's only $4.95, and it's in the college bookstore.) Having bought it, you can read it or not read it. If you read it, you can agree or disagree or forget about it. It's up to you.

But it's *not* up to you whether you sit here and listen today; you damn well have to, if you want to get your diploma. It's a totalitarian situation. I don't like being in that position.

However, having shared with you a few ideas about writing, I'll share one more: a hint about what I think most good writing—maybe *all* good writing—is about, at least in a roundabout way. It's about death. I said before that death is perhaps the most important human experience; that's because death sets a finite limit on the possibilities of life. We all know it's coming; we don't know when or how it may be coming. Good writing is generally a fierce celebration of that stormy and magnificent interval before it arrives. It's a roar of rage against the brevity of life. A good book outlasts a good man, which is a sobering thought. A good book preserves the flickering victories of courage and beauty and love, the little victories we achieve in our brief moment outlined against the void.

Come to think of it, I do have an idea I'm willing to impose on you. I do have a tiny little graduation address. Here it is:

The young cannot generally bring themselves to believe they will become old, and so perhaps it does not seem to you today that life is *so* short, and so uncertain; time is the most precious thing we have. To waste your time is actually, in a small way, to waste your life. But a good book—or a splendid experiment, an elegant solution to an organizational dilemma, a noble building, a graceful boat—says by its very nature that even though the victories we can achieve are fleeting, they are real victories nevertheless, and worthy of our ambition.

You are graduating today from what I suspect is the most interesting, innovative and imaginative little college in Canada—and I don't say this lightly; this is my sixth university. If you have learned here—from books, from teachers, from the complex geometry of scientific thought—if you have learned to seek and love and pursue excellence, then you have learned how to make your own protest against the finite limits placed by death upon the infinite aspirations of mankind. I hope that *is* what your experience at this unpretentious and humane little college has meant.

If you have learned to seek excellence, you have begun to celebrate life. And that celebration, obliquely, will enrich us all.

Just Let the Music Play

THE YOUNG BOAT BUILDER SLIDES THE PLANE down the spruce timber, shaping a bowsprit for a schooner. The shavings peel off as thin and even as paper, and curl up in piles on the floor like ringlets in a barber shop.

"Let the tool do the work," says Murray Stevens. "You just guide it."

Some remarks strike like revelations. Let the tool do the work. And if it won't, it probably needs to be cared for: sharpened, adjusted, oiled, or whatever.

When you've practiced enough, let the guitar play itself. Your fingers will remember. They'll remember how to type, how to drive a car or a nail.

The fingers of Murray Stevens are full of memories. Murray is not your gnarled, crusty old craftsman; he's in his mid-thirties, living carefully and comfortably with his wife and young family in Lunenburg County, Nova Scotia, next door to his father, within walking distance of three or four uncles. His father David builds and skippers championship racing schooners, and still farms in a small way. His uncle Randy runs the family dairy farm. His uncle Harold presides over the family sail loft. Murray is the son of a shipwright, the grandson of a shipwright. And a Stevens ship is a work of art.

See them lying at their moorings at Second Peninsula. The Schooner *Kathi Ann II*, twice an international champion. The schooners *Avenger* and *Skylark*. The *Atlantica,* which David and

Murray built at Expo '67. Look at the workmanship. The glue joints are perfect hairlines. The planks are so smooth and fair, their seams so completely filled by tiny cedar strips, that you can barely tell where one plank ends and the next begins. The paint is impeccable. The very ropes are neatly coiled on the belaying pins.

Murray has his foibles, which have been known to cause annoyance. He is something less than utterly punctual. He is given to offering advice from a great height. On some matters he is not so much meticulous as simply fussy. He does not suffer fools particularly gladly.

He is also kind by nature, shrewd at business, fair in his dealings with clients, thoroughly decent as an employer, responsible as a citizen. He's a good raconteur, a delightful companion.

And excellence is his business.

In this day of mass-produced fibreglass yachts, in which most of the work can be done by semiskilled workers on an assembly line, Murray Stevens has realized that he can only compete at the activity he loves best by performing in a very special way. Nobody today will buy a slipshod wooden boat, but a small and demanding clientele will still commission absolutely superb wooden yachts, custom-built to the owner's specifications, boasting workmanship which compares to that found in fine furniture.

Watching Murray and his little band of colleagues at work is like watching dancers or athletes. Their movements are economical; they work methodically and carefully and yet with a steadiness that carries them inexorably through the work. Their tools are always sharp. Indeed, they have worn a great hollow in the whetstone which lies swimming in oil on the workbench.

Somewhere Leonard Cohen remarks that a saint does not dissolve the chaos of existence; instead he rides the drifts like an escaped ski. For me, excellence is like that: performing with the effortless grace of Cohen's escaped ski. Excellence unites the actor, the action and the thing acted upon in one harmonious, balanced whole, so that Murray Stevens, his plane and the spruce timber become a single thing in which Murray is wholly immersed. At first glance, that kind of excellence seems egotistical, because the workman has no attention for anything but his own job. But in fact that concentration is the exact opposite of egotism, for it is not of himself that the workman is thinking, but of the job and the process of accomplishing it.

One is tempted, too, to think of excellence as a matter of practice, of skills and techniques, but those are only its superficial indications. Fundamentally, excellence is more a question of attitudes and outlook. You develop the skills because you want to do the work excellently. Why else would you bother developing them at all? You are actually seeking perfection: a poem which when once read can never be forgotten; a building which is absolutely square and level, in which every nail is driven precisely home without hammer marks in the wood around it, in which every line is true, straight and pleasing to the eye. The techniques are a result of that ambition.

It takes patience. I am impatient by nature, and I compromise.

Of course I compromise, I tell myself. There are only so many waking hours in a day, only so many days in a life. How much of that time am I to spend on a lousy little book review, or a wooden facing for the kitchen wall? And speed, after all, is also a minor factor in excellence: Of two equally competent workers, the faster one is the more excellent.

So I compromise. And then, for the rest of my life, I have to live with the board on the kitchen wall which doesn't quite fit, or the published sentence which moves awkwardly to its conclusion. Those things exist, irrevocably, as part of the trail I leave in my passage through this world. They are part of my record, muffed opportunities which will never come again.

For me, excellence is also bound up with creativity. The creative personality, I suspect, tends to be creative at everything he or she attempts; the person who cares about excellence cares about it, somehow or other, in every aspect of living. Any job worth doing, my mother used to tell me, is worth doing well. At the time I thought she was just trying to induce me to be more careful to get the egg off her china, but as I grow older I see more and more wisdom in what I once thought was mere nagging.

Still, one sets priorities. If worst comes to worst, as it often does, I will let the dishes go, neglect my correspondence, fail to mow the lawn, leave the spice rack unbuilt. Where I really want to be excellent is here, at the typewriter.

If the gods are kind, I will someday write prose which is as clear and straight and true and mysterious as the bowsprit Murray Stevens made for me. Prose like that will yield exultation to me and rapture to my readers, and I truly believe it will set up a little tinkle in the music of the spheres.

[1977]

Afterword

by Silver Donald Cameron

RON CAPLAN SELECTED THE ITEMS FOR THIS BOOK. When I first saw his list I didn't like it.

Ron's choices seemed too personal, too confessional, too... *egotistical.* Oh yes, personal essays are an important aspect of my work, and yes, a writer's character and values are deeply embedded in every line that person writes. I don't even trust writers who try to appear wholly impersonal: Each of us sees the world from a particular standpoint, and before I give a writer my trust I want to know where that writer *is*.

But that's not an excuse for building a whole book around the writer's precious little ego. Where, I demanded, were the externalized autonomous pieces—the radio dramas, the reportage, the fiction, the commentaries and analyses? Where were the profiles, the travels, the accounts of science and technology?

Well, said Ron defensively, this is the book I want.

Humph.

Ron's selections also made me melancholy. Leonard Bonin is dead, along with his son Mark. So are Carl Vilas, Dan R. MacDonald, Marshall Bourinot and the Drummer. Cancer claimed Ann Brimer before her fiftieth birthday; the echo of her life is the Ann Connor Brimer Award for Atlantic children's literature. Arthur Terrio, whose presence I noted at Artie Samson's funeral, later became my father-in-law. He died in 1990, leaving a large hole in all our lives. The list could go on and on.

The book itself talks a lot about death, too. Look at these pieces: a meditation on suicide, an account of a funeral, a short story about corpses, a lament for a dead musician. Even Olaf finally turned up his tootsies and went to join the Choir Invisible. I think of myself as quite a cheerful fellow: Why am I always writing about death?

More melancholy. The magazines in which most of these pieces were published have also passed into history. *Quest*, *Atlantic Insight....* When I began as a freelance writer, *Weekend* and *The Canadian* were publishing 10 or 12 feature articles every week, and paying a living wage to their contributors. When they died, it was like the collapse of the cod fishery. A few of my old markets survive, fiercely defending their niches—*Saturday Night*, *Reader's Digest*, *Harrowsmith*. But most of these stories simply would not be written today; the market for them has all but vanished.

What a depressing book.

Well no, said Ron, it's not.

It's not? I looked again.

The world has changed during the time these pieces were written, and all change contains an element of loss. But there is certainly a fierce assertion of life in these pages, too. I've celebrated lovers and rebels, scavengers and survivors, artists and volunteers—and many of my people are doing fine. Farley Mowat published a new book last fall, and Claire is publishing one this fall. The Potties have transformed their little house, and Allan Savoury has a bunch of aquaculture leases. Red Angus is retired. Symphony Nova Scotia has risen from the ashes of the Atlantic Symphony. Stan Rogers' songs are everywhere, and the old fiddlers have been joined by a whole generation of brilliant young people.

Not all change is for the worse. I am now the Dean of the School of Community Studies in the University College where I was once the graduation speaker. My son Mark, now a teenager, is turning out to be a neat guy, if not a tidy one. And Lulu remains an inexhaustible marvel.

I also found a powerful sense of community in this book. There's a lot of music in it, too, and a lot of love: the love of man and woman, the love of parent and child, the love of place. If this is a fragmentary autobiography—and in a way it is—it reports that I've loved and been loved; I've had a good life among good people, and I've cherished the experience.

Time and death versus love and art. I didn't choose these themes: They chose me. But if one set out to choose great themes for two decades of work, one could hardly do better.

I don't know whether that underlying unity is what Ron Caplan saw, but I'm glad he put these pieces together. In the end, *Sterling Silver* isn't the book I thought it would be—and that may be just as well.

Silver Donald Cameron
D'Escousse
Cape Breton Island
1994

ALSO AVAILABLE FROM
Breton Books & Music

SILENT OBSERVER
written & illustrated
by CHRISTY MacKINNON
A children's book of emotional & historical substance—autobiographical story of a little girl who lived in rural Cape Breton & in the world of a deaf person.
$21.50

WATCHMAN AGAINST THE WORLD
by FLORA McPHERSON
The Remarkable Journey of Norman McLeod and his People from Scotland to Cape Breton Island to New Zealand
A detailed picture of the tyranny and tenderness with which an absolute leader won, held and developed a community—and a story of the desperation, vigour, and devotion of which the 19th-century Scottish exiles were capable.
$16.25

CASTAWAY ON CAPE BRETON
Two Great Shipwreck Narratives in One Great Book!
1. Ensign Prenties' *Narrative* of Shipwreck at Margaree Harbour, 1780
(Edited with an Historical Setting and Notes by G. G. Campbell)
2. Samuel Burrows' *Narrative* of Shipwreck on the Cheticamp Coast, 1823
(With Notes on Acadians Who Cared for the Survivors by Charles D. Roach)
$13.00

CAPE BRETON BOOK OF THE NIGHT
Stories of Tenderness & Terror
51 extraordinary, often chilling, tales, pervaded with a characteristic Cape Breton tenderness—a tough, caring presentation of experience
$16.25

ARCHIE NEIL
by MARY ANNE DUCHARME
From the Life & Stories of Archie Neil Chisholm of Margaree Forks, C. B.
Saddled with polio, pride, and a lack of discipline, Archie Neil lived out the contradictory life of a terrific teacher floundering in alcoholism. This extraordinary book melds oral history, biography and anthology into "the triumph of a life."
$18.50

THE MOONLIGHT SKATER
by BEATRICE MacNEIL
9 Cape Breton Stories & The Dream
From a mischievous blend of Scottish & Acadian roots, these stories blossom, or explode softly, in your life. Plus her classic play set in rural Cape Breton.
$11.00

DOWN NORTH:
The Original Book of Cape Breton's Magazine
Word-and-Photo Portrait from the first 5 years of *Cape Breton's Magazine*
239 pages, 286 photographs
$23.50

CAPE BRETON LIVES:
A Second Book from Cape Breton's Magazine
300 pages of Life Stories • 120 photos
$23.50

HIGHLAND SETTLER
by CHARLES W. DUNN
A Portrait of the Scottish Gael in Cape Breton & Eastern Nova Scotia
"This is one of the best books yet written on the culture of the Gaels of Cape Breton and one of the few good studies of a folk-culture."—*Western Folklore*.
$16.25

• PRICES INCLUDE GST & POSTAGE IN CANADA •

CONTINUED ON NEXT PAGE

ALSO AVAILABLE FROM
Breton Books & Music

CAPE BRETON QUARRY
by STEWART DONOVAN

A book of poetry that gravitates between rural and urban Cape Breton Island, and the experience of working away. Stewart Donovan has written a relaxed, accessible set of poems of a man's growing up and his reflections on the near and distant past of his communities. A lovely, lasting little book.

$11.00

CAPE BRETON CAPTAIN
by Captain DAVID A. McLEOD
Reminiscences from 50 Years Afloat & Ashore

A rough-and-tumble autobiography of sailing, shipwreck, mutiny, and love.

$13.00

ECHOES FROM LABOR'S WARS
by DAWN FRASER
Industrial Cape Breton in the 1920s
Echoes of World War One
Autobiography & Other Writings

Intro by David Frank & Don MacGillivray. Dawn Fraser's narrative verse and stories are a powerful, compelling testament to courage, peace & community. They belong in every home, in every school.

$13.00

A FOLK TALE JOURNEY THROUGH THE MARITIMES
by HELEN CREIGHTON
eds. Michael Taft & Ronald Caplan

72 folk tales from a lifetime of collecting. Dr. Creighton introduces each storyteller, and then lets them talk to us directly, in their own words. A wonderful portrait of the faith and courage of the collector and the trust of the storyteller. This book is a Maritime treasure.

$23.50

THE CAPE BRETON GIANT
by JAMES D. GILLIS

& "Memoir of Gillis" by Thomas Raddall
"Informative, entertaining, outrageous...!"

$10.00

THE SPECIALINK BOOK
by SHARON HOPE IRWIN
with chapters by Linda Till, Karen Vander Ven, Dale Borman Fink

SpeciaLink is a national network based in Cape Breton devoted to getting *all* children with special needs into mainstream childcare—the real world, rather than segregated settings. The story of the road to these principles, and of the symposium that made them the national agenda.

$18.50

• PRICES INCLUDE GST & POSTAGE IN CANADA •